AVEDONIA

This Is War

Jessica Benjamin

Also by Jessica Benjamin: *Avedonia: So It Begins*

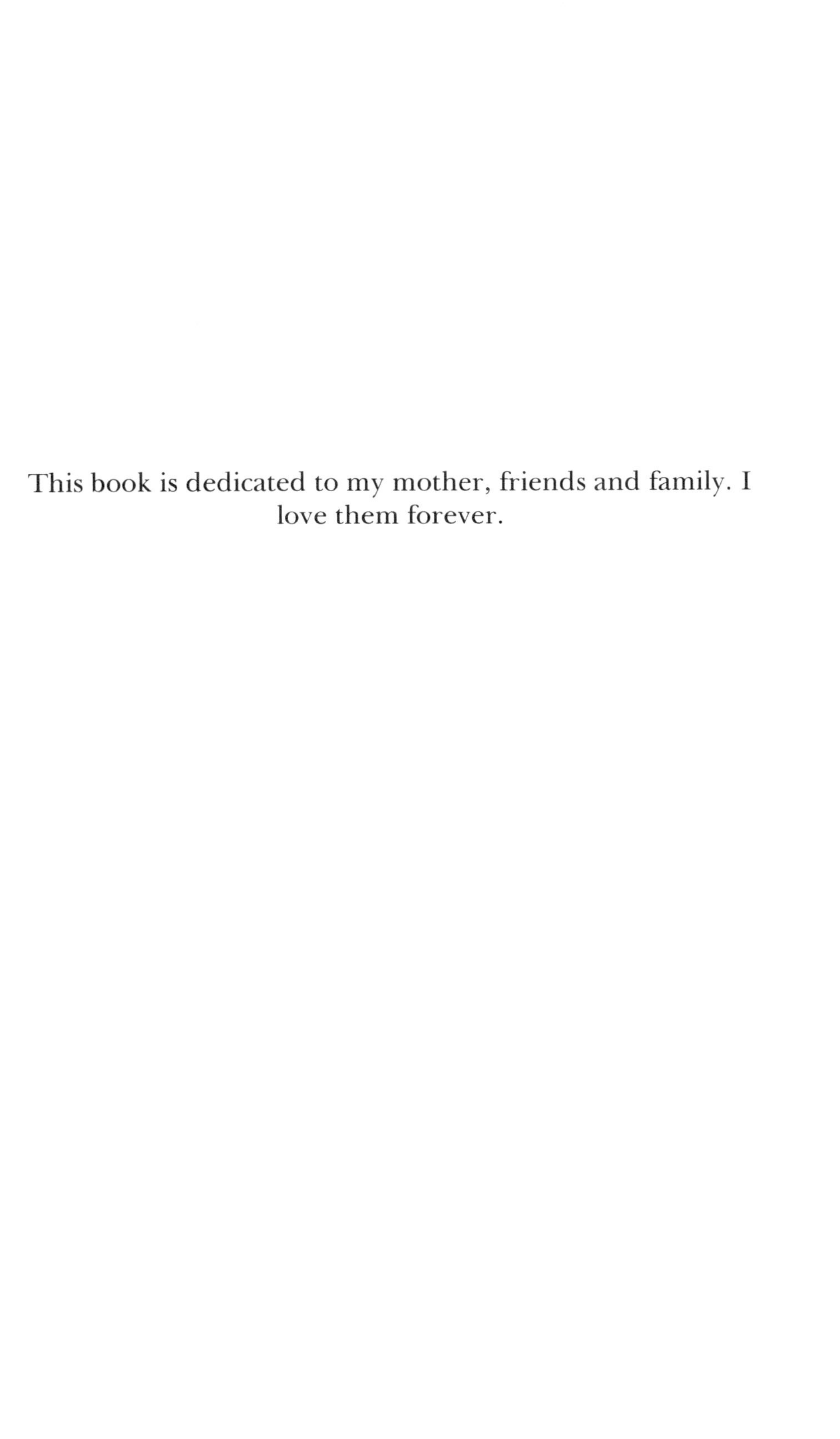

This book is dedicated to my mother, friends and family. I love them forever.

Acknowledgments

I would like to thank my mom for all her hard work, time, effort and support she has given and continues to give me throughout this journey and in my life. I want to thank all those who have supported me throughout this journey... my friends and family. The support and love you all show is amazing, and I couldn't do it without you. Also, I would like to thank all those who have read and enjoyed my first book. I hope you enjoy this book just as much as the first. As this amazing adventure continues, who knows where it will lead.

Hugs and Love Jessica

Table of Contents

The Arrivals

The wind and rain began to pick up in the early morning sky. The Alicorns and Pegusus had a hard time flying, especially the ones with carriages attached. They all pushed farther into the storm to get their passengers to the Secret Palace. Thunder boomed loudly around them as lightening started to slice through the sky all around the travelers. The closer they all came to the island of the Secret, the worse it became.

"Aye, I have not seen weather like dis round ere since de night we brought da little one ere. I don ope da horse can get um ere." Warketh commented, as he puffed on this cigar.

"I know it is quite a storm. But flying is the safest and fastest way to get here. You know that." Vex said, as he watched the skies and waited to hear for the first signs of the flying carriages.

"Well, I wouldn't say dat, but it's a way to get ere. Think we should move the island out of dis ear storm?" Warketh asked as he watched with Vex from the balcony. "Absolutely not! If we were to move now it would throw the horses all off and then we would have people lost and all over." Vex exclaimed as Warketh nodding and shook his head. *"Huh…"* He thought *"We dun moved it before when we was bringin da little one. I need tah keep an eye on him…"*

Suddenly, in the distance there came the glint of lights from the first carriage.   "Incoming!" A guard was heard, yelling across the courtyard.

"Release the Docking Dragons to help those horses." Joshua ordered, as he and his men, along with Warketh, rushed to greet the carriages. The fastest and first of the carriages to arrive was the Dark Prince himself and his wife, Queen Alice. As they landed, the Dark Prince, Doceo, looked at his wife,

"Well, that was one hell of a ride. Haven't been that shook up since our honeymoon." He laughed, as they bounced along the ground. Alice blushed.

"Oh Doceo! Do you have to bring that up now?" She answered, as she gently hit his side.   "Hey,   nothing wrong with some stress relief." He said to her, with a wink.

"Well, that will have to wait. I'm happy to be on the ground." She exclaimed, nauseous and frazzled. Doceo gave a chuckle as the carriage stopped and the door was opened.

"Sir." Joshua said and saluted him. Doceo returned his salute and escorted Alice through the invisible gates, the men that were moving around the courtyard stopped, stood at attention and saluted as they passed making their way to the Palace

"Lord Vex is waiting for you in his office, Sir." Josh

continued.

"Good. Has anyone else arrived before us?" Doceo asked raising his voice over the rain.   "Just the military men and the servants. Albert and Alberta are in your chambers, ready to attend to your needs. Do either of you need Toby's assistance?" Joshua asked.

"No, we are good! Get back to directing traffic and get everyone inside and safe!" Doceo commanded.

"Yes sir!" Josh said, as his eyes turned back to the sky and the others returned to their duties.

"Release more of the dragons. We need to get control of these carriages before there is an accident!" Josh commanded. "Dragon Flyers to your wings! Get those singles in!" He yelled. Soon more lights filled the sky with carriages needing to dock.

Inside, a woman of five foot, five inches with long white hair pulled back in a bun stood holding a towel. She has a broad forehead and gentle red orange eyes that sparkled and accentuated her crow's feet when she smiled. There are many wrinkles on her face. Her lips were thin with creases on either side of her mouth, especially when she smiled. Alberta smiled at Doceo and Alice handing them towels.

"Oh, you poor dears, here, get dry and warm." Alberta said.

"Thank you, Alberta. You are such a sweetheart. I have missed you so much when I was gone." Alice replied.

"I miss you as well, Miss. I am so happy you are back." Alberta said smiling.

"Thank you, Alberta. Honey, go to our room and dry off, get settled and comfortable. Alberta will show you the way. I need to check in with Vex to see why we are keeping the island in the middle of a storm and how things are progressing." Doceo said, as he kissed Alice's forehead and hurried to the office. Alice and Alberta headed towards the stairs, chatting arm in arm.

Outside, the next to arrive were Lucas and Marie De Cartier and their children Jules, Louis, and Amiee, who ran a mostly Vampire territory called Leur Bost on the mainland. Lucas picked up their youngest, Amiee. Marie grabbed Louis's hand, with Jules following. They all proceeded through the gates and scurried across the courtyard and into the shelter of the Palace.

Jim and Athena Valkyrie's carriage landed on the island. They ran the Lycan Territory known as Conriston, on the mainland. Jim shielded Athena the best he could with his coat as they ran through the gates. Once they had passed through security and into the courtyard, the storm seemed to have become more violent on and around the island. Instead of one docking dragon to guide the carriages to the land, they had to use two.

"I think we need to get Akasha and the other Royal Elves working on this storm." Jim said, as he held onto his wife to keep her from being blown backwards.

"Yes, this is definitely no normal storm tonight!" Athena yelled, as thunder crashed and lightning lit up the sky. A strong wind blew against Athena. Seeing this, Joshua took Athena's other arm and helped them across the courtyard and into the Palace.

"Thank you, Joshua dear." Athena said, grateful for his help.

"Of course, ma'am, anytime." Josh replied heading back into the storm.

Josh grabbed his radio off his hip as he exited the Palace and crossed the courtyard.   "Toby!" He yelled.

"Yes, Joshua. What do you need?" Toby responded.

"Is Ahz up and around and still with you?" He asked.

"He is. Why? Do you need him?" Toby asked.

"Yes, I do. We need him to use his magic to calm this storm, at least until some of the Royal Elves arrive." Josh replied.

"On my way Josh! I will grab the "skin bag" first to help as well." Ahz explained.

"Well hurry up! God damn it!" Josh demanded.

Ahzreal took off across the Palace and burst through Vex's office door.

"Sorry, but I need your dead ass to help get this storm under control until the Elves get here." Ahz exclaimed, as he stared at Vex. Vex and Doceo stopped what seemed to be a heated argument and looked at him. Vex with his mouth aghast.

"Well, I will if you show me some damn respect, you Mutt!" Vex replied.

"MUTT! I am of purer breed then you ever thought of being! You skin bag!!" Ahz bellowed, as he started to glow, and fire started coming out of his muzzle.

"ENOUGH! We need to get people here safe! Do your God damn jobs and fight later!" Doceo ordered. The frustration shown clear on his face as he glared at Vex.

"Fine, but this is not over!" Vex hissed at Ahz and glared at his brother as well.

Ahz and Vex went out of the Palace, into the courtyard and approached Josh.

"You and Vex keep things mellow from in here. I will go out to the docking area." Ahz ordered. "Can you keep directing traffic too, Josh?" Ahz asked.

"Sure can! I just need some help with this damn storm!" Josh yelled over more thunder. Ahz nodded and went out to the docks as Josh and Vex stayed in the courtyard.

"Ok all. Slow and steady. We got this." Josh yelled. As they started to chant, on the ground, around and under Joshua, Ahzreal and Vex's feet, alchemy circles appeared and lifted them up into the air. They continued chanting. The storm started to subside as thou the carriages and horses were flying into the calm eye of a storm.

"Ok, lads and ladies, this is the only chance we have! Get those carriages and people down here safe!" Joshua ordered as the docking dragons and dragon flyers took off like a shot to help land the other carriages and horses in the sky, as safely as they could.

The first ones down this time were Delya and John Blackthorn, the leaders of all the Lycan nations. They were followed by their youngest son, Joseph, who was on his chariot that was attached to his Pegasus. The Blackthorns took care of the capital of the Lycan Territories, Wolf Pine on the mainland.

"Holy hell! Next time I am riding with you two!" Joseph yelled towards his parents. "You are damn right you are!" Delya said.

"Where are we going?" Joseph asked. Delya grabbed her son's arm and pulled him through the invisible gate. He then saw the Palace and was in awe.

"You can look later son. Come on. Let's get inside!" John ordered as they proceeded inside. Once inside, they felt the warmth of the fire, and the staff handed them towels to dry off. "I will stay down here. I want to wait for my Little Wolf." Delya said worriedly. She proceeded to the side room to watch out the window. John gently grabbed her arm.

"Dear, you need to get dry first, so you do not get sick." John instructed.

"You are right love. I am just worried." She answered.

"I am sure he is fine. He is a big boy and can handle himself, unlike some people lately." John said, looking at Joseph, who just shrugged. Once this was decided Albert came up and showed them to their rooms.

Behind them came the last Lycan royal family. The rulers of the Oakheart Territory, Matoskah and Aponi Arrowheart and their children, Chaskam, Mitexi, Enapay, Chenoa, Napayshni and Aquene in two carriages. Aponi headed through the gate with Chaskam, Mitexi and Chenoa. Matoshkah waited on the other three children and hurried them through the gate. They all rushed though the courtyard and into the Palace. Happy to be safe inside and out of the raging storm.

Some time had passed and finally the carriages that Ahz, Vex, and Josh were anxiously waiting on were starting to land.

"Finally! Some back up!" Josh yelled as all three Elven carriages were docked at the same time. The storm was still raging around the island. Dior and Akasha Orijeon, Triandal, and Morgana Asari, and Ruban and Lilith Faemenor, who were all the rulers of the Elven Territories on the mainland, stepped out of their carriages.

"Rosco and Poppy, help your brothers and sisters inside, quickly." Morgana ordered her eldest two children.

"Blossom, Lil, and Ruban Jr., you do the same, and stay in there until we come in." Ruban ordered. The children, without hesitation, ran through the gates, across the courtyard and into the Palace. Akasha looked to Ahz and smiled.

"Looks as though you might need a little help around here." She said.

"That would be appreciated. If you think all of you can manage it." Ahz replied giving her a big grin. She shook her head and nodded.

"Ok everyone, take your places." She ordered the other Royal Elves. Quickly the six of them teleported themselves using magic to different areas around the Secret Island. Akasha placed herself in center of the island, Dior took the south side by Squall End Beach, Morgana and Lilith took the north end of the island near Orrinshire. The west was covered by Triandal, near the edge of Rutherglen and Tirion. That left the east to Ruban, which was near the Palace and Secret City, where refugees of Campania were now filtering in for safety.

"OK! Everyone ready!?" Akashas voice was heard by all who were about to tame this storm.

"READY!" They all shouted. A huge bright white light engulfed the island. It extended to a mile around it. The storm, while still there, was calmed to a normal rain and light wind, so the rest of the carriages and horses could arrive safely.

Soon Doceo's daughters, Princesses Lady, Bree, and Exie with their families, started to arrive in a smoother manner. More civilians from Campania, the capital of Avedonia, filtered into the city quicker beyond the Palace walls. Everyone was getting to safety and settling into their new, temporary, homes.

"I have yet to see my niece Jasmica arrive." Vex stated to Josh.

"Not yet, but they will be here soon. I was just

informed by my fae that they are not far off now." Josh replied. Vex nodded as everyone proceeded inside to get dry. The Royal Elves created a circle and sealed barrier to surround the island. It seemed the island was in its own bubble, for the time being. Once the barrier was set in place, the Elven Royals proceeded into the Palace to change their clothes and get dry. Inside Doceo and Vex continued to argue and send out Agents from the Special Forces to gather intel and other agents to evacuate civilians to the Secret. They were waiting patiently for stragglers and Jasmica to arrive.

WE MADE IT

My eyes opened slowly. Seeing the rain trickle down the windows and feeling the carriage bouncing around, the events of the night before came rushing back in my mind. I closed my eyes as I felt my face go very pale again. I shook my head, stretching and looking around, and realizing that I was in my carriage. It was a black, Victorian style carriage with gold etchings on the outside. It has purple crushed velvet interior and black accents. Nothing too extravagant. I had designed it more for comfort than looks. As the carriage swayed in the wind, I looked around more and realized I had had my head in Logan Santiago's lap. He is my guard. I moved a bit, and he rubbed my back gently as he softly snored. I looked across the carriage and saw Shadow Blackthorn, the eldest son of the head Royal Lycan family and my new friend, sleeping peacefully. Next to him, on the pillow, was his little fairy.

I smiled softly as I slowly sat up and stretched some more. I felt light pressure on my right shoulder as a tiny hand touched my face. My smile grew as I turned my head slightly towards my shoulder. I raised my left hand so my fairy could sit in it.

"Good morning, Moonbeam." I said quietly.

"Good morning Moonlily." Moonbeam said with a large smile. Moonlily was the nickname she had given me.

"How are you doing this morning?" She asked me, with a bit of worry in her eyes.

"I am ok. A bit rattled still and tired, but I'm ok." I said with a smile.

"Good. I am glad to hear that you are ok." Moonbeam replied as Guard Tucker, Logans' Fae or Fairy, fluttered in and landed on my hand next to Moonbeam.

"Oh! Good I was just about to ask if you were here, Tucker." I said.

"Yes, I sure am Princess." He replied.

"How far out are we?" I asked.

"We should be arriving any minute now. I was about to wake this big lug up, but I think he might like it more if you do it." Tucker chuckled.

"I am not so sure of that." I replied.

"Oh? Are you two fighting again?" Moonbeam asked.

"Yeah…" I said looking down. "He was acting like an asshole again." I said feeling some pain in my heart about the recent fight.

"I swear he is more stubborn than a damn mule. When it comes to commitment with you, he runs like a damn cheetah." Tucker said.

"Well, it is what it is. But I will wake him. He probably won't remember anyway." I said trying not to think about it too much.

"You know it is not that he doesn't remember. He would just rather not face it or think about it, only when he absolutely must." Tucker replied. I took a deep breath, nodded, and waited till they both flew out of my hand.

"I will wake up Ivy so she can try to wake up Shadow." Moonbeam said. I nodded again and looked out the window, watching the rain slide down it. I really did not want to wake Logan. I was already exhausted and not in the mood to deal with him, but I gently shook him.

"Logan… Logan…" I said, gently shaking him a bit more. His arm wrapped around my waist and pulled me closer. His lips pressed against my ear as he softly said,

"Shhh babe. It's ok. Go back to sleep." I wiggled away some and shook him some more. "Logan. It's time to wake up." I said a bit louder. He just pulled me closer and buried his face in my hair. I sighed and looked out the window again, thinking for a moment. I looked over and caught something move out of the corner of my eye. It was Ivy, stretching on the pillow near Shadow's head. She looked over at me with wide violet eyes. I pried myself away from Logan. He mumbled and went back to sleep. I shook my head, rolled my eyes and slid onto the floor. I held my hand out to Ivy.

Ivy saw this and smiled, fluttering over.

"Good morning, Princess Jasmica. I am Ivy Plumbloom, Mr. Shadow's fae." Ivy said as she curtsied.

"Good morning, Miss Plumbloom. It is an honor to meet you."

"Oh! The honor is all mine, Princess." Ivy replied,

almost jumping up and down with excitement. I smiled as Tucker flew in again.

"No luck on the wake-up call, Princess?" he asked.

"No. He is not getting up for me. He wants to get handsy and put me back to sleep." I replied.

"Well, I guess he will have to be woke up the fun way." Tucker said, rubbing his hands together with a mischievous grin.

"Yes, but let's at least wake Shadow first." Ivy said.

"Ok. Ok. Hurry up though." Tucker said anxiously. Ivy nodded "Excuse me Princess." She said and fluttered over to Shadow's head by his ear.

"Shadow. Time to wake up." Ivy said in his ear. Shadow mumbled and swatted at his head. Luckily, Ivy ducked just in time so that he missed her. She tried again. This time his hand almost came down on top of her. I dove over and shielded Ivy with my arm, pushing Shadows' arm away, as my chest landed in his face. His eyes flew open.

"Ummm. Panda..." He mumbled with his head between my breasts. I looked at Ivy.

"Are you ok?!" I asked.

"Yes, I am fine." She panted and she climbed into my hand. I felt a tap on my shoulder.   "Panda... Panda..." Shadow mumbled again. I moved back.

"Phew, I can breathe again. Panda, I am not sure what you were doing but... it's a nice way to wake up." Shadow smiled and chuckled.

"Howls, I was trying to save your fae, and save you from being electrocuted." I said staring at him. "Sorry about suffocating you though." I said blushing a little.

"Oh… ok. Well, at least I would have died happy." Shadow laughed with a sly smile and a wink.

I shook my head and returned to my seat on my side of the carriage. Feeling this, Logan wrapped his arm around me again, pulled me close and rested his head on mine.

"Thank the Gods Logan didn't see that, or he may have tried to cut my head off." Shadow said with a sigh of relief. Ivy took off and flew into his face.

"Hey! You almost squished me!" Ivy yelled as she started to glow red.

"Oh God! I am so sorry, Ivy. I didn't realize. Please forgive me." Shadow begged, feeling very bad about it.

"I will this time, but next time Mr., I will zap your tush." She replied as she settled on his shoulder and calmed down a little.

"You just need to work on your waking techniques." Moonbeam said as she settled on my shoulder and I nodded in agreement.

"Logan… Logan, wake up." I said as I shook him. "Babe, its ok. I am right here." He mumbled kissing my head. I sighed as I placed a shield around myself. "Ok. You asked for it. Get him Tucker!" I exclaimed. Suddenly, a yellow bolt of light flew from Tucker's hands and into Logan.

"Ahhhh! What the fuck!?" Logan yelled as he let go of me and jumped up, knocking his head on the top of the carriage, and falling back down into the seat. Shadow, the faes, and I all started to laugh so hard, we were almost crying, as my shield dropped, and Logan was looking around. "What the hell, Tucker! What was that for?!" Logan shouted angrily at him.

"Well, Princess tried to wake you, but you wouldn't

budge so, I had to. You know that is the only way I can get you up." Tucker said trying to contain his laugh.

I calmed down my laughing and I looked at Logan.

"Are you ok?" I asked.

"Yeah, I am fine. It was worth it to see you laugh. After, last night, I was afraid you'd never talk again let alone laugh." Logan replied as he leaned in and again kissed my forehead. I looked at him in surprise because he was finally sharing some emotion. I smiled back.

"Damn it, Kage! Don't do that!" Logan said to his wolf.

"There is nothing wrong with showing her some feelings! We do have them you know." Kage explained.

"Yeah, well not in front of the flea bag." Logan exclaimed.

"Oh! I forgot he was here. Ehh, oh well." Kage said as Logan grumbled a little.

"Hmmm… either Tucker woke Logan's wolf up or he rewired Logan's brain because that was new for him to share especially since Shadow is here." I thought.

"I think his wolf, Kage, had something to do with it." Kita replied.

"Most likely." I said.

Tucker popped out and back inside.

"Hold on all, it's going to be a bumpy one." He warned.

"Where in the hell did this storm come from anyway? It's almost like a hurricane." I commented.

"I am not sure, but it sure has been a roller coaster that I would love to get off of!" Moonbeam replied. The carriage was tossed and turned, turbulently. Suddenly, things seemed to calm down and a docking dragon appeared next to the window.

"Ahh! What the bloody hell is that?!" Shadow yelled in surprise as he looked terrified out the window.

"It's Igneel. He is a docking dragon." I opened the window, reached out and gently petted his nose. "You been working hard tonight haven't you." I yelled to Igneel as he nodded to me. "I know. It's almost over. Then you can rest, big boy." I said as he gave a nudge on my hand. I pulled my hand back inside and soon we were on the ground. Shadow and I looked out the window.

"Wow! This place is…. Amazing!" Shadow said in awe.

"Trust me. It only gets better!" I commented. The carriage stopped and Logan opened the door and got out. He held out his hand to help me out.

"Careful not to hit your head, Howls." I said as I took Logan's hand.

Shadow got out, making sure he cleared the door. He saw the thick tropical rain forest all around them. In front of them was a large lagoon area with multiple flowing waterfalls and an inlet on the right side, that led to the ocean.

"It's Beautiful!" Shadow exclaimed. I smiled.

"That it is!" I said, looking around and breathing deeply in the light rain.

"Where do we go? There is nothing here. I do not see a Secret Palace." Shadow asked. "Follow us, but make sure you walk straight, or you will run into the Palace gate and that will not feel great." I warned, as I walked forward and disappeared from his view.

"Yeah, please don't hit the gate. I don't want to carry you down to the hospital wing cuz you knocked yourself out." Logan retorted as he walked through the gate and disappeared. The carriage and faes had all taken off ahead of him. Shadow was left alone.

"Well, I guess we have to just walk into whatever is here." He thought.

"Let's try not to hit a wall. I do not fancy Logan touching us." Maximus, Shadow's wolf, advised.

"I will do my best." Shadow replied as he walked into the unknown.

The Secret Palace

I walked through the gate and felt almost renewed. I was home! I wished it were under better circumstances but either way, I was where I belonged again. I knew every territory, every nook and cranny on the whole island. I breathed in deep as I reached the other side of the gate.

"Aye, der be our Wee One!" Stock said with a huge smile. "Come and give us a hug now." he said.

"Stock!" I yelled happily and ran over to him, leaned down, and hugged him tight. "It's so good to see you. I have missed you." I said.

"I have missed ye as well, Wee One. It has not been da same since ye left ere." He said as his silver eyes had a familiar sparkle in them.

Josh came up beside us clearing his throat.

"Sorry to interrupt Jassy, but your father wants you to

come see him as soon as you get changed." Josh said. He too had the sparkle back in his eyes. The same sparkle we all have when we are home, full of life, magic, and energy. It had dulled, being on the mainland. I looked at Josh and nodded.

"Ok." I said as I turned back to Stock.

"We will have to catch up soon." I told him.

"We sure will, Wee One. Go see ur Poppa and I will catch up with ye soon." Stock said with a large smile.

"Definitely and remember," I said with a pause, "Keep Smiling." We all said it at once and laughed. Josh and I started to walk away when Stock yelled,

"By the way, Wee One. How many ye got with ye?"

"Two. Logan Santiago and Shadow Blackthorn!" I yelled back.

"Aye! Thank ye kindly!" He yelled back, smiling and waving. I waved and smiled in return and started to jog across the courtyard, to catch up with Josh.

Next through the gate was Logan.

"Why does that light have to be so damn bright?" He complained.

"Keep it cumin', Logan." Stock yelled.

"Yeah, yeah, yeah. I am here. Now where the hell is Jassy?" Logan asked. Stock chuckled.

"Ye haven't been ere even ten minutes and ye lost her." Stock chuckled.

"Gods help us if this is how things are going to go again, now that we are here." Logan said. Stock broke out laughing.

"Ye know she be wild. Not one of ya has tamed er yet.

Der only been on of ya dat can keep er to stay put and dat is Teagan." He said. Logan sighed and huffed.

"Ok. Out with it. Where is she?" Logan said. Stock wiped a tear from his eye from laughing so hard.

"She be wid Josh. He came to get er at da gate. Her poppa wanted er." He said.

"Very funny. I think you all are out to give me a heart attack. Between Tucker shocking me awake and you scaring me at the gate and Jassy taking off..." Logan stated, as he shook his head.

"Ahh lighten up. Ye know things round ere ain't dat serious. She be in da safest place she ever could be here." Stock replied as he nudged him in the shoulder.

"I remember that now. It has been a while since things have been this way. The mainland is a hell of a lot different than here." Logan said as he recalled some of the good times and how much easier it was here, for him and the other people, to protect her no matter the cost.

"Yeah, well ye better get down to da barracks before dhey become too serious down der. Dhey dun sent Vex down der and ye be knowin' how much of a cluster fluff that will be." Stock said.

"Damn it! What has he done already?" Logan asked frustrated.

"Vex has been orderin evacs from da mainland already. Though not in da right order, mind ye." Stock replied.

"Shit." Logan said as he kicked the ground with his boot. "I am guessing Warketh got here with the men, if Josh is already here?" He inquired.

"Yesum. Toby has been workin, non-stop, tendin to 'em. We be waitin on ye, but ye know Vex. He had to do it his way and control it while he can. He and da Dark Prince already been fightin." Stock said.

"Yeah, I know all too damn well how he is?" Logan said as his southern accent got thicker, the angrier he got.

"Aye, I reckon if he weren't da Dark Prince's kin, he would be strung up somewhere by now." Stock said with a bit of a chuckle.

"I know dats right. Yall woulda done it way before now." Logan said with a smile as he nudged Stock.

"Ya damn right we would ave." Stock replied.

"Well, either way, let's get this flea bag, Shadow, through the gate so I can get to my real job. I don't want to babysit anymore." Logan said. Stock nodded.

As Shadow walked forward, a ring of pastel rainbow colors surrounded him, and a bright light shined in his eyes. He put his hand up to shield his eyes as he kept walking straight. Suddenly, Shadow heard a deep gruff voice say,

"All Clear!" He looked to his left and saw a stout little man standing there. The man was standing on a crate, looking at a computer screen. The little man hopped down. Shadow's mouth dropped, as he looked down at the four-foot-tall man with soot colored skin, long blonde hair braided in a Viking style. He had a horned helmet on his head and a long blonde beard to match his hair, that covered his armor-clad chest and belly. He had a large shield on his back and two axes swung, one from each his hips. When he picked up his large hammer, Shadow could see he was very strong. His muscular arms shown under his armor.

"Thanks Stock." Logan said.

"Aye, ur' welcome. Godspeed." Stock said. He turned

and hurried off through the door on the left side of the gate. His silver eyes glowed in the darkness on either side of his broad nose. Logan looked at Shadow.

"Stop staring man! Have you never seen a Dwarf before or what?" Logan asked impatiently. Shadow shook his head, no. "Well, now you have. Come on. I have shit to do. By the way, that's Bhostock Hammerborn, King of the Dwarves in Orrinshire." Logan said as he started to walk across the large courtyard with Shadow behind him.

The morning light creeping and lightening the stormy skies above so you could see the Palace clearer now. Shadow looked up, saw it, and stopped dead in his tracks. Logan kept walking. Around the outside of the Palace was a large wall. It ran into the side of a waterfall on one end and wrapped around the opposite way to meet the back side of another waterfall. This Palace design must have been created by someone else because the design was a whole different style than the Autumn Palace on the mainland. This design had the look of an Elvin Castle. Straight out of a fairy tale. There were many archways and open spaces. A lot of windows, balconies, and gazebos. Elvish décor and carvings of nature ran wild throughout the outside of the castle. The tops of the turrets were green, while the walls were white limestone, with beautiful white marble columns. It seemed like there must have been a billion rooms and passageways that someone could get lost in.

Shadow's mouth hung open as he looked at everything, trying to take it all in.

"Oh, my Little Wolf! There you are!" Delya exclaimed, as she rushed over to him. Shadow shook his head and saw his mother coming towards him. He met her and hugged her tightly.

"Are you ok?" She asked.

"Yes, Mum. I am fine." He replied, as the Palace caught his eye again.

"It's beautiful. Isn't it?" She asked.

"Yes, it sure is. Do people actually live in this place?" Shadow asked as he walked with his mother towards the large oak door, with a tree of life carved on it. Delya chuckled.

"Yes, they do. The Orijeons built it to house their granddaughter, Princess Jasmica. She grew up here with her uncle, Lord Vex, and the missionaries, also known as the Secret Service, to the Dark Prince. So, there are many people who live here. In times like these, the city fills up and is used as a Secret fortress to keep everyone safe." She said smiling.

"City?! There is a city too?" Shadow asked.

"Yes. Just beyond the walls there. In fact, there are four territories here too. They have rulers just as we do on the mainland." She said smiling. "We will see that all later. I am sure we will have time. Let's get you inside and dry." She said as they walked forward, and she opened the door.

Through the doors, they were met by servants, guards, and soldiers, running around like bees in a hive. Shadow walked into a large hall that had a huge split staircase at one end and rooms on either side. There was a set of large doors, with one door open, and he could see it had a large fireplace in it. The carpet on the floor was a vibrant shade of green, like the leaves on the trees in summer, with gold embroidery on the sides. It led to the split staircase. Around this hall area were chairs and tables set up to sit and converse. The chairs were not as decoratively carved as the ones in the Autumn Palace. They were simple, yet beautiful, with cushions of different color velvet on them.

There were many columns around the outside of the room. Some were carved to look like trees. They supported the high arched ceiling. Many lanterns and lights were scattered about to give more light to the room. In the middle of the room's ceiling was a large, stained-glass window that let in light from outside.

"Woowww!" Shadow blurted out, as he continued to look around the room.

"Very nice in here, isn't it Master Shadow?" A voice behind him asked. He was nodding and turned towards the voice to see his servant Michael standing there.

"Mike! It's great to see you again. I was beginning to miss you." Shadow said happily. "Great to see you as well, Sir. Shall we get you dried off and settled?" Mike asked, handing him a towel.

"Oh yes! Thank you so much." Shadow said.

"You are most welcome, Sir. Follow me please." Mike instructed. Delya and Shadow followed him across the lobby to a door which held an elevator. As they rode to their floor, in the quietness of the elevator, Shadow figured he could ask his mother some questions that he had.

"Mum. What are all the smells here? They are different than the ones before." He asked. "Well, that would be because there are new creatures here that you have never been around." Delya answered.

"Like What?" Shadow asked.

"Well. Let me see. If I remember correctly, there are Dwarves, Centaurs, Demons, Orks, Merfolk, Dragons, Alicorns, and Pegasus, added in with the other Lycans, Fairies, Elves and Vampires." She spoke.

"What?! Why didn't you tell me about this place?"

Shadow asked.

"Really. There was no point at the time. You would not be coming here unless we were at war, along with much of Avedonia. So, your father and I figured we would tell you when you needed to know… and now you know." She smiled sweetly as the bell chimed and the elevator doors opened. "Ahh yes, here is our floor." Delya said as she walked out into the hallway. Shadow stood for a moment taking it all in. Then, he hurried out of the elevator to follow Mike and his mother, before he got stuck in the elevator.

"Did you know about all this?" Shadow asked.

"Hey, I am as shocked as you are. I had heard stories, but thought they were all rubbish." Maximus replied.

"Here we are, Sir." Mike said, as he opened the door. Delya walked in with Shadow behind her. Mike followed and quietly closed the door behind them.

"Michael, get him some fresh, dry clothes out, please." Delya asked. Shadow looked around his room. To his left was a sitting area with a couch, loveseat and two chairs, which all had purple velvet cushions. There was a fireplace with a television set above it. Behind the chairs was a large window looking out onto the courtyard. There was a desk and chair in front of the windows. The bathroom door was next to a door that led to a closet. There was the servant's quarter door next to that. As he looked to his right, he saw balcony doors next to a four-poster bed, with curtains and a canopy. Another window on the other side of the bed and a door to the next room beside the window. Behind him was the door to the hallway. The ceiling had a light in the center that was spiral shaped. The room had many colors, wooden furniture, and doors. The rug on the floor was fluffy under his feet and complimented the room.

"This place sure doesn't disappoint, does it?" He asked.

"Not at all, my Little Wolf." Delya answered.

"Where are Dad and Joseph?" Shadow asked.

"Joseph is in his room and your father is in ours." She said.

"Thank god, I don't have to stay in a room with him anymore." He thought.

"I know his stench and attitude was cramping my style." Maximus said.

"Well Dear, if you need anything, Michael is just a knock away, on that door." Delya said as she pointed to the servant's door.

"Ok Mum. Thanks. By the way, what is going on? Why are we here?" He asked.

"You get cleaned up and I will go get the other heads of the Lycan Territories and your father will explain it all." Delya said as she reached up and kissed his cheek.

"Ok mum." Shadow replied. Delya walked out of the room, to the hall and closed the door.

Shadow went into the bathroom to get a shower. He saw that it was a large room. On one side of the sink on the counter, Mike had laid out his clean clothes. His toiletries were on the other side of the sink. He walked over to the walk-in shower, and he observed that Mike had put all the things that he required in the shower stall.

"Ahh yes... I sure did miss Mike being around." He thought as he turned the water on and double checked that the towel was within reaching distance from the shower. He peeled off his clothes, dropped them onto the floor and climbed into the hot shower. It felt amazing on his skin and muscles after the cold rain and cramped carriage ride.

"I soo needed this." He thought.

"You! I was the one out half the night trying to get comfortable on that seat." Maximus replied.

"Yeah, yeah, just enjoy it. Though I hate to wash. I was so close to Panda and I can still smell her scent on my skin." Shadow said. Maximus laughed.

"Yeah, well, the poor girl has been through hell, and even more is coming at her. Best not to think we are going to be crossing any lines, any time soon." Maximus said.

"I know. I feel bad that she has so much on her plate and has to shoulder it all herself." He said.

"Don't worry. She has people to help her. Plus, we have other things to worry about, I fear, from the way Mum was talking." Maximus said.

"Yeah true. I wonder what is going on. God, I hope it is not too bad. I'm beat already." Shadow replied.

"You and me both, but we will sleep good tonight, hopefully. Maybe we will have a peaceful rest of the day?" Maximus said.

"Well, we can hope, but I doubt it." Shadow said, as he heard Mike come in, grab his wet clothes, and walk back out as quietly as he could.

"You better get out before everyone gets here." Maximus said.

"Yeah." Shadow sighed, shutting the water off and grabbing his towel. He dried himself off and looked in the mirror. He fixed his hair and put on his underwear, jeans, and button up shirt. He sighed again.

"Here we go." He thought, as he left the bathroom and headed towards the sofa.

Back To Work

Once I was inside the Palace, I was met by Toby, our medic, and Jeni, my assistant and best friend.

"Thank the Gods you are ok!" Jeni said, relieved. She wrapped me in a warm towel and hugged me tight.

"Yes, Jen. I am fine. Though it was a bit bumpy on the way here. I might take my chances in the tunnels with Warketh the next time." I said with a chuckle.

"Well, by that smile and comment I can tell you are feeling better today." Toby said. "Yes, I am Toby. Thank you very much for tending to me last night. I appreciate it." I said.

"Not a problem. It was my pleasure. We couldn't have you all out of sorts, you know." He replied with a wink. I smiled and nodded as I saw Mrs. Blackthorn in the side room.

"Excuse me all, I need to let Mrs. Blackthorn know we are here. I will meet you by the stairs." I said, as I headed to the side room with the large fireplace and big windows. Mrs. Delya Blackthorn was pacing back and forth, and worry was all over her face. "Mrs. Blackthorn…" I said, somewhat quietly so as not to startle her too much. She stopped and turned towards me. As she did, a big smile came across her face.

"Yes, my dear niece, and Princess." She said.

"I just wanted to let you know we got here safe, and Shadow should be in soon. Thank you for letting him ride with us here." I said with a smile. Relief washed over her.

"Oh good. It was no problem, Dear. I am glad you are all here safe and sound." Delya replied.

"See you soon, Aunt Delya. I must get cleaned up and go see my father." I said as I started to walk away, I saw her smile get even bigger.

"See you soon, My Dear Niece." She called from behind me. I made my way quickly across the hall to the stairs.

"Do you need me anymore Miss Jassy?" Toby asked.

"No. Thank you Toby. Please get back to those in need. I am good." I said as I walked up the stairs with Jeni and Joshua behind me.

"Josh, where is Logan?" I asked.

"He just radioed me and told me he is headed to the barracks to get control of things. Your uncle has had control and is knee deep in problems." Josh replied.

"Oh, Sweet Baby Jesus! Why can't he stick to what he knows, which is gathering intel?" I said, shaking my head. "Ok. Well, please let Dad know I am here and will be in as soon as possible. I must clean up and change." I said.

"On it." Josh replied.

Jeni and I continued down several passageways to get to my wing in the back of the Palace. On our way a strong gust of wind came through the archway. I stopped for a moment, suddenly feeling uneasy.

"Are you ok, Jas?" Jeni asked. I shook my head.

"Yeah. Fine I think?" I kept walking but the feeling that something was wrong kept nagging me.

"It is so wonderful to be home again. I have missed this old place, ya know?" Jeni commented. I nodded trying to figure out what was going on.

"Kita, do you feel that too?" I asked. Kita is my wolf, and she knew more and sensed more than I did, or so it seemed.

"Yes, something is amiss." She replied.

"Well, here we are. At least this place is still intact. Jassy, what is wrong?" Jeni said as we reached my bedroom door.

Josh was there at the door already.

"Josh, go get Kye for me, please!" I said with urgency in my voice. Josh's smile faded as he heard my words.

"Right away." He said as he sprinted to find him.

"I guess it's a good thing I laid out your fighting clothes then. By the sounds you are going to need them." Jeni said.

"Possibly. Thank the Gods. I don't think I could have done another day in a dress." I said as I entered my room. I had been wearing gowns and dresses most of the time on the mainland. I preferred pants like my sister, Lady. Most of my life, here at the Secret Palace, I trained and ran around the island and dresses were not that practical to wear here.

My room looked much different than the one at the Autumn Palace. In this room there was a door to a sitting area to the left, the bathroom and closet doors were to the right. Straight ahead was an open bedroom with double doors that led onto a balcony. My bed hung in the middle of the room. Scattered around the room were many bookshelves containing books and trinkets. A full-length mirror sat in the corner, near the vanity, and in the north corner was my magic room that contained my altar. I stopped and took a deep, relaxing breath. All the doors were open, and I could see the waterfall outside that I remembered waking up to when I was young. There was a lagoon below the waterfall, a garden in front of that, and you could access them from my balcony stairway.

Jeni just stared and watched me, as I kept taking deep breaths, with my eyes closed.   "Something   must   be really wrong if you are semi meditating." She commented.

"Yes. I can feel it deep inside. Something is not right." I said as I turned to go back to the closet. Jeni had laid out my black corset, leather pants and boots. I tossed off my sneakers, jeans, and hoodie, which I had traveled in. I grabbed the corset and zipped it up, then I wiggled into the black leather pants. Jeni checked to make sure my laces were tightened properly. I slid on my boots and zipped them up the side. As I went to the mirror, I pulled my long strawberry blond hair into a high ponytail on top of my head and put on my leather arm bracers. As I spritzed myself with perfume and put deodorant on, I looked in the mirror. This was the reflection I knew, and who I was. I am a warrior.

"I have to say, I like this side of you." Kita said as she looked through my eyes.

"It is time to get down to business and I have no time for games. So, you better be ready to work, got it?" I told her.

"Understood. Together we will kick ass and take names." Kita said.

"Good girl." I said as I turned and nodded to Jeni that I was ready to leave.

I walked back down the hallway with Jeni following close behind. Josh heard my boots on the floor coming near the door and opened it for me. As I walked out, I saw him, all eight feet of him, shrouded in darkness and shadows. I gave him a smirk as the red hues of his eyes appeared out from under his black hood, that covered his long, black hair with white highlights. His cape hung down his lean and muscular body. His body adorned with all black leather armor and boots to match. He had a katana hanging on his left hip, and multiple knives hidden throughout his armor. You would never know what he truly looked like under all that darkness unless you knew him well. This was our top of the top, best of the best, Secret Service Agent, mercenary, and assassin, Kyerus Leviathan Graves, "Kye" for short. He could be anything you need him to be. He taught me most of what I knew about fighting, honor, loyalty, and respect, as well as love.

"Well, I know you didn't send for me just to look at me." His gruff voice came from the darkness under the hood.

"Hello Uncle Kye." I said as Kye sighed in irritation. "And no, I did not call just to look at you. I have an assignment for you." I continued. "I need you to make sure everyone made it here safely, especially my sisters." I commanded and looked at him.

"Just when did I become the errand boy?" He said sarcastically.

"You aren't, but I feel that something is not right. One

of the Royals may be in trouble, and you know that easing my mind will stop me from being a whine ass during training." I said smirking at him.

"Ahhh. Well, if that is the case, then consider it done." Kye said as he vanished.

Jeni shivered.

"I am not gonna lie. When he leaves like that, it gives me the creeps." She said as she looked around.

"I can't believe you are still not used to that yet, Jen." I said shaking my head.

"Not sure I ever will be." Jeni replied.

"Well, either way, I need to meet with my father. So, I will catch you later." I said hugging her.

"OK. Be careful Jassy." She said as she hugged me back.

"Always." I said smiling and turned to Josh.

"Dad still in the office?" I asked.

"I believe so. Let me check with Ahz." He said.

"Oh, he is awake. Is he ok?" I asked.

"Yeah, he is all good. He was helping with the storm earlier." Josh said as we started to walk towards the office. Josh picked up his walkie talkie. "Josh to Ahzreal, over." He said.   "What is it? Over." Ahz replied.

"Is the DP still in the oval? Over." Josh replied.

"Yes, he is. Over." He replied.

"Ok I am in route with the LP. Over." Josh said.

"Ten four, over and out." Ahz said.

I sighed some.

"I do not miss using those damned things." I said as we

picked up our pace.

"Yeah, well, not all of us can mind link. Plus, even if we could, can you imagine how confusing that would be, and loud." Josh said as he thought about it.

"Ok, fair point, but sometimes it is easier." I said with a smile.

"That is true." Josh said. We continued to chat quietly as we made our way over to the right side of the Palace, gently jogging, as we used to do. Once we arrived at the large oak doors, Ahzreal and Nolan, my father's other top guard, were there. I smiled at Nolan, he nodded as he looked down at me with a smile. Nolan is eight feet, six inches tall with medium length brown hair swept to one side with it shaved underneath. He has wide set hazel eyes that sat on either side of his broad nose. He has a milk chocolate complexion. He is a demon-lycan hybrid which we usually called a hell hound. He is very muscular, with broad shoulders.

"Good to see you are up and around." I said, as I looked up at Ahz.

"Thanks, I heal fast, so it was not an issue." Ahz said.

"Ok, well thanks for saving us from being toast." I said. Ahz raised his eyebrows.

"You know there are other ways to thank me then just saying it." He said with a wink. I rolled my eyes.

"Keep dreaming, Ahzreal." Josh said as Nolan opened the door for me.

"Exactly." I said as I high-fived Josh and walked through the door. I heard my father on the phone and stopped in the entry way, I glanced behind me as I looked at Ahzreal. He winked again. I thought *Did Ahz get taller?*

Doceo sat at his desk and was chatting on a video call with his brother, Vex, and brother-in-law, John Blackthorn. I turned around and started to study my surroundings, taking it all in again. The walls were lined with books on both sides of the room. Looking to the left side of the room, amid the bookshelves were a set of doors that were open to the balcony. Beside the doors were more bookshelves, his desk in the corner, facing the center of the room. Followed by a window, a painting, and another set of balcony doors. More bookshelves, a fireplace with a picture of my sisters, father, and I, above it and a sitting area in front of the fireplace. Past the fireplace were more bookshelves, the bathroom door, the bar, and the door to the office.

I took a deep breath as he waved me in. I walked in and took a seat in front of him at the desk as he ended the call. He leaned back in his chair and pressed the bridge of his nose between his thumb and first finger. I waited a moment until he looked at me.

"So how bad is it?" I asked quietly, not sure what to expect.

"It's a God damned shit show!" He replied as he raised his voice and hit the desk. I sat up straighter in my chair. I had only ever seen him this mad a few times and I knew better than to be a smart ass at this point or ask any other questions now. Silence filled the room as I walked over to the bar poured a shot of vodka for myself and downed it. I grabbed a whiskey glass and poured him a glass of straight whiskey over ice. I crossed the room and set it on the desk. Then I sat back in the chair. He looked at the glass and then at me, sighing. "I'm sorry, Sweetie. I have been dealing with a lot so far today." He said tiredly.

"I kind of figured that much, Dad. So, what is going on?" I asked cautiously. He took a long swig of his drink.

"Well, it's not good. It's nothing I didn't think would happen. But I had hoped not." He said. I nodded and continued to listen as he finished his drink. "Thank you for that, Sweetie." He said as he loosened his tie. "It seems your mother and Marcus, along with some 50 or so other inmates on death row, escaped last night. The Bacimortes helped them do so. It is rumored they have and are continuing to build, an army to take over the whole of Avedonia." I sat back in my chair, stunned.

"You mean it was not just revenge on me?" I asked.

"It appears not, my Little Monkey. You are merely a part of this twisted puzzle we must figure out." He replied. "And that God damned brother of mine doesn't have the sense the Gods gave to a bedbug." Huffing as he rubbed his forehead again.

I stood up and looked out the window.

"Oh no! It is worse than I thought." I said to myself as a tear ran down my face. I felt sudden pain in many different places in my body, all at once. It felt like an unseen force was beating me up and I couldn't stop it.

"What is wrong, my Little Monkey?" He asked as I looked at him. He came over to me and took me in his arms. More tears came faster.

"What is going on Kita?!" I said as more and more pain hit me almost doubling me over.

"I don't know. It has to be a spell or something." Kita yowled in pain. Doceo lifted my chin as he held me.

"It's ok. You don't have to do all this on your own. We have plenty of people behind us and we will beat her. You are not queen yet, my Little Monkey." He said. "Plus, you are more than qualified for this. You not only have trained your whole life for this, run, and worked in the Secret

Service with your uncle." He said. Looking in my eye he saw the pain coming out of me as the tears poured down my face.

"Jassy, talk to me!" He said as fear rose in his throat. "What is wrong?" He asked. I tried to answer but I couldn't, I felt as though I was being choked as my vision blurred. I no longer could see my father anymore and a different creature appeared in front of me with his clawed hands around my neck.

Doc started to raise his voice as I started to turn red. "Jassy, Jassy! What is wrong?!" He asked as he checked my throat, and nothing was there. "Joshua! Ahzreal! Get in here!" He yelled. They looked at me choking and turning white.

"Dimiserunt eam mane!" Ahzreal yelled as I gasped and coughed, the image of the thing in front of me let go and flew towards the open door. I could see everyone in the room again, as Josh went to the bar to get some water and my color started to return.

"What the hell was that?!" Doceo asked as he looked at them, then at me.

"Are you ok, Sweetie?" He asked. Joshua came over with a pitcher of ice water and glass. "Ahz do you know what that was?" Doc asked.

"Who?!" I croaked as I looked at Ahzreal. As Josh handed me the glass. I took the glass from Josh and nodded my thanks. Doceo and Joshua looked between me and Ahzreal as we locked eyes.

"Did you feel more pain than just the choking?" Ahz asked.

"Yes! Who?!" I asked again. He shook his head.

"Damned that wretched bitch of a witch." Ahz said as

his eyes started to glow. "Where is my brother?" Ahz asked. Josh and I looked confused.

"I am not sure where Kye is. I can send for him." Doceo said.

"No, he is on a mission for me." I croaked out.

"Oh, where did you send him?" Doceo asked as he helped me to the chair, and I continued to drink the water.

"I had a bad feeling that something was wrong on the way to my room. I did a small meditation on it, and it got worse. So, I asked Kye to check to make sure everyone was here so I would not be distracted during training." I explained, as I gulped more water to soothe my burning throat. "He agreed and that is where he is." I finished and took the pitcher from Joshua and started drinking quickly from the pitcher.

"Is your throat burning?" Ahz asked.

"Yes, it feels like it is on fire" I said as I started drinking again.

"It can't be. We banished that fucker!" Ahz said.

"Oh no. Please tell me you are not talking about your sperm doner?" Doceo said. Ahz looked at him and nodded slightly.

"Monkey, did you see who was doing this to you?" Doceo asked. I nodded yes. "Ahzreal, find a picture of him and your family. Nolan, you help him. Then meet us in the war room. Joshua, you stay with us." Doceo ordered.

"Yes, Sir." They said.

"The… the war room?!" I croaked as I was sucking on ice that was in the water.

"Yes, my Little Monkey. Like it or not this is war,

anyway you look at it, whether it be Aldiun, your mother, or both. We must stop it!" He replied with a dark look on his face. I looked back at him, and he could see in my eyes that I agreed, and I supported him. "Let's get down there. There is a lot to be done." Doceo said as I stood up and we, all three, headed down to the war room. I hoped I would never have to see the inside of the infamous war room, but it was inevitable now.

Wolf Pine, Conriston and Oakheart

Shadow sat on the sofa and found it to be quite comfortable. As he waited for his family and the other Heads of the Lycan Territories, he started to dose off. He had just drifted off when the door across the room from him opened and his mother, Delya, brother, Joseph, and father, John, walked in. Shadow jumped as they woke him.

"Sorry to wake you, Son." Delya said as she came in and sat beside him.

"No worries, Mom. I was just catching a nap while I waited. It was a long night." He said as he stretched to wake up.

"We would have been here sooner, but your father was on a call with your Uncle Doc." She said as she fixed the few hairs on Shadows head that were not in the right place.

"Joseph, sit with your mother and brother, please. The others will be here soon." John said as he came in behind his wife and son. Joseph nodded and sat on the couch on the other side of his mother.

"I wish he would just tell us already the suspense is killing me." Joseph said.

"Soon we all will know. Be patient." Delya replied as she grabbed both boys' hands to brace herself for the incoming news.

A knock was heard at the hall door and John opened it. It was Jim and Athena Valkryrie. They were not only Shadow's grandparents, but also the leaders of the Conriston Territory and the previous leaders of all the Lycan nations. Jim came in first, hugged John, nodded and made his way towards Shadow, Delya and Joseph. Shadow could see that he was not his usual self today. He seemed preoccupied with other things.

"Are you all ok?" Jim asked as he looked at his daughter and grandchildren.

"Yes, father we are all in one piece. How are you?" Delya replied.

"We are well. We made it here just fine, Honey." Jim said as he patted Shadow on the shoulder and sat down in the chair near him. Jim looked to his wife, Athena, who was a bit smaller in stature, being only five foot, seven inches tall. Her long brown hair fell over her small frame and shoulders. She came in the room and hugged John, then she fixed her big green eyes on her family. Looking them all over to make sure they were ok. Her deep tan skin showed the creases of age and a few scars here and there. She wore a deep brown leather dress that hung from her right shoulder, leaving just her hair covering her left shoulder. Across the breast area, a top of solid cloth, with fringe and bead work. The dress came to her knees and had fringe at the bottom. Her feet were simply wrapped in tanned, leather looking sandals. She smiled at the boys and her daughter, who stood, and in turn, hugged her and kissed her cheek. Athena then took the chair next to her husband and fixed her large green eyes on her son-in-law by the door.

Right behind them was Matoskah Arrowheart. He was the same height as Athena, but his skin was a deeper brown than hers. He had long, black hair that was braided into two braids that hung over his broad muscular shoulders. He had brown, shallow set, wide, almond shaped eyes that peered out over his cheek bones. He had a broad nose that came to a slight point at the tip. His mouth is strong and stern with full lips and a round face. Around his neck hung a bear claw. He wore a vest with some beads and embroidery on it. His leather pants also had fringe with beads on them.

As he came in, he hugged John and nodded to everyone else as he sat on the love seat. Matoskah ran the Oakheart Territory with his wife, Aponi. She came in quietly behind him and hugged John also. She had a smaller frame, like Shadow's mother, Delya. Aponi is a little shorter though, at only five foot, five inches, with a reddish-brown tone to her skin. She had heavy, creased, dark brown, almond shaped eyes that peer out over her high cheekbones. Her nose had a slight bend in it with broadened nostrils. Her mouth was delicate with full, well-proportioned lips and a strong jaw. Her long, black hair hung down onto her shoulders with eagle feathers hanging in it. She had on a linen embroidered shirt and turquois beaded necklace with a tanned hide skirt, a belt and some leather moccasins that had fringe and beading. She smiled and nodded at everyone and sat down next to her husband.

John shut the door quietly, as everyone watched him. The room was eerily quiet while everyone waited for the update on what was going on. John stood in front of everyone and cleared his throat.

"Brothers and Sisters. I thank you for coming so quickly. Is everyone ok? Was anyone hurt?" John asked looking around.

"We are all well here." Matoskah said as he placed his arm around Aponi's shoulders and pulled her a bit closer. John nodded and looked at his in-laws.

"We are fine, as long as you and the family are OK." Jim said.

"We are all well. No need for worry here." John replied.

"I am glad we all have made it ok. Next, I will address the recent events. I have been speaking with my brother, Doceo, and he has informed me that Luna has escaped the prison as has Jasmica's attacker, Marcus, along with quite a few other criminals. The Bacimortes have assisted them in this. Luna has raised, and is continuing to raise, an army to take over all Avedonia." John paused as he saw many emotions rolling across the faces in the room. Delya grew paler as she was aware of what he was about to ask. John took a drink of water as Delya squeezed Shadow's hand tighter. Noticing this, he squeezed his mother's hand back and patted it gently, trying to comfort her.

"This cannot be a good thing." He thought.

"No! not at all." Maximus said.

"Luna is declaring war on us all. Upon coming here to negotiate a peace pact between us all, this could not have come at a worse time. So, I hate to ask you this, but I must. Where do we stand on this? Are we to stand by neutral? Or do we show loyalty to our brother and sister Avedon, and fight, as we did long before the war between the Elves, Vampires and Lycans?" John asked as he looked around the now silent room. John turned and gazed into the fireplace and gave everyone time to think.

Shadow looked around the room. He saw that people's eyes were closed or glazed over. He mind-linked his mother, Delya.

"Mom, what is going on?" He asked.

"The others are communicating with their wolves and nations, my Little Wolf." She said. *"Going to war is a big deal and we all must agree, or it will create a great divide in our people. Agreeing on what we will fight for will make us a cohesive unit."* She finished.

"Oh, OK. Makes sense. Thank you." He said as he unlinked from his mother.

"Are you ok?" Maximus asked. *"You seem rattled by all this."*

"I am just a bit shocked. I did not think, in my wildest dreams, things would be this bad." Shadow responded.

"I agree it is bad, but if we side with Avedonia, then we have the best chance." Maximus said.

"I agree, but my worry is that I did not know some of these beings even existed. How am I supposed to fight against them." Shadow contested with some fear creeping in.

"Well, you will learn these wars are not fought like the one we have recently fought in. There is a lot of training. The battles are bigger, longer, and not as sporadic. Many more parish in these types of wars. But there is much more at stake too. In the end, remember, do not get overwhelmed. The Gods do not give us more then we can handle." Maximus said.

Shadow nodded and could hear something, quietly at

first then gaining volume. It was drums and rattles. They grew louder and voices joined in. He looked around and no one else seemed to hear it or notice it. Shadow got up and went to the window and looked out onto the courtyard to see if he could identify where it was coming from. Below he could see warriors dancing, drumming, and singing around what looked like a fire. He could hardly believe his eyes. These men were dressed for war. He watched in awe. He had never seen such elaborate war paint and outfits, on his people. John heard this as well and walked over to his son.

"Can you see that too, Dad?" Shadow asked quietly.

"Of course, I can, Son. Those are our ancestors." John said as he patted his son on the back.

"Is this how they always send you messages?" Shadow asked.

"Not always. It is usually more subtle than this, but apparently, we are in the right place, where we should be, according to the ancestors." John said as he closed his eyes and gave thanks to the Gods and their ancestors. The music, dancers and singing then stopped and faded away.

When John and Shadow turned around, all eyes were on them. John took a deep breath   "What say you brother, Matoskah?" John asked, looking at him.

"We fight with our brothers and sisters here and protect our homes." Matoskah said proudly.

"Sister Aponi, what do you say?" John asked.

"I agree with my husband. We will fight to the death if we must, for Avedonia." She said.   "Brother   Jim?" John said.

"We will rain down hell's fury on them. You know I will support your decision, my son, as will your mother."

Jim said speaking for himself and his wife Athena. John nodded.

"Then it is settled. We shall fight alongside brother Doceo and sister Alice and defend Avedonia. Off to the war room!" John said as he crossed the room and opened the door. A loud cry was heard from all, as they headed out of the room, following John toward the war room.

Azmarin, Glenarm, Eelry

Exiting at the side of the Palace, Athena and Dior Orijeon heard the war cry as they headed out to the gazebo to meet with all the Royal Elves. A slight smile crossed their lips.

"I am guessing by that cry; they have made the decision to join us." Athena said quietly. "I would say so. That is what I remember hearing long ago when they joined us to defend Avedonia." Dior replied as they continued their walk to the large gazebo just in front of the tree line. Once there, Akasha said a few words and a round wooden table with six high backed wooden chairs magically appeared. A dark, green tablecloth with gold embroidery appeared on the table. There were dark green cushions on the seats of the chairs. Candles, a pitcher of water and wine, with six water and six wine glasses, sat in the center of the table.

Dior pulled out a chair for his wife, Akasha, and guided it in as she sat. Akasha and Dior were not only Luna's parents and Jasmica's grandparents, but also the head leaders of all the Elven people. They specifically maintained the Azmarin Territory. They were highly respected and were very ashamed of what their daughter, Luna, had unknowingly become. She was now a stranger, and their enemy, therefore they would have to treat her as such.

Dior took a deep breath as he sat his six-foot, six inch muscular but lanky frame, covered in blue robes and leggings, into the chair by his wife. He had long, honey blonde hair from which his elongated, pointy ears stuck out from the sides. His slightly slanted blue eyes looked out over high cheek bones. He had a straight, pointed nose, with a thinner upper lip and fuller bottom one. His oval face had a strong jaw line which shown more prominent by the stern look on his face.

"I still can't believe we are in this predicament with our own daughter." Akasha said quietly.

"I know my love, but it is true. She is not our daughter anymore. She has become someone and something that is foreign to us now. We did the best we could. She was always a troublesome young one. We cannot blame ourselves anymore. We must now worry about our people and the safety of everyone." Dior said as he gently rubbed his wife's back. She nodded as she took a deep breath to compose herself.

Soon a muscular man of five feet, six inches stood in the doorway to the gazebo. He had a green, short sleeved top on with brown leggings and boots that came over his large calves. His long, green cape hung from his shoulders and gloves covered his hands. His brown hair was shoulder length and flopped over to expose the shaved side of his head. This showed off his slightly shorter pointed ears. His honey-colored eyes peered out over high cheek bones and a broader nose that sloped up. He had a square jaw and full lips that usually were curled into a smile, although today, they were not. His name is Triandal Asair, along with his wife, Morgana, they ran the Glenarm Territory.

Triandal waited quietly until Dior saw him.

"Come on in, Trian." Dior said. Akasha gave him a slight smile but remained quiet. Triandal sat next to his brother-in-law, Dior.

"Is my sister coming?" Dior asked.

"Yes… Yes, she will be down in a moment. I believe she was fixing her hair when I left." Triandal said as he rolled his eyes. Dior sighed and rolled his eyes also. Just then a breeze blew through the gazebo, stirring the leaves. Hovering in the doorway was a six-foot, one-inch-tall woman with long, curly, bright red hair that fell midway down her back. She landed on the step and looked at them with her big blue eyes.

"She always has to make an entrance, doesn't she?" Akasha said with a smile.

"Yup." Triandal said.

"She is my sister. What do you expect, Dear?" Dior said. Her full red lips sat perfectly on her heart-shaped face and under her pointed nose.

"Come on in, Morgan." Akasha said. Morgana glided into the room and sat next to her husband, Triandal, before he could get up to pull out her chair. Morgana poured herself a glass of water.

"Would anyone else care for some?" She asked. The others at the table shook their heads no. She sat back in her chair quietly as they waited on the last two to arrive.

Dior looked up and there he could see two elves running across the side yard as fast as they could. Dior chuckled at seeing this. In front was the woman. She was five-feet tall. Her long blonde braids flew out behind her as she ran as fast as her little legs could take her. She was a bit stocky, though you could not tell from her purple robes unless you were looking at her leggings. Once she got to the gazebo she was huffing and puffing as she waited to be invited to sit at the table. Dior met her large purple eyes and smiled. She had a round face with chubby cheeks that were now scarlet in color. Her braids now settled, hanging behind her, were down to her waist.   "Lilith. Were you and Ruban racing again?" Morgana asked.

"Yes ma'am. But I got him today! I Won! Finally, victory is mine!" She proclaimed excitedly. Dior chuckled and shook his head at his sister-in-law.

"Well, how about you come take a load off here and have some water, Sis. You have more than earned it today." He said and Akasha nodded with a smile.

"Thank you very much." She said as she came in and sat by her sister-in-law Akasha. Morgana gave her a glass of water and sat back in her chair. "Thank you, Morgan." Lilith replied.

"You are welcome Lily, and congratulations on your win today. Though I hardly think it is the time for games." Morgana replied.

"Come now, Dear. A little fun is what we all need in these times when things are so tense." Triandal said smiling.

"Indeed, we all have our own ways of relaxing, Dear Sister." Akasha said.

"I guess you are right. I never really thought about it that way. I am sorry Lily." Morgana apologized.

"It's no big deal, Morgan. No worries at all." Lily said smiling as she finished her water.

"I am coming!" A low gruff voice called out. "Don't start without me!" He yelled as he chugged across the yard. A stocky man of five feet, five inches came trudging up onto the step and waited in the doorway. Beads of sweat pooled up on his brow. If it were not for his dark, sooty colored skin, you would see his cheeks beaming red. He has long, shoulder length, white hair, and a long beard to match that fell over his little round belly. His red eyes shone brightly behind his glasses, which he removed to wipe them off. If it were not for his pointed ears and skin tone, you may have thought he was Santa Claus in his red robes. "Oh! Goodness that was a run!" He said as he huffed and puffed.

"Come on in brother." Akasha said with a smile.

"Thank you, Sis." He said as he sat in between his wife, Lilith, and sister-in-law, Morgana.

"I see Lily beat you today." Dior said.

"Yeah, well, she cheated, but yes, she did." Ruben answered his brother.

"I did no such thing, you old son of a gun." Lilith replied.

"You did too. You got a head start." Ruben said.

"Ok, maybe a little one, but it is still a win, so pay up, buster." Lilith said as she pointed to her cheek. Ruben chuckled and kissed her cheek. Everyone gave a bit of a chuckle watching them. Lilith and Ruben Faemenor ran the Eelry Territory together and were quite playful at times.

Morgana gave Ruben a glass of water while Triandal poured the wine. Once everyone had their wine and was seated again, Dior decided he had better start this meeting.

"Well, I think we all could have figured this would happen." He said pausing, as everyone looked down.

"I take it Luna escaped and went after the Princess again." Lilith replied.

"It's worse than that, Lily. She is trying to take over all Avedonia with the help of those monsters." Akasha said.

"Akasha!" Morgana scolded.

"Well, she is not wrong. The Bacimortes are monsters. You have heard them all undermining the Dark Prince for years now." Ruban angrily replied.

"So does that mean I should turn my back on my poor brain washed niece?" Morgana asked.

"She was not brainwashed when she tried to take out Queen Alice, now was she?" Triandal said.

"Well, no, I would say not." Morgana replied.

"Then I highly doubt she is now. She wants power and is not the girl we knew and raised. We have lost that young innocent child, long ago, if we ever had her at all." Akasha said trying to hide her pain. Tears ran down Morgana's cheeks.

"Do you mean she…" Morgana replied slowly.

"Yes, I am afraid so my, Dear Sister. She manipulated and lied to us all, for a very, very long time." Dior said quietly, swallowing hard.

"So, we must treat her as we would any other threat to our people, home and country." Triandal said.

"Are you all sure?" Morgana asked.

"Yes." Ruben said shaking his head.

"Yes." Lilith said, closing her eyes.

"Yes." Akasha said, looking to her husband.

"Yes, we must." Dior confirmed.

Morgana sat back in her chair and took a large sip of her wine.

"This has been hell for us all. We have not only had to condemn her to death, but now we must go to war against her or with her." Dior said.

"I am with Avedonia and the Dark Prince. I will not leave the man who I have helped raise and think of as my son." Akasha said with conviction.

"Nor will I." Dior agreed with her. "You all are free to make your choice as you see fit for your people." Dior finished.

"I am with you brother. We will have our warriors en route as soon as possible. Right, Honey?" Triandal asked, looking to his wife.

"As I have now seen the truth. I agree with my husband and side with Avedonia." Morgana said.

"I have my allegiance to you all as well as the Dark Prince, but I must follow what my husband decides." Lilith said as she looked at Ruben. Ruben sat for a moment thinking it over as he cleaned his glasses quietly.

"That is understandable, Lily." Akasha said as they all waited for Ruben to decide. Ruben thought carefully, weighing his options. He knew the consequences if either side lost. He also thought how much his people suffered under his niece, Luna's, rule when her parents were out of town. She was rotten to the core.

"Well, I have made a decision." Ruben said finally. Everyone looked at him and waited, holding their breath.

"We shall join...you all of course." He said with a smile. "Did you all really think I would join them?" Ruben said chuckling.

"Well, we would hope not, but you know, times like this can change a person." Dior replied.

"Naw. I've been with you all way too long to trade on you now. Besides it was nice to see you all sweat for once." Ruben chuckled.

"Ohh, you little..." Morgana stopped and punched him playfully in the arm.

"Then let it be said and done. We are to inform our people that we are to join the war and fight for Avedonia." Dior said as he raised his glass. They all toasted and drank their glasses of wine.

"Send out your best and fastest messengers to your Territories to let them know the decision and gather the troops. We will all meet in the war room." Akasha said as they all nodded and stood. The table, chairs, and table accessories all magically disappeared, as all the Elves left the gazebo to do what they must, to get the news out before they reconvened in the war room.

TIRION

Meanwhile, across the Secret Island, in the Territory of Tirion, an elderly guard of five feet, nine inches, limped into the best run he could. He ran down the elaborate, yet congested hallway, to the throne room. His long white hair, with streaks of gray, trailing behind him as he burst through the doors. There were four, high backed chairs, two larger than the other two, with red and gold trimmed cushions. The room itself was surrounded by windows with a balcony around the top, adorned with many banners of all the Territories.

In one of the smaller chairs, a tall, shirtless, muscular man with piercing black eyes glared at the guard as he was surrounded by what some would have called, his harem.

"Excuse me, Your Grace." The guard spoke quickly as he almost threw himself on the floor to bow.

"Gerard! What is the meaning of this?!" The man said

glaring at the guard.

"I have urgent, important news and documents that you all must receive." Gerard said unsteadily, as he trembled just hearing the anger in the other man's voice. The man in the chair stood up. His six-foot, six-inch lengthy, muscular frame towered over Gerard, who was still kneeling. The man's long slender finger tucked his fine dark brown hair behind his pointed ears as he stared down at him. He raised a perfectly arched eyebrow, as he heard Gerard's words and rubbed his strong pointed jaw carefully. He turned and snatched his shirt off the back of the chair he was sitting in. The women's faces grew annoyed and disappointed as the man replaced his shirt.

"This better be worth it or you will pay for ruining my day, peasant." The man hissed. "Yes, it is of great importance, Your Majesty." Gerard said.

"Just breathe G. It will be ok. Prince Raven will get in touch with King Callen soon." Lex, Gerard's wolf said.

"I will mind link my family and get them here." Raven said as he sat back down.

"Ladies, I am sorry, but please retire to my room. I shall be with you all soon, I hope." He said charmingly.

Once all the women left the room, he closed his eyes. Gerard wobbled some as he tried to stay still so he would not be reprimanded.

In another part of the castle, by an indoor pool, was a woman laying on a lounge chair. Her long legs fell on either side of it and an empty bottle of vodka sat on the table next to her. Her big brown eyes shot open as she was linked into the conference.

"What is the meaning of this?! I told you NEVER, to wake me!" She screeched as she sat up in the chair. Her black

hair a knotted mess on her head.

"I am sorry, Mother, but Gerard says he has very important news we all must hear." Raven replied.

"What, did the old bastard break wind and scare himself?" She snottily replied.

"I do not know but he insists we all be here before he tells us."

"Gahh, I will make him pay for ruining my beauty sleep." She fumed.

"Now, my Dear Verona. We must keep our tempers in check." A man's calm voice came through.

"FINE. I will be there in ten minutes and you all best be there ON TIME!" Verona demanded as she unlinked herself from them and stormed off to her room. The man sighed.

"Did your brother accept the link, Raven?" Asked the man.

"NO, of course not. You know how Teagan is. He is probably meditating or something stupid." Raven replied in a snotty tone.

"Ok, I will go get him then. See you soon." The man said as he left the link.

"Of course, you will. You will always go above and beyond for the Golden Child." Raven thought.

"We will show them all one day we are just as worthy, Rave. Don't you worry about that." Razor, Raven's wolf, replied.

"You stay put. I need to go find my brother." Raven said to Gerard as he got up and left the room.

Teagan's father stood up in his room and walked over to the mirror. He stood six foot, three inches tall with broad, muscular shoulders that made his white cotton shirt look tight on him. He had sandy blonde hair that was slightly below his shoulders. It was pulled back into a ponytail. He tucked a piece of his hair, that had come loose from the rest, behind his ear as he looked himself over in the mirror. His blue eyes sparkled like the sea against his tan skin and high cheek bones. He had a rounded nose and rounded jaw with a clef chin. He was a pure Lycan and proud of every bit of it. He had on dark colored pants, and he put a blazer on over his shirt. His name is Callen Ringclaw and he is the leader of Tirion Territory with his wife, Verona, and sons, Teagen and Raven. He took one last look in the mirror as he headed out into the hallway to look for Teagen.

"Hmm. I wonder where he is?" He thought.

"Probably in the garden by the waterfall with the jasmine flowers." Anton, Callens wolf, said.

"Well, it's a place to start." Callen replied as he headed down one elaborate hallway after another.

"Is all this junk necessary in the house?" Anton asked.

"I don't think so, but it keeps Verona off our backs and happy, so we deal with it?" Callen replied as he continued to walk.

"I do not know why you continue to appease her! You don't even like, let alone love, that drunken floozy." Anton replied.

"Easy Anton, she is the mother of our children." Callen said as he was about to approach the garden. Anton huffed and shut off the connection at that moment. *"Of course, he is out in a rainstorm. Why wouldn't he be."* Callen thought as he pulled his coat closed and ventured out into the cold rainstorm.

Sure enough, as he walked up the path, there was his son, Teagen. Those that knew him well called him Tee. Teagen sat shirtless with his legs crossed. He is six feet, one inch tall, with collar length blond hair that is tucked behind his ears. Raindrops are trickling down his muscular, toned, tattooed body, broad shoulders and down his abs. He has a nicely proportioned face with deep set blue eyes that were closed right now, slightly high cheek bones and a rounded nose. His strong jaw line was softened by his blonde goatee which wrapped around his full lips. He sighed as he heard footsteps approaching him.

"You better answer them." Conri, his wolf, said. Teagen sighed again. *"I ignored their call and if they are sending someone to get you, it must be important, Tee."* Conri concluded. As Teagen was about to open his eyes his brother, Raven and his father approached him.

"Oh, please don't tell me he is moping about that little bitch still." Raven said. Teagan's eyes shot open. Before anyone could have tried to grab him, he had closed the distance between himself and his brother and had his hands around Raven's throat.

"You keep your vile fucking mouth shut! If you choose not to, then I will make sure it stays that way indefinitely. I never want to hear you speak of her that way again. Do you understand me?!" Teagen shouted as Raven started to turn red.

"He is not worth it, Son. Let him go." Callen said as he placed his hand on Teagan's shoulder. Teagen took a deep breath and released his brother. Raven coughed trying to catch his breath. Callen reached out his hand to help Raven up. Once he was back on his feet, Raven glared at Teagen.

"Now apologize. Both of you." Callen said looking at the men. Teagen stood with his arms folded saying nothing.

"I will do no such thing. He attacked me!" Raven proclaimed. "If he would just get over her and move on, then he would be fine. There is more than enough beautiful woman around and he thinks he must settle on one." Raven said glaring again at Teagen.

"Listen to me, Raven and listen well. There is only one woman for me and, until she returns, I will never be whole again or at least the same." Teagan replied.

"I don't understand it." Raven replied.

"You will one day, Son." Callen said as he patted his shoulder.

"Now let's get to the throne room before your mother does and she tests my last nerve." He said as he started to walk back to the castle. Teagan and Raven followed their father.

Once they reached the doorway a servant handed them each a towel to dry off with. As they entered the throne room, Callen saw Gerard still kneeling and trembling.

"Jesus Raven! Did you leave him like this?!" Callen asked as he rushed to Gerard's side to help him up.

"He is right where he belongs. The useless old fool." Verona exclaimed as she entered the room. Verona Ringclaw was very well known for her temper tantrums, and dislike for those who she thought were below her in class. She was not a kind woman unless you could help her financially or with her social status. Callen on the other hand was kind, caring and thought of all people as equals. Although his temper was even worse than Verona's, when he finally lost it, but it took a lot for him to lose it.

"That's enough! Gerard and his whole family have been, and continue to be, unwavering in their loyalty and service. You could learn a few things from them." Callen said as he approached his wife and sat on his throne.

"Humph." Verona said as she sat and scowled at Gerard.

"Raven. Apologize to Gerard for your inconsiderate behavior." Callen ordered. Raven stopped in front of Gerard and looked at him with a bit of disgust.

"I am sorry." He spit out and continued to sit on the throne next to his mother where he had been sitting earlier. Teagan sat next to his father with a towel hanging around his neck. The room fell silent for a moment as everyone got settled.

"Well, out with it, you buffoon! I do not have all day for this!" Verona said glaring at Gerard.

"That is enough Verona! You are wearing my patients!" Callen said as he gave her a warning. Verona looked at the wall, pouting like a spoiled child.

"Now Gerard, what is it you must tell us." Callen said.

"Yes sir, there is a messenger from the Main Palace. They informed me that the Royals have returned to the Island." Gerard said.

"Is she with them?!" Conri said happily.

"Which Royals have returned?" Callen asked.

"All of them from all the Territories on the mainland. Also, there are two letters here for you, Sir." Gerard said as he stepped forward to bring them to King Callen. Verona reached for one of the letters and Gerard pulled them back. Verona erupted, stood up, and she struck Gerard across the face, knocking him to the floor.

"You ignorant fool. HOW DARE YOU TAKE THAT AWAY FROM ME!?" She screeched. As she was about to bring her fist down on him, Callen caught it.

"I'm...I'm. Sorry Miss, but I was ordered to give them only to King Callen." Gerard stammered. Callen looked at his wife with fire in his eyes.

"You DO NOT EVER strike anyone in my presence or out of it! You are to act like a lady and not a spoiled brat or an animal! Do you understand me?!" Callen bellowed.

"Ye..yes." Verona replied as she was now pale, with fear in her eyes. She sat back down. Both boys knew their father was near the end of his patience for the day, and the best thing they could do was not to interfere.

Teagan saw the blood on the floor and jumped up.

"Get a chair and medic in here, quickly!" He ordered. He noticed that not only was Gerard bleeding from the scratch on his face from his mother's nails, but also from his forehead. Gerard must have hit it on the floor when he fell. Teagan placed the towel from around his neck on Gerard's forehead.

"You ok G?" Teagan asked as he helped him to the chair that one of the servants had brought over.

"Ye..yes, young Master Tee. Thank you." Gerard said.

"If I could, I would rip that bitch apart." Lex said angerly.

"Calm down this is nothing, Lex." Gerard replied.

Once the medic arrived Teagan picked up the letters and handed them to his father. "Hmm… one is from the Dark Prince. The other from Luna, using her maiden name." Callen said, a bit confused. He read the one from Luna first and his face started to become darker, and his eyes turned a deeper shade of blue. He closed it and read the one from the Dark Prince, Doceo Avedon. His eyes were such a dark blue they looked like the color of the sea during a turbulent storm.

"That ungrateful, manipulative whore!" Callen raged as he stood up and started pacing, trying not to let Anton out.

"How dare she even think she could do this and get away with it!" He continued shouting.

"What is going on?" Teagan asked. Callen took a deep breath.

"Something treasonous!" Callen replied as he took some more deep breaths and sat back down. Everyone looked at him, waiting for an explanation and orders. "Luna has not only tried to kill Queen Alice, but Princess Jasmica, as well!" He said. Teagan and Conri growled in response.

"Is that beast, Alice, still alive?!" Verona asked, shocked.

"She is very much alive and has been returned to us after being put through hell." Callen replied through gritted teeth.

"Pitty, I like Luna much better." Verona replied fanning herself and sticking her nose up in the air.

"Luna is now bringing war upon all of Avedonia!" Callen said with rage building in his voice again. "Let it be known, here and now, we will be siding and defending Avedonia with the Dark Prince!" Callen declared as he stood. Verona cleared her throat.

"You speak for yourself! This warrants discussion. I will be supporting Luna above Doceo and his wife." She said sternly.

"That is, it!" Callen said "I will take no more of your insolence and idiocies! You have gone against me and tested me for the last time, Verona! We are through! Pack your clothing and belongings and get out! I will have the papers sent to you once you get wherever you are going." Callen declared as he turned to walk out.

"But where will I go!?" Verona screeched. Callen turned and leaned down over her and looked in her eyes.

"Frankly, My Dear, I don't give a damn! Go to your precious Luna! Here is the letter with the coordinates. I am sure she will take in someone as loyal as yourself!" He spat out at her as he tossed the letter, and it landed in her lap. Callen spun around. "That also goes for anyone else here and in the Territory. If they wish to support Luna, I will arrange transport for them, and they can go to her!" Callen decreed. "G once you are bandaged up, you get on to spreading the word. We support the Dark Prince of Avedonia. Those who wish not to, shall leave. They cannot stay here." He said. Gerard stood quickly.

"Yes Sir!" He said, saluting as the medic pulled him back down to finish his stitches. Callen nodded and left the room.

Verona, Teagan, and Raven sat in silence.

"Well, I guess you better get packing mother." Raven said.

"Brother, we have a decision to make and must talk about this." Teagan said as he looked at Raven.

"Yes, shall we go to your room? I wish not to speak in front of my ladies." Raven replied. The medic and Gerard stood and walked out of the room quietly.

"Yes, I believe that is the best place. Away from prying ears, so we may speak freely." Teagan said as he stood.

"Aren't either of you going to stand up with me?" Verona asked as she grabbed both her son's arms. Raven looked down at her... patting her hand.

"We will see mother. Now go and pack." Raven said as he pulled himself loose from her hand. Teagan said nothing and just pulled his arm away from her and walked towards his room. Raven followed him. Verona fell to her knees and whaled like a child.

"Can you believe it. She has returned. I knew she would be back!" Conri rejoiced.

"Calm down, Conri. She is back, yes, but there are other things we must worry about. Plus, she has three mates in total. We do not know if Logan has wormed his way into her heart." Teagan said.

"But that does explain why she has not come here yet." Conri said. Teagan rubbed his chin, thinking as he walked and remembered his mother's words.

"I have got an idea that could give us a big advantage, if Raven is with us." Teagan said with a large grin as he got to his double bedroom doors.

"Your father is in your office." Conri replied.

"Thanks for the heads up." Teagan said as he pushed open the door, holding it for his brother to enter.

Teagan's room was a very Zen, balanced and feng shui place with different Asian influences. It had lounge sofas and pillow piles to sit on in front of the large window that looked out onto a courtyard garden. Split off this room to the right was his office and to the left was his closet and bathroom. Around the back was his bedroom. It was a large square area. The colors seemed to vary depending on which room you were in, but you could not help but be relaxed within the whole of the area.

"I always forget how mellow it is in here. I should really stop by more often and relax." Raven remarked.

"The door is always open. You know that." Teagan said as he closed the door. "Would you like something to drink?" Teagan asked as he moved over to the small built-in bar on the wall.

"A beer would do wonders right now. Especially after what we just witnessed." Raven replied as he relaxed on one of the lounges. Teagan nodded and got Raven a beer and poured himself a whiskey.

"Here you are." Teagan said as he handed the beer to Raven. Raven took it and took a long swig from the bottle.

"Ahh. That's better." Raven said enjoying his beer as Teagan sat on the lounge across from him. Raven looked down and then at his brother. "I am sorry I said those things about Jasmica. I was angry with Mother, and how Dad treats you better than me." Raven said.

"I am sorry I tried to kill you. My temper got away from me." Teagan said. "Well, now that that is out of the way," He picked up the remote, pressed a button to activate the sound proofing of his office, so that his father could not hear them. "Let's talk about this mess we are in here." Teagan finished, taking a sip of his whiskey.

"I take it we have someone trying to eavesdrop?" Raven asked.

"Yeah. What else is new? Just father. He can know when we decide to tell him." Teagan said.

"Can't say as I blame him, after all he has been through with mother." Raven replied, taking another drink.

"Yeah, well I still don't like it." Teagan replied. "Now you know where I am on all this." He continued.

"I know I was surprised you didn't tear out of here when you heard she was back." Raven said with a chuckle.

"It took all I had, not to, but I knew if she had not come here yet and Doceo was sending out notices, something else must be going on. So, I firmly planted myself and tried to pay attention." Teagan said grinning.

"Well, I will not be going to help Luna, that is for damn sure. She only uses people, and she hates half of what I am." Raven said.

"That is good to know as I have a plan that just might help us." Teagan said. Teagan got up and opened the doors to his office. "You can come out now Old Man." Teagan said.

"Who are you calling Old Man?" Callen replied as he came out.

"You, because you are!" Raven said laughing with Teagan.

"Well, this Old Man can still kick your little asses. So don't start with me today." Callen said. "So, what have you both decided upon?" he asked.

"Raven and I are with you father, but I have a plan." Teagan replied.

"Oh?" Callen asked looking at Teagan.

"Well only if Raven is willing. We both have had training and are still in the Secret Service. If we make mother believe Raven is with her, he could spy on Luna and her minions and relay their information to us through his birds. It would put someone on the inside. Not that we will not have more than one person in there, but it gets someone in easy, at the top. He will not have to work his way up the ranks!" Teagan explained and finished his drink. "What do you two think?" He asked.

"That just might work!" Callen said.

"I am game. I am good at lying to people who don't know me, and kissing mothers' ass when I need to." Raven said.

"We will have to run it by Doceo and the others, but I don't see where anyone should have a problem with it. But either way, we should get going to the war room. We have been told to meet there in the letter." Callen said pulling the letter out of his pocket. "I kept it so that your mother would not get ahold of it." He said with a sly smile.

"Good. Let's go then, before we are missed." Raven said. All three men got up and walked out the side door of Teagan's office, down the stairs to the ground below where G met them with their horses. They galloped off into the forest, headed to the Secret Palace and the war room.

RUTHERGLEN

Warketh and Stock were moving quickly through the underground tunnels of the island. The only thing that could be seen was their glowing eyes and the blue glow of their enchanted boots that Akasha gave to them so they could move faster. They came to a three-way split in the tunnel.   "Aye" Warketh said

"What? Ye ol' coot?" Stock asked.

"Which ye be wantin, da Mers or da Cents?" Warketh asked.

"Hmm? Dats a good question der?" Stock said stroking his beard. "Truth be told neither but…" he paused.

"Well, if ye take da Cents ye will be home first ta tell da news to the clan and ye won't be gettin wet." Warketh said trying to convince him. He knew Stock loved to be the first to tell anyone news. Plus, he and Pirereon, the leader of the Centaurs did not get along.

"Aye, I do like da sound of dat. You gots a deal!" Stock said.

"Right, try not to get trampled over or an arrow in yer arse." Warketh said as he chuckled.

"Enjoy ye bath, ye old coot." Stock said.

"Godspeed." Both said at the same time as they parted company.

"I fooled him. We got wet suits now. No bath fer me." Warketh thought with a chuckle.

Stock went to the left, north and started up under the forest hills and meadows. He moved as quick as his shoes could carry him, knowing the message he was carrying was of the upmost importance. After a few more splits in the tunnels and hills, he came to the entrance to the Rutherglen Territory.

"I best fill up me shoes first before I get out dere." Stock thought. He pulled out a glowing blue vial from his pouch. He sat on the floor of the tunnel and took off each shoe and carefully filled them to the top. He had only used one quarter of the magic powder. He knew if he had to run away from or with the Centaurs, he would need all the help his little legs could get. He replaced the cork on the top of the vial and secured it in his pouch. After replacing his boots on his feet, he took a deep breath and pushed open the huge stone doors. He peaked out into the night, noticing the rain had stopped. Slowly he crept out of the door and tried to shut it quietly, but the stone was slippery on this side, and it slipped out of his hands and slammed shut, echoing in the tunnel and throughout the silent forest.

"Oye! I hope dat doesn't alarm anyone." Stock thought. He turned around and waited for the many sounds of the night i.e., crickets, owls, and frogs, to start again. He made

his way through the forest to where the messengers of the Centaurs could be found. He ran through the trees, catching glimpses through the thick canopy of the night sky. As he made his way to a meadow, he saw the moon hanging high in the sky and the stars were like a sparkling blanket across the horizon. He walked out of the trees towards the small pond, cautiously looking around for any signs of the Centaurs.

"Pire... Telephinee" He called out, looking around. "Anybody ear?" He asked. "I gots a message ear for ye from da Dark Prince. Its Urgent!" He called. Just then he heard hooves take off. "Well, I'll wait ear, I guess." Stock said.

Stock waddled over to the pond and cupped some of the cold water in his hands, splashed his face and took a sip of it. "Ahh, I needed dat der." He exclaimed out loud as he listened to the crickets, frogs and owls sing in the clearing. He noticed a good size rock with a flat surface and moved over to where it was. *"Huh. Tis a bit bigger den I thought but I tink I can manage."* He said. He did his best to hoist himself up. "Whoa!" he exclaimed as he lost his grip and fell into the mud. *"Aye, best try it again."* He thought. He jumped with all his might and grabbed on tight, kicking his feet, trying to get himself up and with one final kick, he managed to get on the bolder and sit down. *"Phew, I be needin to get some more exercise."* He thought as he swung his feet over the side. He star gazed while he waited on the Centaurs to come back.

He had just started to dose off when the sound of hooves hitting the ground, as loud as thunder, woke him up. He jumped down from the rock and hid himself between the bolder and his shield. Stock knew that sometimes, when it was slippery, the Centaurs couldn't stop quickly and would slide. He didn't fancy the idea of getting tripped over tonight.

"Whoaaaa!" A strong, loud voice boomed. Stock peaked out from around his shield. He was surrounded by Centaurs, and right in front of him stood Pirereon himself. He was ten feet, six inches tall from head to hooves. His long, medium length, brown hair swayed in the cool nights' breeze. His green eyes sparkled in the torch light that he was holding and popped against his darker complexion. He looked around a bit, his face very stern and well carved like it was made from stone. From his high cheek bones to his pointed nose and strong jaw, that his pointed beard rested upon. He was perfect. His broad muscular shoulders were covered by shoulder plates. A large axe rested on his back and bracers covered his arms. He had some brown chest hair that came down his abs and faded to white where it met his horse half. He is a white palomino horse with gray spots on his hind quarters. He paced with his large Clydesdale-like hooves. Pire, as he was known to his friends, nodded as he saw Stock. The herd behind him parted and up came Pires wife, Telephinphae, known to those close to her as, Telephinee, as many had a hard time pronouncing her proper name.

Telephinee is eight feet, six inches tall from the top of her head to her hooves with a brown body and black socks. She had long curly blonde hair. A flower crown rested on her head and flowers decorated her hair. Her aqua colored eyes, that many would have compared to the color of the sea waters in the Caribbean, peered out over high cheek bones next to her rounded nose and full lips. Shoulder plates covered her delicate but strong shoulders, and leather bracers covered her arms. She wore a corset tank top dress and had a large sword on her back. She was known around the island for her beauty and kindness. She walked slowly up next to her husband and saw Stock. She gave him a warm smile and bent down slightly.

Together Pire and Telephinee ruled the Rutherglen Territory and the Centurion Herds.   "Hello there, Stock. How are you?" Telephinee said.

"I am as well as I can be. How might ye all be?" Stock replied, with a slight bow to them both.

"I am well, thank you." Telephinee replied.

"Ehh. I'm alright. What is it you want Dwarf?" Pire said trying to keep his disdain for the dwarves from showing. Telephinee elbowed Pire and he grunted some.

"Well, I have ear a letter from da Dark Prince." Stock said holding it up and out as high as he could. Telephinee reached down and took the letter carefully from him.

"Thank you, Stock." She said with a smile.

"Bring some light over here," Pire commanded, as two more torches were brought forward. Both Pire and Telephinee read the letter together.

"We shall fight with the Dark Prince. We will assist him with whatever he needs." Pire said as he started to turn towards some of the herd that was behind him. Telephinee nodded.

"We shall see you in the war room, Stock. Thank you for bringing us this news." Telephinee said.

"Twas my pleasure, Miss Telephinee. I will be going now." Stock said.

"Good idea. Godspeed." She said as she waved elegantly.

"Godspeed." Stock replied and scurried out of the clearing and back into the forest.

"It is time to show what we are made of! Men and women of able body, it is time! We are going to war to save our home and Avedonia! Back to the village and light the lanterns to let everyone know in Rutherglen to come together!" Pires' loud voice boomed as the Centaurs cheered and started to circle.

"Let's Ride!" Telephinee exclaimed over the crowd, and they all took off, in a cloud of dust, towards their village to light the lanterns and spread the word. Stock had just made it back to the tunnel entrance, panting heavily, as he closed the door behind him.

"Phew, I made it out in one piece." He thought. He refilled his shoes again, as he knew he had a long trek to get home to the Orrinshire Territory where he, his wife and his clan lived. He took off running again, headed for home, to break the news to the others.

SQUALL END

Back in the tunnel, Warketh ran to the right, South toward the water. He could hear the dripping of water as he got closer to the entrance of Squall End.

"Best be gettin' a patch crew and da metal piping laid down ear soon." He thought, as he kept running. In no time, he came to the tunnel entrance he was looking for. Light shown on his now dirty face as he pressed a button. A large vault door opened to a steel and glass room in which two guards stood at their posts to monitor the room. As he scooted inside, the door closed behind him. Straight ahead was a large glass door that looked out onto the ocean floor. On the wall to his left hung wet suits of many shapes and sizes. To the right were air tanks and other scuba gear, along with the buttons to get out of both doors. His boots echoed in the chamber as they clanged on the grated floor. He scurried over and grabbed his suit off the hanger. Then tramped back across the room, gathering the rest of

his gear and sat it on the bench in the middle of the room. Warketh removed his armor and most of his clothes and boots. He sighed, looking at himself and then to the suit. *"I am not sure dis is gonna work, but if it do… I knows it will not be pretty."* He thought to himself. Warketh slowly started to put one leg into the suite. He felt it getting tighter and tighter as he pulled it up his leg. *"Ok, one in. Now da next."* He thought. He put the other leg in and got it up to his knees. He stood up, wiggling as he worked the suit on like a pair of pantie hose. He almost fell over once, as he struggled to get his arm in. "Damn blasted thing!" He cursed and mumbled as he struggled. Finally, he got the suit on, and it was time to zip it up. "Oh boy." He said as he tried to zip himself up.

"Umm" He grunted. "A lil' elp ear." He asked. One of the guards came over to assist him.

"Ugg, I think ye need a bit of a diet, Sir, or a bigger suit." Said the guard as he struggled to zip up the wet suit. "Suck it in, man!" The guard shouted. Finally, the zipper slid up and Warketh was in.

"Aye, I think I should have had one less sausage and stout for dinner." Warketh said with a chuckle. The guard nodded and wiped his brow. "Thank ya, Son. I got it from ear." He said. The guard went back to his post. Warketh went to put on his flippers, and the rest of his gear. As he started walking towards the end of the room, he caught his flipper on the floor. "Ahhhhh, what da… bastardly flippers…" He grumbled, as he rolled down the room. The guards started to run after him. "Someone! Stop meh!!" Warketh yells. One of the guards was a Drow elf and he used his magic and stopped him.

"Are you ok?" the second guard asked.

"Aye, just a wee bit dizzy." Warketh replied.

"Ye must be careful der sir." The first guard said as he helped Warketh up and checked his equipment.

"Aye." Warketh replied. "Like I meant to do dat and make a damned fool of me self." He said back.

"Well, ye be set to go. Are ye ready?" Asked the first guard.

"Aye" Warketh said as he started to walk again, with the assistance of the second guard who had stopped him.

Once Warketh was in the chamber and both guards were back to their posts, the first guard hit the out button and a loud alarm sounded, signaling the air lock door was being closed on one side and opened on the other. As soon as the first set of doors closed behind him, water started to fill up the enclosure he was in. Once the water was to his chest he checked once more to be sure his helmet was secure and waited till the room was full of water, the doors opened and Warketh swam out. *"Huh, dhat is pretty nice, n dis is much better den trying to hold me breath or use a straw to breathe."* He thought as he grabbed an underwater scooter. He made sure it was fully charged and started off towards the Kingdom of the Merpeople. He raced past many fish and reefs. Soon the underwater Palace, with its wall and the gate that surrounded it, came into view. It looked almost like it was glowing in the moonlight. Soft voices could be heard through the water, humming a quiet lullaby. One of the mermen at the gate swooped in and stopped him.

"What can we do for you, Little Fella?" He asked.

"It be me, Warketh Battleforge! I am no mear lil' fella!" He protested with a tinge of anger in his voice.

"Oh! I am very sorry, Sir! I did not recognize you in your suit. Very fancy." The guard apologized and complimented Warketh.

"Thank ye. It be much easier to travel ear now. Anywho, I got da message from da Dark Prince fer King Sebastian." WarKeth said.

"Ah. OK, follow me then." The guard nodded and Warketh followed him through the gate. Warketh never got over how beautiful this place was with all the brightly colored coral and still brighter fish. Smaller homes made of white stone lined the seashell streets. In the middle of the town was a large stone Palace with many archways and tunnels. In many areas the rooms and tops of the arches looked like large seashells. The Palace rose high up above everything else. The guard and Warketh swam through the large white doors, into the great hall where King Sabastian and Queen Sakura sat so still and quiet, as though they were asleep. The guard cleared his throat.

"Excuse me, Your Majesties. I hate to wake you, but we have an urgent and important visitor from the surface."

King Sebastian yawned and stretched, and bubbles moved around him and tousled his long pink and blue ombre hair. He settled back down onto his throne and his long, shimmery, teal tail and hip fins rested underneath him and the wide flat fins of his tail rested on the ocean floor. Warketh stared at his beauty like he was seeing it for the first time. He was enchanting with his pale, shimmering skin that was almost like glass. He had on a seashell crown and necklace. His trident sat within grabbing distance, as his sea blue eyes settled on Warketh.

A warm smile came across his stone like face.

"Warketh! So good to see you. To what do I owe the pleasure of this late-night call?" Sebastian asked.

"Nice to see ye as well. I do apologize ear for da lateness, but it has taken me a bit to get ear." Warketh replied.

"Is that Mr. Warketh I hear?" A beautiful voice, like a melody from a song, said.

"Yes, Dearest One. He has come to see us." Sebastian said. Next to Sebastian, the woman's dark brown, slanted eyes fluttered. She had long, black hair that extended down to her lower back, just above her pink hip fins. Her long, flowing, pink and purple tail twitched with excitement. Her skin was an olive color which made her green and purple shell top, explode with color. Her face had very delicate features. Her coral crown sat on her head, as a pearl and shell necklace graced her neck and chest. She was an Asian beauty, more beautiful than the cherry blossoms in spring, for which she was named. No man could resist her, even if he wanted to. She smiled sweetly at Warketh.

"Sorry to wake, ye, Miss Sakura." Warketh stammered.

"It is quite alright." She said. Warketh cleared his throat remembering not to look her in the eyes for fear of being bewitched by her.

"I have a letter ear from da Dark Prince." Warketh said as he swam forward holding out the laminated letter to Sebastian.

"Oh! Thank you very much." Sebastian said as he gracefully took it from Warketh.

"This is not good." He said, continuing to read the letter, as he furrowed his brow. "I shall rally the troops and we will meet you at the war room, Warketh. I will not let them fight alone. My loyalty has, and always will be, with the Avedons." Sebastian stated. Sakura nodded faithfully in agreement. She stood by her husband's decisions and never went against him.

"Aye. See you there. Godspeed to ye both." Warketh said as he turned to leave. "Godspeed." The King and

Queen replied. Warketh left the Palace. The singing immediately stopped and large horns began to blow throughout the city. He swam through the gate and headed back towards land so he could return to the Palace and proceed to the war room.

ORRINSHIRE

Stock huffed and puffed and finally made it to the end of the tunnel and the entrance to his own Territory. Orrinshire was under the mountains covering the northern most part of the island. Stock pushed open the large stone door and walked into the large entry way. The hall had many extremely high archways that echoed loudly. He shut the door gently and ran down the stone brick hallway, deeper into the mountains and underground. His heavy footsteps echoed around the chamber. As he ran through the hallways, the torches on the pillars lit magically by themselves. He continued running down deeper in the hallways until he could hear the clang and clank of hammers on metal. The cold underground air started to quickly heat up, the closer he got to the village.

All the village houses were built into the rock walls and floors. Lights twinkled through the oddly shaped holes that were used as windows. Railroad tracks ran down the middle of the village, to the metal factory at the end. The large furnaces not only heated the village area but also made the whole area glow with a reddish tint. In the village, the sound of hammers and drills was even louder. There were young dwarf children running every which way in the streets, as their parents and other adults continued working hard to make their many wares. Upon seeing Stock, the children rushed to him. He patted their heads as he slowed down to walk with them heading towards his house. His home was much the same as the others, just a little bit bigger than most.

"Thompson!" Stock yelled to a guard of the families, "Blow da horn fer a meetin'. I have some important news." Stock said. Bhostok Hammerborn, known as Stock and his wife, Thezzosli, known as Thezzie, ran the Dwarven Clan and Orrinshire. Thezzosli was the daughter of Warketh Battleforge and was his only child. Together, all three made big decisions for the clans.

Hearing her husband outside, Thezzosli came out of the house. Thezzosli was smaller than both her husband and father at only three foot, five inches. She has a stocky build and soot colored skin. Her eyes glowed bright green and were surrounded by a warrior princess tattoo. She had a round button nose and full lips. Her long, brown hair was micro braided, and the color matched the long brown beard on her chin. {Note: Beards on male and female Dwarves was common in the Dwarven Kingdoms. Newcomers and outsiders thought it strange at first but soon became accustomed to it.} She had on a leather dress, with an apron full of jewelry tools and her battle axe strapped on her back.

"Look, Pappa Stock! I gots a chin air today!" One of the children said happily.

"Aye, so ye do! That is a mighty fine one der." Stock

said.

"It's bout time ye got ear." Thezzosli said in a soft yet gruff voice.

"Aye, don't be startin' on meh today. My dogs be barkin and I be runnin all night and most of the mornin." Stock replied.

"Oh, ye better have a good reason." She replied.

"Ok kiddos, I need to be goin in. I'll see ya all soon." Stock said as he headed into the house with Thezzosli. Once he was inside, the horn sounded and echoed throughout the tunnels and village. The sound shook the walls and both Stock and Thezzie vibrated across the floor and fell on top of each other laughing.

"Da never gets ol' does it?" He asked as he chuckled.

"Never ever." Thezzie said wiping her eyes from laughing so hard. Standing up, they heard people gathering out front of their house.

"Welp, time to address mah people." Stock said with a sly smile. Thezzie punched him in the arm.

"Uff.. Now don't ye be gettin' frisky now." Stock said as he winked at her and walked out the front door. She followed him out onto the porch.

Once Stock did a head count, he cleared his throat, and everyone got quiet.

"Thank ye all fer commin'." He said. "I have an announcement fer ye. Da Dark Prince be needin' our assistance. War be a brewin' on da horizon." Stock said as murmurs sounded. "I am ere askin' ye if ya be on board? Or if ye be hidin' like a lil pansies, up in ear?" He asked, looking around. Thezzie went into the house and brought out his chair and placed it on the porch. Stock smiled

"Thank ye, love." He said and kissed her cheek.

"Ye be welcome." She replied. He sat there for about an hour or so. As soon as everyone sat down on the ground, that was the signal to him that they were ready to vote. "Are ye all ready to be votin'?" He asked.

"Aye." Everyone shouted.

"Nay, an we be stayin' ere? Show of hands." He asked. He looked around and no hands or sound were heard. "Yay, we be goin' ta war?" Stock asked and a loud resounding,

"YAY!" Was heard and all hands were raised in the air.

"Tat be da spirit." He said. "I will bring back da list o' things we be needin'. Back to work, ya'll." He replied to the crowd. "Let's be gettin' to da war room, Thezzie. The ol' coot will be mettin' us der." He said. Thezzie nodded and lifted the chair, dropping Stock on the porch, as she brought the chair back inside. He stood up and brushed himself off.

"Guess she's still a bit sore bout me being late." He thought.

"Well, we goin' ore ye just gonna stand der like a lump of coal?" Thezzie asked. "Comin', Dearest." Stock said and they both started to run out of the village then turned Southeast in the direction of the Secret Palace and the war room.

The War Room

Ahzreal and Nolan reached the barracks and headed down the stairs to Ahzreal's quarters. As he opened the door, everything was a mess and covered in dust. There was just room enough to open and close the door.

"I guess they used this place for storage once you disappeared." Nolan said.

"Yeah, I am guessing all my things from the other Palaces are here too." Ahzreal replied looking around. There were at least four beds on the left side of the room. His desks were lined against the back wall. The rest of the room was filled with trunks, boxes, artifacts, and décor that was too big to fit into boxes.

"Well, this should be like looking for a needle in a haystack." Nolan said. "A dusty haystack at that." He said looking around.

"Yeah well, we better get looking. The sooner we find it,

the sooner we are out of here. We need to find my large red trunk." Ahzreal replied.

"Ok, let's get to it." Nolan said.

"You take the left and I'll take the right and we can meet in the middle." Ahz instructed. "Sounds good." Nolan replied as they both set out to start digging through the room.

***

Meanwhile, my neck was now glowing with a red imprint on it from being choked.

"How is your throat doing, Honey?" Doceo asked.

"It's not burning anymore, so that is a plus." I replied.

"That's a plus." He replied.

"She is not croaky anymore either." Josh noted.

"Also, a good thing." Doceo said with a smile. The three of us traveled lower into the Palace until we were at ground level. Doceo walked up to the wall and pressed a stone. It popped out to reveal a button that slid open the door. Once it was open, we walked down a spiral staircase to an underground tunnel that was lit with lights on the walls. We followed it in silence. I did not want to be in this tunnel. I didn't want any of this to happen if I was being honest. I felt the regret building in myself for even leaving the island in the first place.

"It is not your fault, you know." Kita said softly. *"But if I had just stayed here then…"* I replied.

"Then what? You would still be dealing with this, or worse, you would be doing it all alone because she would have harmed your father. And you would not have even met me yet. I do not see how that is any better." Kita replied. I sighed.

"You are right, Kita. I am sorry. I am overwhelmed right now."

I said.

"It's ok. You got a lot of people here to help. We can do it. You told me it is time to work. Did you ever doubt yourself in training?" She asked.

"No." I replied.

"How about when you gave an order to the Secret Service, did you doubt yourself then?" She asked.

"No, not one time." I replied confidently.

"Then don't start now. You know what is right and what you need to do, so do it, and stop doubting yourself. I always have your back and so do a lot of other people." Kita said.

"You are right! Thank you, Kita." I said.

I realized we had made it to the door of the war room. A side panel on the wall popped out and Doceo put in the code. The door rumbled as it opened. We all walked in, and I stopped for a moment. There was a lot of commotion going on. People were all talking at the same time and papers and maps were flying around. The wall to the left of me had maps of all Avedonia with red stick pins in it. Cubicles filled the center portion of the room with people, desks, and computers in them. To the right was a glass wall and behind it was our meeting room. I walked forward and down a cubicle row to the back wall that was full of monitors. Each one had a different scene on them, from news stations to surveillance. As I looked at one of the monitors with live coverage, I noticed it was of Newham. It was under attack and the sight made a tear run down my cheek. The very people we had sworn to protect were being attacked. At that moment it was all real. A fire was lit inside me that had never been lit before. My people were being hurt and they needed me. My father, Doceo, walked up behind me and placed his hand on my shoulder. I wiped the tears from my cheeks and placed my hand on his.

"I swear Father, even if it kills me, I will save and help my people, until my last breath." I said, as I turned, looking up into his eyes. "Luna will not win. I will not let our people suffer under her or because of her." I finished. He smiled and kissed my forehead.

"I know you will not, my Little Monkey. That is why I choose you. Let's go get the reports that have come in and see what we are dealing with." He said in a stern voice. We walked over to the meeting room and through the door. Inside there were groups of tables along the walls for each territory to sit at. In the middle of the room was where Dad and I sat. Across the back wall were more monitors, with a larger screen in the center of them all. Next to that was the water inlet and tank for the Merpeople to enter and participate in the meeting. On the left wall was a large white marker board and in the front of the room, behind our table, was the same map as in the front room, of Avedonia, without the red stick pins.

I took a deep breath and made my way across the room to my seat. Alice and the De Cartiers were already waiting in the room for us. Lucas and Marie De Cartier were pure vampires and had been allies with us longer than anyone could remember.

"I am glad to see you are sticking with us." Doceo said as he stopped by their table to talk with them. He and Lucas shook hands and hugged. Lucas is a little shorter than my father, at six feet, six inches tall with tight, curly dark brown hair. His eyes are black with red flecks in them. He has an oval face with a broad nose and wide nostrils. He has a large mouth with large lips and his skin was black as night itself. He was a handsome man with a muscular build. He had on a dark blue suit with a white shirt and red handkerchief.

"Of course, we are. I could think of no other place my people and I would be, My Friend." Lucas replied.

Maria nodded as she stood and hugged my father after Lucas. Maria is only five foot, five inches tall with long black hair that's straight as string. Her dark brown eyes always seemed to have a sparkle in them. She has a broad nose like her husband. Her mouth is smaller, but she still had very full lips that she always had red lipstick on. She is of an average build and very curvy with a plump behind. She has a lighter skin tone than her husband, but she was still dark complected. She had on her usual business suit, that was black with a red rose on the lapel of the blazar.

I smiled at them and made my way to where Alice sat in the middle of the room staring at the floor. My father continued to chat with Lucas and Maria. As I got closer, Alice looked up at me and a large smile of relief covered her face. She reached out and hugged me tight.

"Oh Sweetie. Are you ok?" She asked, concerned. I hugged her back. Up until this point, I had not realized how much I needed a hug from a motherly figure. I nodded yes..

"I am as ok as I can be, Momma Alice. How are you?" I replied. She nodded and released me so I could sit down.

"I am doing well, Sweetie. Just a lot of nerves going on from what is happening and the not knowing." Alice replied with a bit of a smile.

The door opened and in walked my grandparents. Seeing my Ohmah, Akasha Orijon, gave me the greatest relief that I had had all day. I stood and ran to her like a child. She caught me and hugged me tight, holding me close, as she always did. The smell of her perfume, Japanese Cherry Blossoms, comforted and calmed me.

"I am happy to see you also, my Little Princess." She

said.

"I am so glad you are here." I replied.

"I would not be anywhere else unless someone killed me." She replied with a smile. "Now get up there and do your thing." She said to me. I went back up to middle table where my father had joined Alice, and I took my seat.

One by one, I saw our Secret Service men coming in and giving their written reports to the people at the desks. They were to compile all the information for Doceo. The Elven leaders filed in and sat down at a table. Then the Lycans came in and sat down at a table. Shadow waved to me, and I waved back. Warketh came puffin' in after them.

"Warketh!" I said, raising my voice over everyone talking.

"Aye." He said, turning towards me as I motioned him over to me. "Well, ello der Little One. What can I do fer ya?" He asked. I said a few magical words and some wet wipes appeared in my hand.

"Hello Warketh. I think you might need a couple of these for your face. All I can see is your teeth and eyeballs. You are covered in dirt." I replied and handed him the wipes.

"Oh! Right. Sorry bout dat. I been in da tunnels." He replied with a chuckle. He took the wipes and cleaned up his face and hands. He tossed the dirty ones in the trash. "Der, all better now." He replied.

"Much." I replied as I kissed his now clean cheek. He smiled and waddled off to his seat. Stock and his wife, Thezzie made their way in and sat next to her father, Warketh. I waved to them both and they returned the wave with large smiles. A large whooshing noise came from the front of the room and there sat King Sebastian and

Queen Sakura with their tails in the water. Both had large smiles on their faces as we waved to each other. At this point I was almost bouncing up and down in my chair as more and more of my adoptive families showed up. Each of them had been around and helped raise me, minus the Lycan families. I then heard the clicking of hooves on the hard stone floor and through the door came Pire and Telephinee. Both were grinning from ear to ear as they noticed me at the table by my father. They waved as they took their places near a table. I breathed a sigh of relief as I waved back knowing I would not have to go against any more of my family, or adoptive families, as they were there in the room to support me and my father.

Doceo started drumming on the table nervously as he took a head count of who was there. *"Come on Callen. I know you will be here."* He thought.

"Don't worry he and his sons will be here." Alpha reassured him. *"I can feel they are close by."* Alpha said.

"It looks like we have a good turnout. I expected as much, but you never know these days." Doceo replied.

"Indeed." Alpha replied as the door swung open. In the doorway stood King Callen with his sons, Raven, and Teagan, behind him.

"I am beginning to think you are psychic." Doceo said to Alpha who just chuckled. I turned to look to see who had come in and smiled as they started toward us.

"Brother!" Callen boomed as he and Doceo embraced.

"It is a relief to see your old ass." Doceo replied.

"Well, you should know, after all these years, I am always with you, especially in a good fight." Callen laughed.

"Very true. I see Verona jumped ship." Doceo commented.

"Yeah, I cut my baggage loose, finally." Callen said.

"Ahh, we will talk later about that." Doceo said.

I didn't see anyone come near me, but I could feel someone staring at me. I turned my chair, and I was looking at a man's waist. Slowly, I looked up as my heart started to race and my breathing quickened. I closed my eyes before I met his. Teagan was staring down at me. When I finally opened my eyes, our eyes met, and I felt like I was on fire. *"Who is that and what is going on?"* Kita asked.

"Mate...." A voice said.

"Whoa, hold up. We have more than one?" Kita asked.

"Three" The voice replied.

"Oh great!" Kita replied.

I stood and gently reached up and touched his face to check to see that he was real. His goatee was just as soft as I remembered. A tear slid down my cheek. He reached up his rough thumb and gently wiped away the tear that was trailing down my face. The whole room was watching us, but neither of us noticed. I stretched up and hugged him tightly. He wrapped his arms around me and held me tight, like he would never let me go. At that point, I didn't want him to. In his arms, my whole world was balanced, and I could see everything clearly and feared nothing. I was whole again.

Shadow was watching this, a bit confused as to who Teagan was and what was going on. *"Who is he?"* He thought.

"Maybe her brother? Or a cousin?" Maximus said.

"Maybe." Shadow said. Vex and Logan came in the room and saw Teagan and I hugging.

"Well, good to see some things never change, A Logan?" Vex said nudging Logan. "Break it up you two. We have a meeting to conduct." Logan said as he got between Teagan and I. Feeling Logan touch me, I was snapped back to reality.

"Logan, you could ruin a good wet dream. You know that?" Teagan stated, annoyed. "Yeah, I know. I am great at it." Logan said glaring at Teagan.

"Not here boys." Doceo said sternly as I looked to my father a bit confused as to what was going on with me.

"How about we take our seats so we can start." Alice chimed in.

"Yes, great idea, Dear." Doceo replied. Teagan leaned down and kissed my cheek.

"I will see you later and we can talk." He whispered in my ear. I nodded yes and smiled.

I sat and Logan gently pushed my chair in for me.

"Everything ok?" he asked me. I smiled and nodded.

"I am good." I replied.

"What in the hell happened to your neck?" He asked.

"I am not quite sure. I only know I was choked by something or someone." I replied.   "What!? I swear I will kill Josh if he let you be in danger." Logan replied.

"No, no. It was an unseen force. I am sure it will be explained when Ahz gets here." I explained.

"It better be." Logan said as he stood behind me.

"Well before you get too comfortable, you best be giving me a hug." Vex said as he set his papers down on the desk next to me. I stood again.

"Of course, you get hugs." I said as I hugged him tight.

"Now that is better." He said.

"How are you Uncle Vex?" I asked.

"I am tired but doing ok." He said.

"You didn't mess anything up too bad, did you?" I cautiously ask.

"No, I never do." He said smiling.

"That's debatable." Logan commented quietly. I chuckled a little hearing, Logan. I sat back down, and Logan pushed my chair in for me again.

"What you got there?" I asked.

"Reports from the field. They are not good." Vex replied.

"Is Kye back yet?" I asked.

"Not yet but I am sure he will be soon enough." He replied. I nodded. Vex nodded at Doceo who stood and cleared his throat.

"Ok everyone. Let's take our seats." Doceo said in a raised voice. Everyone in the room moved around and sat in their spots. It was time for the good, the bad and possibly the ugly to come out.

The Reports

"Ok, I believe we are all here now. Let's get this thing going." Doceo said. "First off, I want to thank you all for answering the call to arms and supporting us." He said looking around as everyone clapped and nodded. "Let me get this out of the way first. I know that, despite current events, everyone on the island is very excited, so let's clap and cheer …. Your little Princess has returned to the island!" Doceo shouted. I stood up and everyone clapped and cheered loudly letting all their excitement be known. I blushed, smiled, bowed, waved, and returned to my seat. Once things were quiet again, Doceo started talking again. "Ok, now that that is out of the way. Vex and Logan, you're up." He said as he sat down in his chair.

"Thank you, brother." Vex said as he stood up. I sat next to him looking through the reports and noticed none of them really were clear, complete or had much knowledge of anything. "Well, this is what we know." Vex started.

"A bunch of nothing really." I interrupted, as he turned towards me.

"Well…Uhh, we do know some." He stammered.

"None of these reports are clear or complete." I stated.

"Well, they are not overly thorough. No, but they give us a bit of an idea." Vex said. Logan just grinned behind me, knowing I was not happy with Vex and his reports.

"We need more than a bit of an idea. This is possibly the most important information we can get." I replied, getting more heated. Doceo just watched, knowing this had always been an issue with the men's reports since she had left the island and Vex had handled the Secret Service alone.

"I told you she wouldn't be happy." Logan said.

"Give me a moment all. I need to get this together." I addressed everyone. Those who lived on the Island were used to this conversation between my uncle and myself. However, the Lycan heads all looked surprised and wondered why I was being so disrespectful to whom they thought was the head of the Secret Service.

Seeing this, Doceo clarified. "Sorry all. The head of the Secret Service was not briefed before the meeting because we have not had the time to do so. So, your Princess needs to look things over quickly. Please feel free to go back to chatting amongst yourselves." He said as he sat back down. I grumbled under my breath.

"Who hired these people, a monkey?" I muttered to myself. "Logan, get me a notebook and pencil." I ordered. Usually, I would have said please but I was in a very cranky mood. He nodded and walked out of the room to get me what I needed.

"Is this really necessary? I have all the notes here." Vex said holding up a note pad. I snatched it from him and read it.

"Okay. Well, what about James' report? That is nowhere in here." I said.

"James made a report?" Vex asked."

Yes!" I said raising my voice a little.

"Oh, I must have missed it." He said. I sighed in annoyance. Logan came back in and sat down the paper and pencils on the desk. I looked up at him and smiled.

"Thank you." I said and he nodded to me. I went back to reading the reports and compiling them together.

"Father. Do you think I should go up and talk to Jasmica about my idea now? Since she is compiling information and all." Teagan asked Callen.

"Yeah, probably a good idea. Come on." Callen said. As they approached the front table, Doceo smiled at them.

"What can I do for you gentlemen?" He asked.

"Teagan has an idea that he thinks will help us. But I wanted to come speak to you before he voiced it to be voted on." Callen replied.

"Oh?" I asked raising my eyebrow and looking up from the paperwork.

"Go ahead son." Callen said as Teagan cleared his throat.

"Well, my mother, Verona is siding with Luna. So, my thought was that we convince her that Raven here..." Raven stepped forward. "Would say he sided with Luna. He could work as a spy for us. Then we wouldn't have to have someone work their way up through their ranks to the top." Teagan said looking back and forth between Doceo and Jasmica, as both thought about this. Doceo sat back rubbing his chin, thinking about this idea. "

Well, whatcha think, my Little Monkey?" He asked me.

"Honestly, I think it is a great idea, IF Rave can lie to his mother." I replied.

"I can lie to her and schmooze her into believing anything I want." Raven replied, "Plus. You know Jassy, if people don't know me, I can lie like a rug." He boasted.

"That is true." I said nodding.

"Well, you are the boss in this department, Honey. I am on board if you are and there are no objections from you, Vex." Doceo said looking at him.

"No objection here, but I think we need more than just Raven in there." Vex said.

"Of course, but it is a start to getting inside and obtaining more information than we have right now." I said.

"Ok, well write it down, Cranky Ass." Vex said with a smile. I glared at him and looked back at the paperwork. Callen, Doceo, Teagan, Raven and Vex continued to talk and I went back to work.

I wrote feverishly, taking in all the pieces of information in front of me. I had noticed some blacked-out information, which I would have to look into later. I noted their names on the paper as well to get the carbon copies. Logan caught the papers as I flung them behind me once I had read them.

"Damn it woman!" He said as one wacked him in the face. "Can't you just hand them to me like a normal person." He complained.

"Now when in the hell has she ever been normal?" Vex asked.

"That's true." Logan answered as I flung another report at his head. "Jesus!" He called out. Teagan and Raven chuckled.

"If you want me to hand you them, then maybe you should ask nicely and not make fun of me when I am already in a mood." I replied, not taking my eyes off my work. Logan rolled his eyes as I tossed another sheet at him.

"Someone is in the doghouse again." Raven said with a chuckle.

"When aren't I? But least I'm in the house, unlike some of us." Logan replied, glaring at Teagan.

"I wouldn't get too comfortable." Teagan said glaring back.

"Boys. Not now." Callen said. Logan and Teagan still eyed each other but said nothing more.

"Guess this is going to be an ongoing trend between them." Callen said quietly to Doceo.   "Yeah, unfortunately there is at least one more that will be joining that fight and until one of them wins her over. You bet it will." Doceo replied as he sighed.

Finally, I finished and slid it gently over to my uncle as I rubbed my temples.

"You already now?" My father asked.

"Yeah, that should give you all the information we have. You are right. It's a shit show and a half." I replied rubbing my temples. Doceo nodded and stood up.

"Attention! Everyone. Back to your seats." He said. Everyone scurried around to their seats and patiently waited to hear what we knew.

"Vex, the floor is yours." Doceo said as he sat back in his chair.

"Thank you again." Vex said as he stood up. "Well, first off, I am glad to see you all here." Vex said smiling at everyone. "Luna and her minions have retreated to the Bacimorte's Territory of Pernrith." He continued and he heard a collective sigh of relief. "We still have control of Campania, but the Autumn Palace was destroyed in the explosion. Be advised that because of last night's events, we have begun evacuations of civilians from the Capital. They are still arriving here on the Island." Vex said as he looked around. He nodded to Logan. Murmurs were heard from the others.

Logan stepped forward. "The events of last night have had very few casualties on our side. Though it does seem that the enemy did take a significate loss of forces." Logan reported. "We have not yet infiltrated the enemies ranks. But we are working on a plan to do so, which Vex will speak on soon." Logan continued as the others nodded. Vex came forward again. "Early this morning the Newham Territory was attacked." Vex said. Murmurs again were heard, and I rubbed my forehead. "I am happy to report that the heads of that Territory Treyton and Willow Griffin, along with their son, Zyair, are safe. They, along with other human civilians, are on their way here." Vex said as the murmurs quieted.

"From the last report on this Territory. It has fallen to Luna and her forces." Logan said. Everyone in the room started chatting at once. Doceo stood.

"Calm down everyone!" He yelled. Once they had quieted, Doceo continued. "There will be time to speak on things after the reports are finished." He said and sat down again.

Quiet filled the room and Vex continued. "It seems Luna and the Bacimorte family have built up quite the army, but we cannot know for sure, until we are inside their ranks, how big they really are. Besides the normal way of infiltrating their ranks by recruitment and training, an idea has been proposed. I would like to ask Captain Teagan to come forward and present his idea to the council." Vex said. Teagan nodded and came forward.

"Hello everyone. First, I need to give you some background. My brother Raven and I have been part of the Secret Service since we were in our late teens. So, we do have all the training needed to carry out the mission I will be suggesting. Also, my mother, Verona Ringclaw, has decided to side with Luna. My father, my brother and I will be staying loyal to Avedonia." Teagan said as he took a sip of water. He never really liked the public speaking part of his position unless it was giving his men orders or talking to them directly. "Here is what I have proposed..." Teagan said as he walked over behind his brother, placing his hands on Raven's shoulders. "Raven here, my brother, will convince my mother, Verona, that he is on her side. Then he can infiltrate the enemies ranks, at the top, and we do not have to wait till someone else can work their way up through their ranks." He finished and sat back between his father, Callen, and Raven.

Murmurs started again as the heads of territories chatted among themselves at their tables. Doceo sat back and let them converse for a few moments. He then noticed Ahz and Nolan come into the room. He motioned them over to us. As they got closer, I could see the cobwebs and dust on Ahz's fur. Once he was right next to us, most of the room went silent. I looked back and everyone was staring at Ahzreal. He cleared his throat.

"It's ok everyone. I am not a ghost, just a little dusty. See?" Ahz said as he shook, and a dust cloud came off him. My eyes immediately started to water, and I started to cough and sneeze multiple times. Quickly, Kye came in the room and magically pulled my chair to him, away from Ahz. Everyone chuckled at Ahz and then they went back to talking.

"Are you trying to ..." I said as I began a coughing fit. "...kill me Ahz?" I asked as I sneezed again.

"Oh Shit! I forgot. Sorry Princess." Ahz said. Ahz looked past me and asked,

"Brother?"

I looked behind me and Kye was standing there like he was in stone.

"No fucking way!" Kye said in surprise. He was looking from Alice to Ahzreal.   "Nooo...." He said, then he bent down so he was nose to nose with me, and I looked into his eyes.

"Little One, are they really alive or have they finally come for me?" Kye asked me in a hushed tone.

"Uncle Kye. They are very much alive. I am sure Ahzreal will fill you in later." I replied. Kye nodded.

"Well, I'll be damned." Kye said as he looked at Ahz. "It's great to see you both breathing." He said. Kye walked over to Alice and kissed her hand. "Wonderful to see you, Ms. Alice." He said.

"I am most glad to see you as well, Kyerus." Alice replied.

Kye walked around the table and looked at his best friend. Ahzreal and Kye were like brothers. They had been raised together and each one knew all there was to know about the other. Kye poked Ahzreal in one of his runes.

"Ouch! Damn it, Bro. You know that one hurts." Ahz protested.

"Well, I'll be dipped in Shit! You are alive!" Kye said with a huge grin.

"Yes! I am alive, you Asshole!" Ahz said. Kye reached up and punched Ahzreal in the face, knocking him over the empty spot at the table.

"Why in the hell did you not come and tell me you were alive!?" Kye shouted. Ahz stood up and shook his head.

"We better get out of the way." Doceo said looking between Kye and Ahz.

"Good idea, Dear." Alice replied as they both moved over next to me. Ahz back handed Kye with his gauntlet hand, making a loud thump as it hit Kye's face.

"Because I was under a spell and when I was out, I couldn't exactly leave!" Ahz replied. Kye pulled out his throwing knives and tossed them at Ahz who caught them all.

"You should know that doesn't work, Bro." Ahz said as he jumped over the table and Kye caught him in midair. Kye flipped over and was now on top of Ahz with a hand full of armor. I ran over to them and placed my hand on Kye's shoulder.

"I ought to kill you myself!" Kye raged.

Before he could say another word, he stopped, feeling my hand on his shoulder. He looked at me. "Yes?" He asked in a cranky tone. I smiled at him.

"I know this is a lot right now and you two have a lot to discuss. But… Umm… Well, we are at war right now and we are on the same side here. I know you want to kill him, but we really could use him alive, Uncle Kye." I said as sweetly as I could, as I fidgeted a bit with my sleeves.

"Go on." He replied knowing there was more.

"So… Umm… It would be great if you could do that, and we could hear from both of you about the information that you have found… Please?" I asked giving him my best innocent puppy dog eyes. Kye sighed.

"Fine! But this is not over, Ahzreal. We have a lot of talking to do later." Kye warned as he released Ahz.

"Yes, we do!" Ahz replied.

I sighed in relief as my father and stepmother came back beside me. Logan brought my chair over and pushed it in under me. Ahz handed the knives back to Kye, who took them and put them back in their holders. Doceo and Alice sat down and looked at everyone else who was just staring like they were watching a tv drama unfold.

"Well. Now that that is out of the way. Did you find what you were looking for Ahzreal?" Doceo asked.

"Yes, right here." Ahz said gesturing to Nolan.

The Enemy's Abode

Meanwhile, Luna and her minions were returning to the Bacimorte's Castle in the Territory of Pernrith.

"Damn Doceo and his explosions!" Luna raged as she walked up the black stone staircase. "I cannot believe I forgot about that! Tony!" She yelled. Anthony Bacimorte, also known as Tony, stood five feet, nine inches tall with light brown hair that was parted in the middle and fell just below his shoulders. He has a statuesque appearance with olive skin that is smooth and flawless with a large, nose and narrow honey, brown eyes. His body is slender and well-toned. He's wearing a black velvet cape with a brocade, deep red vest with a white shirt under it, black dress pants and black shoes.

"Yes your majesty." He said.

"Did we get anything from the Palace before it blew up?" She asked.

"Marcus is checking with the General to see if they were able to salvage anything of importance. Why don't you take a nice relaxing bath? It will be a bit before we know anything." He suggested.

"Hmm, that does sound nice. I do deserve it. After all I have been through." She said. "Yes, most definitely. You poor thing." He replied.

"Ok. Send Angie to get me if there is any news before, I am done with my bath!" She ordered and walked into her room. Tony nodded and headed downstairs.

Pernrith is usually run by Anthony and Angelina Bacimorte and their son Marcus. Though now that Luna was there, she ruled it. Pernrith is mostly a Vampire Territory. The people there are very stuck up and stuck in their old ways. Demons and Elves are the only races they think as equal to themselves. Most other species are mere peasants unless you are a Lycan or a human. Lycans are considered slaves and humans are no more than food for the Vampires.

The streets of Pernrith at night are dark and foggy and the red night sky that seemed to cover the area gave it an eerie feeling. During the day, the Territory looked like a normal medieval town other than it was deserted and quiet. The town was surrounded by a large, black brick wall with a heavy black gate. The Castle had a mote and a draw bridge, that was usually up, to protect it.

Marcus Bacimorte is five foot, eight inches tall with short black hair and olive colored skin. He has medium sized brown eyes, a large nose and strong square jaw line. He is very muscular, with medium width shoulders and tattoos on his arms, back and chest. He wore a dirt covered, white shirt and black pants with dress shoes. He walked across the Castle courtyard and into the General's office.

Behind the large oak desk sat a tall man of six feet, with a military haircut, fire red hair and pointed ears. He had large muscular hands that made the pen in his hand look tiny. His broad shoulders filled out the dress shirt nicely and covered his tattoos, except the one on his neck. His almond shaped, orange eyes seemed brilliantly bright against his pale skin and were focused on the task in front of him. This was the General. His friends called him Brad and he is a Vampire/Elf Hybrid.

He heard Marcus come in, he looked up and sat back in his chair, staring at him.

"To what do I owe the pleasure of your visit, Master Marcus?" The General's deep low voice asked.

"I came to see what you have to report." Marcus said.

"I am just finishing my report now. If you are willing to have a seat, then I will have it to you shortly." The General replied.

"I prefer verbal reports to reading." Marcus retorted.

"Well, that is too bad now, isn't it? Seeing how the only verbal reports I give are to your father and her highness, Luna. I am afraid you will have to wait." The General said with a smug grin on his face.

Marcus was about to give him a piece of his mind when his father, Tony, walked in. The General stood up immediately and saluted him.

"Sir!" The General said.

"At ease, soldier." Tony said. The General nodded and sat back in his chair. "Have you got the report done yet, Brad?" Tony asked.

"I was just telling your boy here that I was almost finished." Brad replied.

"Ahh, anything good?" Tony asked.

"Not much really. We lost quite a few men in the explosion." Brad replied.

"She is not gonna be happy about that." Tony said shaking his head.

"Nor am I. We were unprepared for this mission, to say the least." Brad retorted.

"I know but it could not wait any longer." Tony replied. Brad sighed as his desk phone rang.

"General speaking…Uh huh… Uh huh… Are you sure?... Positive? … One hundred percent?... Ok, we will be right down." Brad responded and hung up the phone.

"Anything important?" Tony asked.

"Well, if they are right, then we just got a huge break, and her majesty will be overjoyed! If they are wrong, there will be hell to pay." Brad replied.

"Can both of you identify Jasmica and her guard Logan?" He asked.

"Of course, I can identify Jasmica." Tony replied.

"Yeah, I know what that damned asshole looks like." Marcus replied.

"Ok, come with me please." Brad said.

Brad stood, grabbed his hat, and placed it on his head. Then he swung on his black coat that was decorated with patches and medals.

"Did they get her?" Tony asked.

"They think so, but I am skeptical at best. I love my men but a lot of these heathens that have been brought in are not smart enough to kick rocks." Brad replied. They continued to chat while they walked out of the room, down a spiral staircase, to an underground hallway and on to the dungeon.

"Yeah, sorry. They are all we could find right now." Tony said.

"They will have to do but we need more qualified individuals if we are going have a chance against Doceo and his army." Brad replied.

"We will work on that. I am sure once word gets out, more people will be coming to our aid. Besides, we still have our secret weapon." Tony said.

"Yeah. When is that going to be activated?" Brad asked.

"When her Majesty feels it is necessary." Tony replied.

The three men continued down the dark hallway that was lit only by torches hanging on the walls, every few feet. They soon emerged into a large tower room that had jail cells in it. The room smelled musty and old, and water dripped from a nearby faucet and echoed in the room. The floor was stone with at least an inch of dust on it.

"Wow, this old place is still the same." Tony remarked.

"Yeah, we have not had to use it in forever, but it is still sturdy, so we left it." Brad replied as he walked towards a crowd of men. "Out of the way, all!" Brad called.

"Attention!" A Lieutenant called out. General Brad and Tony saluted the men as they continued to walk through the path to the jail cell. The guard at the door saluted them, unlocked the door to the cell and all three men went inside. It was a small room that had a small slit of a window at the back. A straw bed to the left and a bucket in the right front corner. There were torches on the wall on both sides of the door, that lit the room. Back in the right-hand corner they saw a woman curled up on the floor. Her knees pulled to her chest with her head resting on them and her hair covering her arms and face.

"Let me handle this one." Tony said, as he approached the woman.

As Tony got closer, he could hear quiet sobs from the woman but could not see her face.   "Aww,   Jasmica, Honey. Are you ok?" He said in a soft comforting voice. The woman lifted her head and looked up slowly. "It's ok, Dear. It's Uncle Tony. You are safe now." He continued. The light was causing a red cast in her hair as it started to fall away from her face. She looked at Tony. Her eyes were bloodshot and swollen. Tony walked closer to her and brushed her hair away from her face. "Shh, it's ok." He said. Tony looked at the woman's round face and dark, red toned eyes. Then he took her hand and noticed that she did not have sleeve tattoos. He was positive then, that this was not Jasmica, it was her twin, Mena. "Oh, Mena, Honey. I am so sorry." He said as he pulled her close. Mena started crying harder as she looked behind Tony.

"They..." She cried more. "They killed him!" She cried harder as she fell against Tony's shoulder. Marcus and Brad turned around to see a head on a spike in the left front corner of the room.

"Well, that sure as hell is not Logan, nor is that my Jasmica." Marcus said.

"I am so sorry, Mena. This was not meant to happen. Especially to you." Tony said. "Now let's get you somewhere proper to stay." He continued. Mena nodded as he walked her to the door of the cell. She was in shock and her heart hurt way too much to be angry right now. "Open the door!" Tony commanded and it swung open. Marcus and Brad followed Tony and Mena out of the cell. As soon as Tony and Mena were out of sight, Brad erupted like a volcano.   "WHO   IN   THE   HELL   IS RESPONSIBLE FOR THIS!?" He bellowed at the men.

There was silence as the men looked around. "WHO IS IT?" He yelled, asking again. "If you do not tell me who is responsible for this then you will all be punished!" Brad commanded in a loud tone. No one moved. "Have it your way then. You will eat hardtack bread and pottage until the responsible parties come forth." He taunted. The men groaned and grumbled. "And! You will only be sleeping four hours max a night, with drills every day, all day, unless you are out in the field. This will continue until you give the responsible party up!" Brad threatened.

As he and Marcus turned to leave, they heard a few men stumble forward.

"We are the ones who got er." One very grungy looking man said. When Brad turned around, he was face to face with four of the foulest smelling men he had ever come across. They were inmates from the prison. Between them they may have had a dozen teeth in their heads. Their hair was greasy and matted and their clothes were soiled and full of holes.

"I take it you four are from the prison?" Brad asked.

"Yeah, so!" The heavier one of them said.

"You caught the wrong woman and brought us the wrong head!" Brad said raising his voice.

"Your point?" The short one asked.

"Uggh! Lock them up!" Brad commanded as the four men were grabbed by trained soldiers and lead to their cells. Brad and Marcus walked up the tunnel towards the Castle.

"Luna is going to be pissed." Marcus said. Brad nodded his head in agreement.

Luna climbed out of her bath feeling refreshed and clean. She dried herself off and dressed. She left her room and made her way through the maze of hallways to the main staircase. At the bottom of the stairs, on a round sitting area that was covered in red velvet and black trim, was Angelina Bacimorte, laying across it, staring at the fireplace. Angelina, also known as Angie to her friends, had very few friends because she had a very bad attitude. Many considered her to be a snob and a spoiled brat. Her olive skin was as smooth as porcelain. Her long, black hair was pulled back from her face in a hair pin and the remaining hair fell in large curls down her back. She has an oval face with almond shaped red eyes, a broad, pointed nose and full deep, red wine-colored lips. She wore a corset top that was deep red like her husband, Tony's, and a long black skirt that gathered in the front and rested on her thighs showing her high heeled ankle boots. She heard Luna's footsteps coming closer and she turned to face her.

"Did you have a nice bath, Your Highness?" Angie asked.

"Yes, it was quite rejuvenating." Luna replied.

"That's good because you are going to need it." Angie replied. Just then Tony and Mena walked into the entry area.

"Mena! What are you doing here?!" Luna exclaimed, shocked. As she heard her mother speak, Mena looked up and saw red.

"YOU!" Mena screamed. "How could you do this to me!?" She screamed at Luna.

"Do what?" Luna asked, confused.

"Don't you dare play dumb with me. You left your grandchildren without a father and me a widow!" Mena cried.

"I had nothing to do with that! What is she talking about?" Luna demanded as Brad and Marcus walked into the room. Brad cleared his throat. "General! What is she talking about?!" Luna asked.

"Well, it seems some of the prisoners mistook her for her twin. They took her and killed her husband." General Brad said.

"WHAT!?" Luna screeched. "YOU INCOMPETANT ASSES! I ASKED YOU TO DO ONE THING AND YOU FUCKED IT UP!" Luna raged.

"I am sorry, Your Highness. It was NOT MY men but the heathens that were from the prison." General Brad corrected her.

"I don't care. Do you have any good news for me?" She asked.

"I am afraid the only good news is, we conquered Newham." He reported. Luna huffed and grumbled in anger.

"Mena Dear, could you tell me where the Island is?" Luna asked sweetly.

"I don't know. No one does until we are on it." Mena replied.

"What do you mean? It's not like it moves. It's land, for God's sake!" Luna protested. "Actually, it does move, frequently, and can be moved around to different spots. Why would I tell you, anyway? So, you could hurt my twin?" Mena spoke.

"Are you going to join me and my cause to get rid of those beasts or are you siding with them?" Luna asked impatiently.

"If you think that I would side with you, you might as

well kill me too. I would never side against my twin, my family and who I am, and I will never tell you anything!" Mena spit out in anger, raising her fist towards her mother.

"So be it. That is your choice. I have ways of making you talk!" Luna said as she glared at Mena.

"Do your worst. I will never tell you anything!" Mena replied as she started to lunge at her mother. Luna stopped her in midair.

"Aught, aught, ahhh. Getting to me is much harder than that." Luna said with a sly grin, "General. Throw her back in the dungeon with her husband's head. She is of no use to me now and schedule her for the works. That should loosen her tongue." Luna said as she started up the stairs.

"The works? Isn't that a bit extreme, Luna?" Tony asked. "It is your daughter after all." He finished.

"My daughters are dead to me if they are against me!" She yelled. "Would you like to join her, Tony, or maybe you would like to conduct the torture?" She asked.

"No." Tony said.

"Then I would suggest you do as you are ordered and shut up!" Luna commanded.   "I think it is time we wake up the secret weapon now. I am dying to meet him and know his strength." Luna said as she and Angie cackled with laughter.

"I thought he was only in an emergency." Marcus asked.

"You foolish men. Do you really think, with all your incompetence, you could take them on alone?" Luna scoffed. "I think not. You are all just weak and useless. No. I need a Demon Ruler to do this. He will whip you all into shape and deliver me a proper army to destroy all of them and make them follow me!" Luna said.

"I will see you two down there." Angie said, looking at her husband and son. They just nodded.

One of the guards came and took Mena back to her cell. Marcus, and Tony made their way to the chambers below the Castle. On the floor of the wine cellar was an inverted pentagram with runic writing around it.

"What is the devil's star doing down here?" Marcus asked.

"We need it to release Alduin." Tony replied shaking his head. Candles were lit at all five points of the pentagram. Luna stood at the head of the star as Angie, Marcus and Tony stood on three other points. There in the center of the star was the chest that Alduin had been trapped in. Luna started the ritual. But to no avail. "Damn it. We need one more person." Luna said. *"Hmm, maybe Mena can be of use to me. She has the Lycan blood in her that I need to mix with Ahzreal and Alduins."* She thought. "Guard! Bring me my daughter and make sure you have her bound up tightly. We don't want her running off." Luna commanded.

Suddenly, there was a loud commotion in the hall. There was a woman cursing and struggling.

"Let me go you, assholes!" Mena yelled. "I will kick your asses if I ever get out of these cuffs." She continued as they carried her into the wine cellar. Luna sighed.

"Put her on that point there." Luna said as she pointed to the empty point of the star. Once they had her on the point, Luna approached her. Mena's face was now swollen and bruised. "Aww, poor baby. Are you ready to join me yet?" She asked. Mena spit blood in Luna's face, from the beating she had just received. Luna struck her hard in the face with her fist. "You ungrateful Little Bitch." Luna raged. "It doesn't matter. You will help me if you want to or not." Luna said. "Hold her still." She ordered. Luna turned and grabbed the ceremonial dagger and walked toward Mena. Luna spoke a paralyzing incantation, stopping all Mena's movements. *"NO!"* Mena shouted in her head.

"I cannot get out! They have the cuffs on us." Jillian, Mena's wolf, replied as Luna came closer and with one swift movement, she cut Mena's throat.

"Drop her." Luna commanded. When they did, Mena's blood ran down to the point near her, into the center of the room and into the small vial on the box. Luna smiled as the wind started to pick up and the candles in the room flickered. Luna saw a shocked look on Angie's face. "Don't worry. She will not die for a while." Luna said and took her spot at the head of the star. Mena watched in horror at the events that were unfolding. Luna started the ritual again. Moving forward, she dumped the rest of Ahzreal's blood in with Mena's. The front vial was a quarter full. Speaking a few more incantations, the lights flickered and the ground rumbled. Luna walked up to the box and pierced her wrist, giving enough blood in the vial on the front of the box, to be filled halfway. She smiled as she felt his presence becoming stronger. She took the vial of Alduin's blood and filled the vial on the box to the top. Once she was on her point again, she concentrated. "Rise! Return to us, oh, Mighty One, and be free of the chains that bind you. Conquer the world with your new Queen!" She chanted. Lightning and rain started outside, and blood fell from the ceiling. Then flames shot out of the box as it bounced around on the floor.

Suddenly, the box exploded, and a loud deep voice was heard yelling. Once the smoke and dust cleared, there stood a man like figure. He was eight foot two inches tall with muscular arms and dark blue skin. There were rune markings on his neck, chest, back and abdomen. He had long legs that were extremely muscular with claw like feet. His horns on his wide head scraped against the ceiling and his red eyes glowed. He smiled with a mouth full of razor sharp, pointed teeth. He would have been handsome had he not been so evil.

"Ahhhh." His loud, deep, raspy voice said. "Who is the one who has freed me?" Alduin asked.

"It was me, Luna Orijeon." Luna said with pride.

"Orijeon? Were they not the ones who put me in that hell hole?" He questioned.

"Yes, well, my parents are stupid and do not know what is best. They are stuck too far up the Avedon's asses." Luna replied.

"That may be true. But just because they are your blood does not mean I will not slay them all the same, as I would all the Avedon family." He stated.

"Kill them all! Let us raise an army to fulfill your dream and we can rule, side by side." Luna suggested.

"Hmm, well you are a pretty, little thing. Will you listen and obey my every command, without question?" He asked.

"Yes, My Dearest." She replied.

"Will you satisfy my every need sexually or otherwise?" He asked her.

"Without hesitation, My Love." She replied.

"So, you pledge yourself to me?" He asked.

"Heart, mind, body and soul." She replied. He grinned evilly, showing his teeth.

"Will you die for me?" He asked.

"Yes." Luna replied.

"Then, it is settled. Sign here and we shall start our engagement." Alduin said.

"Umm, not to interrupt, but aren't you married to Lilith still?" Angie asked.

"No, she just kept my name. We divorced during the war, but no one knew. She betrayed me!" Alduin replied clenching his fist.

"She is a dumb woman. I would never do such a thing to you. I love you." Luna said as she signed the paper next to Alduin's name. The paper disappeared as he pulled her close.

"How about we retire to the bedroom, and you show me just how much you love me." He suggested.

"With pleasure, but first could you do me a small favor?" Luna asked as she took his hand and kissed him gently.

"I might be able to. It depends on what it is." He replied.

"Go find the Secret Island and give Princess Jasmica a warning." She requested. "Hmm..." He replied.

"Just scare her a little. It should be easy for you. They will not be expecting you." She pleaded.

"Fine. Considerate it done." He said as they started to walk out of the room. Alduin stopped for a moment looking at Angie, Tony, and Marcus "All of you, clean this mess. I do not want this cellar stained. I expect an immaculate home." He commanded as he left with Luna.

"Well, they are two peas in a pod." Tony said.

"Yes, well, love is love. Now, let's get this cleaned up.

Before they throw us all in the dungeon." Angie replied.

"Guards! Get her medical care and put her back in her cell." Marcus ordered, pointing to Mena as she lay still on the floor.

THE AMULET

Nolan handed Ahz the large frame he had been holding. Ahzreal brought the photo over and set it down on the table. Before he could even ask me anything I said.

"That's it!" And pointed to the picture. "That is what choked me." I said my eyes wide.   "DAMN IT ALL TO HELL!" Ahz yelled as fire flew out of his mouth.

"No way! That is not possible! We killed that Bastard! I helped you!" Kye said in disbelief.

"Akasha, can you come up here please?" Doceo asked.

"Yes…" She replied as she came up to our table. As she approached, she looked at the photo and her eyes grew large as it became clearer. "Please tell me she did not do what I think you are going to tell me she did." Akasha said. Vex shook his head.

"How could she have done it though?" Vex asked.

"You don't teach dark magic, Akasha, and I didn't think Elven magic was able to do this." He stated. Akasha closed her eyes.

"Dior!" She said in a raised voice. My Ohpah came running up.

"Yess…." He replied. "Why is there a picture of Alduin here?" He asked a bit confused. "Listen. If this is who she saw attack her, he is back and he is not one to be messed with!" Ahzreal replied.

"We know it took close to the raising of hell last time to get rid of him." Akasha said.   "Wait. Is he the one that started the last war?" I asked. Doceo sighed.

"Yes, Honey, he is the reason the last war started. He wanted to take over and rule. It took all that we and my parents had, to defeat him." Doceo replied, slamming his fist on the table.

"Is it possible?" Vex said in a low voice. Dior and Akasha looked at each other, closed their eyes and nodded.

"Yes, it is possible. We used Elven magic and Demon magic to seal him away. All he needed was one magic to be broken and he could be released." Dior explained.

"It is possible, Brother. We all discussed it, at the time, but it was the only way. As we did not have anyone strong enough to completely banish him." Doceo said, hanging his head. The room suddenly got loud as everyone tried to talk at once. Everyone in the room was listening.

"We do now!" Queen Sakura said, as her shell necklace glowed, and the room went quiet.   "We   do?"   Vex asked.

"Of course, we do. Do you all not remember the prophecy?" She asked.

"That's right!" Akasha replied.

"Born of two but made of three, she shall come. Slayer of evil ones and helper to all. To her all shall seek refuge, receive salvation and freedom." Both Akasha and Sakura spoke.

"Sebastian Dear, could you bring up the box, please." Sakura asked.

"Dior.." Akasha said.

"On it already." He interrupted. A light breeze filled the room and in the back of the room, in front of the monitor wall, a box appeared.

"Everyone! Get your pieces." Doceo order. Vex magically disappeared to his office and came back again with a piece. Doceo pressed a button on the table and raised a pedestal with a pillow on it, in the middle of the room. Warketh rummaged in his pocket, by his heart, and pulled out a piece. Stock pulled one out of his pouch and Thezzie took one out of her apron.

I sat in awe of everything. My head was spinning.

"What were they all talking about?" I thought. I heard a loud clang, as Pire put his shield on the table and pulled a small piece from the center of it. Telephinee shook her hair and out of a flower and into her hand, dropped another piece. A sudden wave brought up a chest from the water and placed it next to the Elven chest. Callen pulled out two pieces from the hidden compartment on the hilt of his sword.

Seeing their father get up, Teagan and Raven headed over towards me. I was standing there, still confused, watching what was happening. Shadow and Joseph looked on in confusion and shock too.

Shadow and Joseph came over to where I was standing

with Teagan and Raven.

"What in the hell is going on, Panda?" Shadow asked. I shook my head and shrugged, still confused. "Do you two know?" Shadow asked.

"No, but I think we are about to find out!" Teagan replied.

"Just how long were they all gonna keep this from us?" Joseph asked. We all shrugged and kept watching.

Delya pulled off her earrings and handed them to her husband John. Akasha and Jim took off their necklaces. Matoshka and Aponi pulled out small metal fragments from a pouch on their hips. The Elven leaders each touched the box and said a few words. When it finally opened, there were six pieces inside. The De Cartiers pulled out four pieces, one for each of them and one for each of the Bacimorte's leaders, who had stupidly left theirs behind.

All the rulers walked forward towards the pillar, placing their fragments down on the pillow. Magically they hovered to their correct spots, but one was missing.

"Doceo, Dear. We need your piece." Alice said.

"Well, I am not the one who has it." Doc replied as he looked back at me.

I touched the necklace my father gave me when I was sixteen. I held onto it tightly and closed my eyes remembering what he told me when he gave it to me.

"This is a special present, My Little Monkey. You must never lose it. Though it may not look like much, it will grow with you. One day it will be very important, and I will need it back. Now take good care of it." Doceo had said. I slowly walked toward my father. Doc held out his hand. I took the chain off as he smiled at me, and I handed him the necklace with the

piece of metal on it.

"Good Girl. Thank you for keeping it safe for me, Honey." He said as he took the necklace and kissed my forehead. I nodded and smiled. Then I turned and returned to our table, where the others were standing. Doc walked up, put the last piece in place and they all started to glow. "Ok Boys! Do your thing!" Doc said as he hurried back beside us.

Both Kye and Ahzreal nodded and started chanting. The pieces started to meld together, slowly. They turned and twisted, melded, and reformed around the gems that I had not seen in there before. Shadow, Teagan, Raven, Joseph, and I were all wide eyed, as we watched what was going on in the middle of the room. Suddenly, a bright burst of light came from the center of the room, and everyone shielded their eyes. As the light dimmed, we were able to see it come floating, slowly, down from the ceiling. A complete and beautifully crafted amulet dangling in the air, above the pillow, spinning slowly in a circle and sparkling in the light. I walked slowly and cautiously toward the pillar.

From its silver chain hung a silver crescent moon that was intricately detailed with spirals cut into it, so you couldn't see through it. Next to the moon, three eye rings down, hung a pendent. Once I was close enough, I could see the pendent clearer and the writing around the outside of it read; *'Cum omnibus vobis salvus erit'* which was Latin for *'with you all shall be saved.'* In the middle of the pendant was a five-pointed star and each of the points had a specific colored gem in them. The top point was a diamond, the right-side top point was a sapphire, the bottom right point was a ruby, the left bottom point was an emerald, and the top left point was yellow topaz. All of this surrounded a beautiful, rounded amethyst, which you could see **Avedonia,** written diagonally under it. It was the most beautiful piece of jewelry I had ever seen. Everyone was watching me, like they were waiting for me to do something. I turned around to my father.

"What is going on here?" I asked, looking at my father.

"I think it would be best if your Ohmah explained." Doc said, looking to her.

"Very well." Akasha said. "The rest of you get comfortable and listen up. I will refresh some of your memories and inform the rest of you who do not know." She said with a smile.

Blast From The Past

Akasha raised her hand so everyone could magically see. It was a place some had not seen for a century. It was the Palace my Grandmother Avedon had spoken of many times. My father grew up there. Grandma Avedon's cottage had always sat on that spot, at least it did, if it didn't get blown up in the explosion. It was a huge medieval castle made of stone, with large stone turrets, and a huge stone wall surrounding it, and a mote to protect it. I gasped as I saw it because it was so beautiful and majestic. Akasha zoomed into one of the windows of the castle. In this room, I recognized the table. It was the same one we had sat at in the Autumn Palace. The people around the table, some I knew and others I had only seen in photos. I sat next to my father and listened to Ohmah.

"A very long time ago, long before this island ever existed, Avedonia was all one land mass. Except for a few squabbles from time to time, everyone seemed to get along." Akasha recounted as some of the older leaders chuckled. "One day the demon lord, Alduin, decided he wanted more power, as most demons do. No offense, Ahz and Kye." She explained.

"None taken. We know how he was." Ahz replied, and Kye nodded.

"He created an army and started attacking territories, much like Luna is now. Word traveled through the land quickly and all the heads of the territories gathered in Campania at the castle. Armand and Ava Avedon were in control then and the young Doceo and Vex were working hard to learn the ropes." She continued. I smiled hearing my other Grandparent's names, as their faces appeared in front of me. "We banded together and threw everything we had at him, but we were losing terribly, until two young demons came to us, Ahzreal, Alduin's son, and his best friend, Kyerus. Ahzreal had just been cursed by his father to live eternity as a Lycan and Kyerus had lost his whole family to Alduin. They wanted to help us stop Alduin." Akasha said, smiling at Kye and Ahz. "This would be no easy task. We devised a plan for one final standoff with Alduin and his army. We were all feeling good about it. The night before the battle, Ava had a premonition from the Gods. She often had premonitions that rang true. She called an emergency meeting and told us that we must use Elven magic and Dark magic to seal him in a chest within his tomb because, strength wise, we were no match for him on our own." Akasha recalled, shaking her head. "We did as she instructed us to do. Once the plan was in motion, Kye and Ahz fought him with everything they had. They wore themselves out, but also weakened and tired Alduin. When the time was right, we struck, using the two magics together. We trapped him within a chest in his tomb. We were all aware that someday someone would be ignorant enough, or dumb enough, to release him. But it was our only option at the time." Akasha relayed. My eyes were huge, as I watched it all unfold in front of me. To me and everyone watching, it was like viewing a movie. "We all met together after Alduin was contained. Ava had another premotion. This time it was a prophecy. Ava told us what the Gods had said: ***"Born of two but made of three, she shall come. Slayer of evil ones and helper to all. To her, all shall seek refuge, receive salvation, and freedom."*** She had also received special instructions for the two demons who had helped us. They were to forge a special necklace that would one day tell of a special individual that would save us all from Alduin. Every territory leader received a piece of the necklace to keep safe until it was needed again." She said pointing to the necklace. "At the time, we were all puzzled by the riddle, until the day Luna gave birth to a set of twins. No royal family member had ever had twins, up until then. That was also the same day Jasmica and Mena were born." Akasha said, looking at me, as the smoke faded away. "This necklace has only been reassembled once before when you two were sixteen. Mena had gotten her wolf and we needed to see if she was the one who could save everyone." Akasha said hanging her head.

"That was the year Mena got very sick and almost died." I said, shocked.

"Yes, My Little Princess. The necklace rejected her, and she immediately fell ill as soon as she touched it. Out of fear, we did not want to put you in danger, so we disassembled it again, until today." Akasha said finishing.

"Thank you, Akasha." Doc said giving her a warm smile.

"You are very welcome." She replied as she went to her seat. Shadow, Joseph, Teagan, Raven, and I sat in our seats with our mouths open, stunned.

The Test

"I thought I knew all the history!" I thought to myself. My mind started racing. *"I memorized it! Knew it like the back of my hand!"* I complained.

"Jassy!" I heard my father's loud voice say.

"Yes, Father..." I replied.

"I hate to ask you this, but I need you to see if you are the one the necklace was made for." He asked and I nodded, yes.

"By the way, when in the hell were you all planning to tell us young ins about all this?" I asked with my arms folded.

"I was going to tell you when you took over the kingdom completely. Until then, I really didn't see the need to worry you with this." Doc replied. I sighed and shook my head.

"I need a minute for all this to sink in. I am going to get a drink of water and take a breather." I stated and I stood up. I looked around and noticed Ohmah and my father starting to come towards me. "Oh no! You guys all hang out here. I will be right back." I said as I walked away quickly.

I walked out the door of the meeting room and through the adjacent room to the tunnel that led to the war room. I took a deep breath, let it out and it echoed through the hallway. I leaned against the wall, slid down, and sat on the cold hard floor. I closed my aching, burning eyes that were still sore from the dust cloud Ahz had previously made. Soon, I heard footsteps. I opened my eyes and saw the outlines of men coming towards me.

"Oh great, here come the guards to get me." I thought.

"Can't they just give you time to breathe?" Kita asked.

"Apparently not." I replied.

But to my surprise it was not the guard but Shadow, his brother, Joseph, Teagan and his brother, Raven. Shadow squatted down next to me.

"Hi Panda. How are you doing?" He asked.

"Well Howls, my thoughts and emotions are a bit all over the damn map right now." I replied.

"From your mouth to the Gods' ears." Raven said as he slid down and sat against the wall across from me.

"We would have been better off to hear all this shit from them way before we were in the middle of all hell breaking loose." Teagan said, as he sat down next to me.

"Most definitely! My head is still spinning." Joseph said.

"Your head is always spinning." Shadow said to Joseph.

"Is not!" Joseph retorted sourly. I chuckled a little as I stared at the floor. I could feel everyone looking at me.

"So Small Fry, what are you gonna do?" Raven asked.

"Small Fry?" Shadow asked.

"Yeah, that is his nickname for me because I have always been smaller than him." I said to Shadow, and he nodded. Teagan placed his hand on mine and held it gently.

"You don't have to try the necklace on if you don't want to, Bay...Hun" He said as he corrected himself. I sighed.

"I know, but at the same time, I know I must. I must stand up and save my people, and if this is the only way, then I will risk it." I explained.

"Ok then, I guess it is decided, Panda. Let's get you back in there and see what happens." Shadow suggested. I took another breath and nodded. The guys all stood up. Teagan extended a hand and helped me up off the floor. We all started to walk down the hall towards the war room. Shadow, Raven, and Joseph were ahead of Teagan and I. Teagan reached down, grabbed my hand, brought it to his lips and kissed it gently.

"You know if you get too sick, I will have to take you away to my place until you are better." Teagan said quietly. I let out a small giggle and smiled shyly at him. As we reentered the noisy and chaotic war room, we all continued to talk amongst ourselves. We walked by the fridge and Logan handed me a bottle of water. He put his hands on my shoulders and started to guide me towards the meeting room.

"You ready for this?" Logan asked me.

"No, but I am as ready as I will ever be. Why didn't you

tell me?" I asked.

"I was sworn to secrecy, just like the mate thing." Logan replied. "I am sorry, Babygirl, but some things I just couldn't tell you." He explained. I sighed and walked through the meeting room door.

"And we are on the shit list again." Kage said shaking his head.

"Do we ever get off it?" Logan asked.

"Not lately." Kage replied. Logan sighed and walked into the meeting room with me.

As I walked in, everyone got quiet and stared at me. I stood in front of our table and stared at the amulet that was still hovering and spinning above the pillow in the middle of the room. My father looked at me, giving me the best smile, he could muster. Trying not to show the worry that was building up inside him.

"I wish she didn't have to do this." Doceo thought.

"Well, you knew this time would come." Alpha replied.

"Of course, I did but...You know that she will be in great danger if she is not the one. If she is the chosen one, she must do this." Doc replied.

"Yes, but you and I both heard her. She is willing to die for her people. You also know if they choose her, she is strong enough to accomplish what she must do." Alpha replied. Doceo sighed, knowing Alpha was right but still not liking it.

"Ok Kita. You ready?" I asked.

"Yeah! Let's do this!" Kita replied, trying to pump up our courage. *"But let's try not to die though, if possible."* She joked.

"I agree. I would like to keep living too." I replied as I took a drink of the water and set the bottle on the table. I walked slowly towards my father.   "So, what do you

say, Honey? Are you willing to give it a try?" He asked.

"Yes, I will, if it means saving my family, friends, and the people of Avedonia. I will do whatever I have to do." I replied. He nodded and held his hand out for me to go ahead towards the necklace. I continued to walk forward, though it felt like I was moving like a turtle. When I finally made it to the pillar, I gazed at the amulet again, taking in every detail of it. I slowly reached out to it. I wanted to close my eyes but at the same time, I wanted to see what would happen. I stopped just before touching it, closed my eyes for a moment, took a deep breath and centered myself as Uncle Kye had taught me. I focused on my breathing and the stillness around me, then I reached up and gently took the amulet in my hand. I opened my eyes as it sat in my hand. I didn't feel any different, I wasn't ill or anything.

"Maybe we have to put it on?" Kita said. I shrugged.

"What the hell? Why not?" I replied. Everyone watched and held their breathe. The elder leaders knew that once she put it on, only Kye or Ahz could get it off her. Kye nodded to Ahz, and they both started to move towards me, slowly. I noticed them coming closer but shrugged it off. I unclasped the necklace and slid the chain around my neck. As soon as the clasp was fastened, a whoosh of light and wind surrounded me, and I was lifted into the air. I looked around in shock, not sure what was going on or what would happen next.

THE MOON GODDESS

I felt the wind throwing me around in circles, lifting me higher and higher. I looked around and I could see Ahz and Kye trying to fight the wind to get to me. I could not move my body to try to get to them. I was scared to death. Suddenly, I felt energy flowing into and through my body. Flashes of images danced through my head like a flip book. The room around me went dark. I kept spinning, the images kept coming and confusing me more and more.

Suddenly, everything stopped, and I was standing on the ground feeling safe, as peace came over me. I could hear a familiar, calming voice singing gently. The longer I heard it, the calmer I became. Around me I could see a vortex of wind that Ahz and Kye were still battling. I clearly heard the voice that was singing, calling my name.

"Jasmica, come here my child." The familiar voice said. I turned and walked towards the voice.

As I walked, I saw a beautiful Palace. The floors and walls were outlined by yellow light. It was like the whole Palace was made of glass and lights. I looked to one side and saw the universe; all the stars were twinkling. In the center room stood a beautiful woman. Her face delicate and smooth. Her long blonde hair was pulled back in the front as the rest flowed over her delicate shoulders. On her curvy body hung a white tunic that flowed onto the floor. I felt drawn to her, so I continued to walk toward her.

As I walked, I noticed there was a gorgeous white wolf walking with me.

"Kita?" I asked.

"Yes, it is me." She replied.

"You are absolutely stunning!" I said as I knelt and touched her soft fur. She giggled and licked my face.

"Jasmica, come here please." I heard the woman say. I stood back up and continued toward the woman in the room. Once we were near her, I could clearly see a crown upon her head. Kita bowed down to her. I looked up at her, in awe of her beauty. "Hello Jasmica. Do you know who I am?" She asked.

"Umm. Well, I would say you are one of the Goddesses." I replied.

"Yes, very good. I am the Mother Goddess, also known as the Moon Goddess." She replied.

"Oh, so you are the one I have heard saying things to me from time to time." I said with a smile.

"Yes, My Daughter, I have. Do you know why you are here?" She asked.

"Well, one of two reasons, A. I am the chosen one or B.

I am dead from putting on an amulet." I replied. Kita chuckled a little. The Moon Goddess gave a soft chuckle and smiled warmly.

"You are not dead." She replied. "You and your twin are the chosen ones." She said, still smiling.

"But Mena got sick when she put on the amulet." I stated.

"Yes, because she chose not to accept her task and she was not pure of heart. So, she couldn't take on the task." The Goddess replied.

"Oh." I said.

"I will ask you, the same thing I did her." The Goddess spoke. "Are you willing to do what you must to save everyone? Even if it is hard and it could mean death and/or heartbreak for you?" She asked. I looked at her, took a deep breath and nodded.

"Yes, I am willing to do what it takes." I replied. She smiled at me and nodded.

"Good. Remember I am always with you. Kita and I will help guide you as much as we can. Never forget... you can do this. The amulet will help strengthen your magic, but you do not need it to call upon the elements to help you. No matter what is thrown at you. Remember, you can do this! You are strong enough! You are good enough! If you get knocked down, get back up and try again. Never stop trying." The Goddess said as she gently kissed my forehead. I nodded. "Now get back down there and put hell, back where it belongs." She commanded. I felt Kita and I become one, as I floated back down into my body.

I opened my eyes and I felt Kye and Ahz's hands on my arms. I looked at each of them, smiled, and gently lifted my hands. The vortex of wind disappeared and there we three stood. My eyes now had a blue ring around the irises.

"It stopped." Ahz said, looking around.

"Are you ok, Little One?" Kye asked me. I looked at him and smiled.

"Yes, Uncle Kye. I am fine." I replied as he noticed my eyes and he smiled.

"I would say that you are... You are perfect." He replied taking my face in his hands and kissing my forehead, like a proud father. Murmurs started, as I walked towards my father. Behind me, Ahz and Kye high fived as I approached my father. I could see the look of relief on his face.

"You ok, My Little Monkey?" He asked.

"Yup! Never better." I said with a smile. He pulled me in and hugged me tightly.

"I have never been happier to hear that than right at this moment!" He replied. "She is ok! She has been accepted!" He yelled as he let me go and the whole room rejoiced.

Once things had died down from the cheering and we were all seated again, I looked at Kye.

"Now I think it is time we hear your report please, Kyerus." I proclaimed. He took a deep breath. *"This should go over well."* He thought as he nodded and walked to the middle of the room.

KYE'S REPORT

"Hello everyone." Kye said as he glanced around the room. "I was sent on a mission by Princess Jasmica to make sure everyone got here ok. I wish I could say that I can ease your mind Princess, but I cannot." He said as he looked sadly at me. "As I made my way around the Palace, I found everyone except..." He paused.

"Except whom?" I asked, knowing if he was pausing, this was not going to be good.   "Your twin, Mena, and her family." He stated. My eyes grew large.

"I knew something was wrong." I said as I stood and started to pace. "Kye, please tell me you found them, and everyone is ok." I pleaded. Doc moved restlessly in his chair.

"I cannot do that." Kye replied. I stopped dead in my tracks and looked at him. I heard everyone murmuring and talking.

"Calm down everyone. Kye is here, so I know there must be more to it than just that Mena and her family are missing." Doc said, pulling me back into my chair.

"Breathe, Sweetie, just breathe." Dad said to me. Vex patted my hand.

"I am sure she is fine. Mena is tough." Vex said as I nodded and looked back at Kye. "Yes, I left the Secret and retraced the route you all took last night. Not far from where you took off, I noticed a carriage down and could smell Alicorn blood in the air. I landed on the sight and found a decapitated body, a decapitated horse and a badly beaten, dismantled carriage. I looked around and saw the grass had been trampled down in this area, so I took a seat and closed my eyes." Kye explained, as he told his tale. "After concentrating for a few moments, it grew dark, and I used my mind's eye. I watched as the carriage and the two Alicorns were being shot at and the passengers fell out, hurdling towards the ground. One of the Alicorns was shot and continued to fall quickly. The second Alicorn, that was not hit, circled back around, and caught some of the passengers and brought them to the ground safely in front of me. He carried Mena and the children. The Alicorn that was hit, slammed into the ground, where I had found it. The carriage followed, making a loud smashing sound. I could see the second Alicorn pushing hard to get to the last individual that was falling out of the sky. Sadly, the individual made impact with the ground before the second Alicorn could get him. It was Trey and he was moaning, on the ground, in pain, but not dead. Mena rushed to him. She knew that a single Alicorn could not carry all four of them to safety, especially with the condition Trey was in. I could see flames in the distance and heard loud voices yelling and footsteps coming towards all of them." He paused and took a drink of water.

"Mena made a makeshift carrier and attached it to the one good Alicorn. She sat the two smallest children in it. Then she put the oldest one on the back of the Alicorn. It was Mena's Alicorn, and she ordered it to go to the Secret Palace and bring the kids to safety. I watched as tears came down her face and the Alicorn flew out of sight in the direction of the Secret Palace." He explained. He paused for a moment so we could all digest what he was saying.

"Please tell me my grandchildren have made it safely?" Doc asked.

"I put together a team and they are out looking for them now. I believe the storm may have blown them a bit off course, but I made sure that was my first order of business before I continued to see what else had happened to Trey and Mena." Kye replied. Doceo nodded and rubbed his head as more murmurs surrounded him.

"So, what happened next?" I asked, trying to stay in my chair. Doc stood and started pacing like I had previously done.

"Yes, continue please, Kye." Doc said. Kye took a deep breath and looked at Vex, myself, and my father. Ahz could tell this was not going to be a good thing and walked over and held my hand, patting it. Logan started rubbing my shoulders.

"What in the hell are they all doing?" Kita asked.

"I think they are trying to keep me calm." I replied.

"Well, it's not working" Kita said as she growled slightly.

"This is where things got ugly." Kye said, taking another deep breath. "Luna's possie caught up with Trey and Mena only moments after the kids had disappeared. Trey was unable to move at all, from what I could see. Mena tried to drag him to the bushes so they would not be seen, but to no avail. As soon as the men saw them, one rushed forward, knocking her down and cutting off Trey's head. Enraged, Mena tried to shift into her Lycan form, but she was sitting in a patch of wolf's bane, so when she lunged forward, she only had herself, not her wolf. The largest of the men caught her. She fought the best she could, but they managed to cuff her and take her away." He said closing his eyes.

"WHAT!?" I yelled. "We have to save her!" I yelled as I tried to jump up. Logan pressed my shoulders and Ahz and Vex held my arms tight. I continued to struggle against them. "Let me go!" I yelled.

"Jassy, calm down. You being mad will not help." Ahz said.

"I am angry, but I need to go get her. She could be in danger!" I replied.

"Jassy, Honey. We don't know where she is yet. You have to calm down." Vex pleaded with me, as I got my wrists loose and started to stand again.

Logan turned me around to face him and looked deep into my eyes. He leaned over me, his hands on both my wrists now. I looked back at him as I started to feel a bit calmer.

"Breathe and calm your ass down!" Kage ordered. I could hear Kita whimper a bit. I nodded and took a couple deep breaths.

"Is that what that mate thing does?" I asked.

"At times, yes." Kita replied. I felt Logan and Kage mind link to me.

"Just breath, Babe. You know it will be ok." Logan said as I sighed.

"I do not recall saying you could come in here." I replied.

"Stop being so damn stubborn. This is important! You need to know how to handle your emotions. With Kita, they will be much stronger." Kage said.

"Thanks captain obvious. I noticed that already." I replied.

"How do you deal with her?" Kage asked.

"It's not easy some days." Logan replied.

"Listen, I get what you are both saying. Can we please get back to the meeting. My head is hurting and it is too crowded." I said. Logan nodded. He and Kage unlinked from me. I rolled my eyes and turned back around to look at Kye.

"He better not do that again, or use it wisely when he does." I muttered to Kita.

"Great. He has wormed his way in." Teagan said as he watched Logan and Jasmica.   *"Don't worry. They have always been close. But you and Jassy have a bond that is much stronger than she and Logan. Things are changing rapidly with her acceptance. That is all I can say for now, but just wait. We will win her over like we always have. No worries there."* Conri said as Teagan nodded. Doc stopped and looked at Kye.

"Do you know where they took her?" He asked.

"Yes, I found her in a terrible state." Kye said. I stood up immediately.

"Is she here?" I asked.

"No, I could not get her out on my own, in the state she is in." Kye replied as he hung his head.

"What do you mean?" I asked.

"Well..." Kye swallowed hard. *"Damn it, she is gonna lose it."* He thought. I started pacing with my father. "She is at the Bacimorte's Castle in the dungeon." Kye said.

"In the dungeon! Why would they keep her there?" I asked, a bit confused.

"Let me tell you the whole story. I followed the vision until I got to the Castle and snuck in. I maneuvered around the Castle everywhere but could not find her. I figured Luna may be a bitch, but she wouldn't keep her in the dungeon. So, I went to the dungeon. First, I found four of the men that took her, locked in cells. Then I looked around some more. When I finally found her, it was because she had been screaming. I made my way towards the screams as fast as I could." He said trying to talk fast because he knew his time was limited.

I had stopped pacing and clenched my fists as I listened. Ahz and Logan made their way to the door to block it.

"This is going to hurt." Kage said as he watched.

"Yes, it is. I think we will be seeing Kita soon." Logan replied. Doc had stopped pacing as rage was boiling up inside him.

"I found Mena in a cell. A man was coming out of a cell zipping up his trousers. I was not prepared for the atrocities that I saw when I peered into the cell." Kye paused.

"Go on." Alpha said through Doceo, as his eyes grew redder.

"I convinced the guard I was there to issue a psychological beating and he let me inside her cell. She cowered away from me, into the corner. Her dress had been ripped and soiled with dirt, blood, and semen. Her hair was missing in patches and matted together in other places. She was bruised from head to toe and had a fresh gash, that had been stitched up, across her throat. She softly cried in the corner. From what I could see she had been put through hell. I could tell, by the way she was moving, she had broken bones that were not healing well and that she was weak and ill. I knew without help I would not get her out of there alive. I reassured her I would be back with help as soon as I could. Then I came straight here." Kye reported as he hung his head. The whole room erupted in shouting, yelling, and talking. Alpha growled and snarled loudly as Doceo did his best to keep him in. Behind him he heard a snarl and growl he had never heard before. He turned and saw that Jassy had completely shifted into her Lycan form. He stopped for a moment to admire her. So, this was Kita. She had long, pure white fur with royal purple eyes that sparkled. She must have been six foot, two inches of pure muscle. He knew she was going to be hard to stop.

Before he could try to grab her, she was gone, charging towards the door. Logan shifted into Kage to stop her, but she threw him off to the side like he was a rag doll. She continued to move forward and wrestled with Ahz as he tried to reason with her. He started to cast a spell just as a strong wind sent him flying out of the way. She ripped the door off its hinges, and she ran through the war room, bursting through the vault door.

"Stop her!" Doc yelled and shifted into Alpha.

Soon, all the Lycans were out the door running after Kita.

"We have to stop her before she gets out of the Palace." Vex said.

"What are we going to do?" Pire asked.

"You saw the way she threw Logan and just blew poor Ahz away." Morgana replied.

"I have an idea. I hope it will stop her. Akasha come with me." Kye replied and they both vanished. Running down the hall, Kita was running one Lycan after another into the wall, until they all fell behind her.

Suddenly, Kye appeared in front of her, and Akasha was behind her. She started to skid as she tried to maneuver around him. Akasha magically made roots grow to Kye's feet to anchor him and he held up his arms to brace himself for the impact. Kita ran into him like she had hit a brick wall and she stumbled back. He caught her and wrapped his arms around her. He looked into her eyes and started to cast a spell to make her sleep. She tried her best to fight, but the roots were growing around them both to contain them, like a cage.

"Let me go!" Kita growled. Kye continued his spell until her eyelids started to flutter. Soon, she was fast asleep and starting to phase back into her normal body.

Snoring filled the tunnel and echoed off the walls as Alpha and Conri caught up to Akasha, Kye and the now sleeping Jasmica.

"You can let us out now, Akasha." Kye said in a smushed tone.

"Oh yes. Sorry, Dear." Akasha said with a small giggle. "Guess I got a bit carried away." She said as she released the roots from both Kye and Jasmica.

"Let's get her to her room and dressed so she can rest. We could use some fresh clothes and we will get Toby to tend to the wounded. Then we can resume the meeting." Alpha ordered. "Will do." Kye replied as he scooped up Jasmica.

"Hey Conri. I think you still have some spare clothes in her room. I am thinking you will need them unless you brought some of your own." Kye said.

"Thanks, I will definitely need them. Hopefully, I have

two sets, as I think Razor may need some too." Conri replied, chuckling.

"Yeah, at least some shorts or something." Razor said as he limped up to them. Kye laughed a little.

"Ok, follow me." He commanded.

"Wait!" Akasha yelled. The three stopped. Akasha summoned a blanket and draped it over Jasmica's sleeping body. "Can't have everyone seeing her like that." She commented.

"Yeah, like that would be the worst that happened today." Kye replied, shaking his head as he headed up the spiral staircase with Jasmica in his arms. Conri and Razor followed him. Akasha shrugged and headed back to the meeting room.

The Plan of Action

As Kye approached Jasmica's room, Joshua opened the door for him.

"Thank you, Josh." Kye said as he walked by him with Jasmica. Joshua nodded, watching Conri and Razor follow Kye inside. Josh closed the doors behind them. Jeni came in the bedroom from the side passageway.

"Oh My God! Is she ok?!" Jeni exclaimed.

"Yeah, she will be ok, Jen." Kye said and he gently set Jasmica down on her bed. Jasmica moaned softly in pain. "Jen, please go check and see if there are any of Teagan's clothes in the closet." Kye asked. Jeni nodded and started to head to the closet.

"No worries, Jen. I know where things are in here. It seems nothing has changed." Conri said as he headed into Jasmica's closet.

"Ok, go ahead then." Kye said. Conri went into the closet and sure enough, his clothes were still in the dresser and hanging in the closet.

"Razor, come in here. I got some clothes for you." Conri called out.

"Shhh." Jeni called out.

"No need to shush, Jen. She is out cold. She phased for the first time today. So, she will be sore when she wakes up. The key word is when." Kye said as Razor went into the closet.

Conri phased back into his Elven form as Teagan. Razor phased back into his Elven form of Raven. Both men got dressed and Kye waited for them. Jeni knocked on the door to the closet. "Is everyone decent in here?" She asked.

"Come on in Jeni. Just doing up our shirts." Teagan replied.

"Try not to stare too much." Raven joked.

"Ewe! I have known you since we were kids. It would be like staring at my brother." Jeni replied as she came in and stuck her tongue out at Raven. Raven smiled back at her and shook his head. Jeni walked across the room to the dresser, grabbed Jasmica's pajamas and walked back out to get her dressed.

"Ok, who is helping me dress her, because she is dead to the world right now and much too heavy for me to handle alone?" Jeni asked. Kye chuckled as Teagan and Raven walked out of the closet.

"I told you she was out!" Kye said.

"I will help you." Teagan volunteered.

"Good. Raven, you, and I can head down to the

meeting room." Kye said.

"Sounds like a plan. See ya later, Jen." Raven said as he and Kye walked out the door. Teagan turned towards Jasmica who was snoring loudly.

"You take the left and I will get the right side of the bed." Jeni said. "OK, no problem." Teagan said. Jeni crawled on the bed and lifted Jasmica's right arm.

"Ouch! No touchy!" Jasmica mumbled in her sleep. Teagan and Jeni chuckled. Teagan put her left arm in the night shirt.

"Ok. You get her pants on, and I'll button up her shirt." Jeni instructed. Teagan nodded and set to putting her pants on.

"Owe! Stop it, meanies!" Jasmica mumbled as they both chuckled again.

"I'll lift her, and you can pull her pants up, Jen." Teagan instructed. Jeni nodded as Teagan lifted her and Jeni scooted her pants on her.

"Damn it you two! Stop touching me!" Jasmica whined. She started to whimper and cry.

"Shhh, Babe. I know it hurts, but you needed to have clothes on." Teagan said softly as he gently stroked her hair from her face and wiped her tears. Feeling his touch, she calmed down as the pain started to dull a little.

"Maybe you should stay with her, Tee." Jeni said.

"I wish I could, Jen, but I need to get down to the meeting room. They need me down there." He replied. He continued to stroke her hair. "Stay with her and I will come back up when we are done." Teagan said.

"Where is Logan?" Jeni asked. "He is uhhh... broken I would say." Teagan said with a bit of a smile.

"What did you do? Tell me everything!" Jeni said excitedly.

"I didn't do anything. Kita tossed him like a rag doll, so I imagine he is out of commission now. Why?" He asked.

"Well, he is one of her mates, so he would be able to help her with her pain." She explained as Jasmica snored quietly.

"Does she know?" He asked.

"Yeah, now she does. I am not sure she has figured out that she has three mates, but she knows he is one. Though, as you can imagine, he sucks at it." Jeni replied.

"He never has been good at being a one-woman man." Teagan replied.

"Oh, how well all women around here know. I mean he has his good points but...yeah." Jeni replied rolling her eyes. Teagan shook his head.

"So, I am guessing he has not changed any?" He asked.

"Naw. You thought he would?" Jen asked.

"Well, I had hoped he would have grown up some. But I guess not." He replied as he stood and turned towards the door. "I better get back down there." He said as he walked out. Jeni nodded and shrugged her shoulders.

Teagan walked into the hall and looked up to see Raven standing there, leaning against the railing.

"Are you ok?" Raven asked as Joshua shut the door behind Teagan.

"Yeah, I just hate to leave her in pain." Teagan replied. Raven nodded and they started to walk down the hall together.

"She will be ok. You remember the first time we

phased? It is not the most pleasant experience." Raven said.

"Yeah, I know. That's why I want to help her, but we need to get Mena home too." Teagan replied.

"Listen man, I understand. If she really needs you, I can handle this." Raven offered. "No, I will go to the meeting. That way I can fill her in later." Teagan replied. "Thanks, though, Bro." He said as he punched Raven in the shoulder playfully.

"No problem, Man. You got your girl back home and that means I got to step up. I don't mind, as long as she can keep you from being so sad or moody." Raven replied with a chuckle.   "Yeah, she is usually good at that." Teagan replied with a big grin.

The brothers continued making small talk as they walked down the hallways to the spiral staircase and down the long hall to the war room.

"Damn. She did a number on this door." Raven said.

"Yeah, she seems to be one hell of a force to be reckoned with." Teagan replied. They continued through the war room to the meeting room. Doceo nodded at them.

"Please take your seats, Gentleman." Doc said. Teagan and Raven sat down by their father, Callen.

Once Doc saw everyone was seated, he started talking.

"Thank you all for coming back. We have a couple things to get done. First, I have added a few more men and extended the search radius to find my grandchildren. Our main goal is to get them home safe and sound." Doceo said as Warketh raised his hand. "Yes, Warketh." Doc said.   "We have deployed some Dwarves to look in da areas as well." He offered. Doc nodded.   "Thank you, Warketh." Doc said.

"Ye be welcome." He said and sat back down.

"Next thing on the agenda is that we need to vote on the mission to send Raven undercover into Luna's castle." Doc said.

"I think it is a great idea, if we can pull it off." Pire said.

"Sounds like a good plan." Dior said.

"Aye, I agree." Stock replied.

"Let's send the boy in." John said as Nolan walked up to Doc.

"Excuse me, Sir, but the Griffins have just arrived." Nolan said.

"Thank you, Nolan. Once they are checked over and settled, have them come down here, please." Doceo asked. Nolan nodded and walked off to tell the Griffins.

"Sounds like a good plan to me." Lucas said and nodded.

"Ok, good. After we are done here, Raven, you set out to start your mission and we will send a few of your fellow service men to infiltrate lower ranks." Doceo instructed him.

"Will do, Sir." Raven replied.

"We will start to bring together a team and a plan as soon as the Griffins arrive down here. Please mingle and chat amongst yourselves." Doc said. He went to his chair and sat rubbing his forehead.

"How are you holding up, Old Boy?" Vex said.

"I could use a stiff drink and a Tylenol." Doc replied.

"Amen to that." Vex said.

"I was hoping we wouldn't have to deal with this until

we were all old, gray and nearly dead." Doc said.

"Well, we are old and gray and technically as vampires, we are dead. So…" Vex said smiling.

"Alright, Smart Ass. I don't need your shit today." Doc replied. "Can you go up and check on Jassy, please?" He asked.

"Yeah, no problem. I will be back soon." Vex replied as he stood up and headed out the door to check on her.

Not long after Vex left, a round man of five foot, eleven came strolling into the room. He had short brown hair, a round face with chubby cheeks, and a button nose. His hazel eyes had a bit of a twinkle. He wore a business suite that was dark brown with a red tie. The man was Treyton Griffin. He and his wife, Willow, ruled over the Newham Territory which is composed of humans. Willow is five feet, six inches tall and was a bit thinner than her husband. She has sandy, blonde hair, deep-set brown eyes, a heart shaped face with a sharply angled nose and long eyelashes. She wore a black pant suit with high heels.

They walked into the room as Doc stood to greet them. Treyton shook hands with him, and Willow hugged him.

"Are you both ok?" Doc asked.

"Yes, we are doing fine." Treyton replied.

"Is Zyair, ok?" Doc asked.

"Yes, he is here safe and sound." Willow replied. "Is everyone ok here?" She asked. "Not really. Mena has been taken prisoner by Luna and her minions. Her children are missing, and her husband has been murdered." Doc said rubbing his forehead.

"Oh My God! That is terrible!" Willow replied.

"Yeah. Then Jassy got her wolf and phased for the first

time today. Luna is throwing us all into a war. It has been a lot, to say the very least." Doceo said.

"Well may the Gods find favor with us and let things work out." Treyton replied.

"Here, here." Warketh said.

Vex came back in and sat next to Doc as the Griffins took their seats.

"How is she doing?" He asked.

"She is whining in her sleep. Jeni got some pjs on her and other than that, she is still sound asleep." Vex replied.

"Ok, good. At least she is sleeping it off. I will have Nolan get Toby up there to check her out." Doc said as he turned towards Nolan and motioned him over.

"Yes, Sir." Nolan said.

"Can you have Toby go to Jasmica's room, check her over and give her something for the pain." Doc instructed.

"I will get right on it." Nolan said and turned to leave.

Doceo then returned his attention to everyone in the room.

"Could you all please take your seats again?" Doc called out. Everyone moved around to their seats and got settled. "Thank you all for your patience. Princess Jasmica will not be rejoining us today as she needs to rest. That being said. We need to figure out a way to get my other daughter, Mena, back home and safe. I will turn this meeting over to Vex." Doc said as he took his seat and Vex stood.

"Thank you. I have been mulling it over and I believe it would be best to send in three men total. One to retrieve her and the other two as a distraction." Vex suggested. "Any thoughts?" He asked.

"Aye, ye be needin bout five in total if ye be doin dat." Warketh commented.

"You better be sending in at least six Elves and one of us Demons to deal with the magic around the outside of the Castle and Alduin." Ahz mentioned.

"So that is like eleven people?" Vex asked.

"Wow, you can count?" Callen said with a chuckled. Vex glared at Callen.

"I agree. Five in would be the best option. Then they can hit the dungeon all at the same time and keep it quiet." Teagan agreed.

"A few of us could help patrol the outside area." Pire said.

"I agree. Between the Elves and Centaurs outside the Castle, that should be enough lookouts." Kye said. Doceo nodded and rubbed his chin as he listened.

"I do not think that we need that many people in there. It is easier to get in a smaller amount of people rather than a larger group." Vex argued.

"Kye, what do you think? You have been in there recently." Doceo asked. Kye sat and thought for a moment.

"Well to be honest, Vex is right about it being easier to get in with a smaller group, BUT with all the people that are coming and going around there, a diversion would be the best option to keep people busy, while we get Mena out. I mean, if only one of us was needed to get Mena out, she would be here right now." Kye said.

"Hmmm… Did you have something in mind?" Doc asked.

"I can take three men with me, two as a distraction and to keep watch inside. Another man and me to carry Mena out safely. Meanwhile, a group of others can stage a small attack to keep the guards busy. That way we are not trying to get so many people inside and there will be more people outside." Kye replied. Doceo sat back in his chair and thought about it.

"Well, if da tunnels are clear, we can get ye closer, under or in da dungeon." Warketh suggested.

"Mena is not that heavy. Why do you need another person to help carry her?" Vex questioned.

"For one, we don't know exactly what is wrong with her. Second, we don't know how much she has healed, so we don't want to make it worse." Kye replied. Vex nodded and thought about it.

"Makes sense to me." Doceo said.

"I think the one to go with Kye should be a Lycan, for his strength." John said.

"That is a good idea." Kye replied.

"The ones we are sending in should be picked by Kye and they should be assassins, like he is." Treyton suggested.

"Agreed." Doceo replied.

"Well, I am not sure about sending in more assassins then just Kye. Possibly Jassy should go with them to manipulate the elements of the stones, and then we wouldn't have to send others inside." Vex suggested.

"I am not taking Jasmica with me. I refuse!" Kye replied with anger in his voice that Vex would even propose that.

"Are you trying to get her kidnapped too?!" Pire yelled.

"Well, no, but it would be easier." Vex replied.

"We are not sending Jasmica anywhere near that place

right now, until she has done more training and especially since she just got her wolf. That goes for everyone else as well. She is not to go anywhere near battle until her training is completed and I give the OK. Am I clear?" Doceo ordered and looked around as everyone nodded in agreement.

"We are going with Kye's plan. Kye get your team together. Warketh and Stock get to those tunnels. Raven, you get back to your mother and head off to Luna's with her and we will be in contact soon. The rest of you get a few of your men together in the courtyard. We will meet there and send them off. Kye, you oversee this mission. Teagan, please come to see me once you have said your farewell to your brother. Thank you. Everyone is dismissed." Doceo commanded. Everyone in the room stood, conversing with each other and exiting the room to get their assignments completed. Teagan hugged Raven.

"Be careful, Bro, and Godspeed." Teagan said.

"I will, I promise." Raven responded.

"You better be. I don't want to lose my youngest son. I love you, Son, and Godspeed." Callen said.

"I love you too, Dad. Godspeed." Raven replied as he headed out the door, followed by Callen. Teagan walked up to the front of the room where Doceo, Alice, and Vex were seated and talking quietly. He cleared his throat.

"You wanted to see me, Sir?" Teagan asked.

"Yes, I need you to help me with something. I know you and my daughter are close and are mates. I was wondering if you can help me by not only helping in training her, but also keeping an eye on her. This is gonna be rough and she has a long road ahead of her. She is gonna need you. What do you say?" Doceo asked. Teagan grinned.

"Did you really think I wouldn't be doing all that anyway, Doc?" He asked. Doc looked up at him and chuckled.

"I forgot who I was talking to." He laughed more. "I am used to having to give Logan instructions and forget that I don't need to with you." Doc revealed.

"Yeah, I heard he hasn't changed much. But to ease your mind, I will always look out for her, whether she chooses me or not, I made my choice long ago. Even when she was taken to the mainland. I vowed to wait for her and always protect her." Teagan said, looking Doceo in the eyes. Doceo nodded.

"Thank you, Son. I feel better knowing she is in your hands. Of course, I realize everyone on the Island will protect her, but you put my, Dad side, at ease." He said as he stood and shook Teagan's hand.

"Well, go ahead and help her get some rest. I know she is hurting." Doc said with a smile.

"Yes Sir!" Teagan said as he turned and headed out of the room.

"I like him. He seems like a good boy for our Jassy." Alice said with a smile as she stood up.

"Trust me, Honey, he is the best one for her. I like Logan but he is not right for her. Never has been. That is why I would never allow it until she got her wolf. While it is her decision, I am still a father who wants the best for her." Doceo replied.

"That is the truth for all of us. But you made a great choice with him. She is going to need him a lot. Logan can't handle this. I know he can't." Vex replied. Alice shook her head in agreement.

"Logan is a bit of a mess. I am finding out." She said.

"You don't know the half of it." Vex said. Doceo nodded in agreement.

"I will fill you in later, Love. Let's get things settled with the men upstairs." He said as the three left the room and headed upstairs.

Rest, Relief And Safety

Teagan walked up the stairs and finally made it to Jasmica's room where Josh was standing guard at the door.

"Hey, man." He said.

"Hey, Tee! Long time no see. How are ya?" Josh replied reaching his hand out. Teagan took it and they did their secret handshake.

"I been better and worse. I guess that means I am ok. How about you?" He replied.

"I am as good as I can be, all things considered." Josh replied.

"I hear you there. How is she doing in there?" Teagan asked.

"In pain, but Toby has been in and out checking her vital signs and such. He is in there now. I am sure he knows better than I do right now." Josh answered.

"Ahh, may I?" Teagan asked as he motioned towards the door.

"Go right ahead man. You know I will always let ya in." Josh said opening the door.   "Thanks Buddy. Hang in there." Teagan said as he walked into the bedroom.

"No problem, you too." Josh said and shut the door.

Teagan walked down the small hallway and saw Toby standing beside her bed. Jasmica laid in bed, asleep, hooked to an I V, and whining in her sleep. He slowly walked in.

"Even in pain, she is beautiful." Conri said.

"Indeed, but I hate that she is in pain." Teagan replied.

"We can fix some of that." Conri replied. Teagan nodded. Toby looked up when Teagan entered the room and smiled.

"Thank the Gods for reinforcements!" He said with a chuckle. Teagan smiled.

"Always have to come help her as much as I can." Teagan replied.

"Well, go for it, Kiddo! I'll take all the help I can get at this point." Toby said. Teagan nodded and walked around the bed and gently sat down on the side. He took off his boots and gently climbed in bed next to Jasmica. He took her in his arms, resting her head on his chest.

***

As I felt someone touch me, my pain started to fade, my eyes fluttered open. I lifted my head and looked up to see Teagan's face. He smiled softly and kissed my forehead as I closed my eyes and a tear trailed down my cheek. Being in his arms felt so amazing. It felt like I was home. Like, no matter what, I would get through this and be safe.

I knew he would die before he let anything, or anyone, hurt me. My whole body relaxed and leaned into his. We melted together perfectly. It felt as though the last fifteen years of separation had not happened and we had been with each other the whole time. It was magical. I rested my head back down on his chest. He ran his fingers through my hair, stroking my head softly and pulling my hair back from my face.   "Shhh, Baby. Just rest." He said softly.

"What did you all decide to do about Mena?" I asked gently.

"You rest and worry about that later. We got it in hand. She will be safely at home soon." He replied. Unlike with Logan, I took that answer as truth and just enjoyed the peaceful space he had created for me in this moment.

Another tear came down my cheek.

"Why are you crying?" Kita asked.

"Because I am happy. I haven't felt this good in so very long. I forgot how amazing he made me feel and how loved I felt with him." I replied. Kita smiled and nodded.

"This is how your mate should make you feel. I looked through your memories and honestly, right here with him is where you need to be. But I will let you figure it out on your own. I am here if you need me." Kita replied.

"Thank you, Kita. Get some rest. I am ok." I said as I felt Teagan gently wipe the tear from my face.

Kita nodded and laid down.

"Are you ok, Babe?" Teagan whispered as he rested his lips against my forehead. I sniffled and nodded.

"Yes..." I whispered and I closed my eyes. "I just missed you." I said quietly.

"Trust me darlin', I have missed you more than you

know." He replied. I looked up at him and smiled. "I promise you. No matter what or who you choose, I will always be here for you. I will never let you go again." He said as he looked deep into my eyes.

I knew that he meant every word of what he was saying to me. He was being honest, and I could put stock into what he told me, one hundred percent. He kept every promise he ever made to me, or anyone. Teagan is everything our family and kingdom stood for. He was honest, loyal, respectful, trustworthy, and loved harder and truer than anyone I had ever known in my life. Another tear ran down my cheek as he gently took my face in his hands, doing his best not to hurt me.

"I know you have a lot going on. I don't expect you to just drop everything you have made with Logan or anyone else. But I will tell you here and now. I will wait and honor whatever choice you make. You are my life and always have been. So, while it will hurt if you don't choose me, I will always be with you. There is no one else for me, anywhere. I know that in my soul. You take your time. I have waited this long and will wait until you are mine again." Teagan said, still looking deep into my eyes as a tear escaped his eye and rolled down his cheek. I reached up and gently wiped it away and smiled. I was still confused, and he knew it. As much as I loved Teagan, the feelings for Logan were also strong. It was a choice I would have to make soon. But I also knew there was one hell of a storm brewing that I had to get through. As I went to speak, he placed his finger on my lips. "Shh, just rest, Baby. You don't need to say a thing. I don't expect an answer right now. Just relax and be safe for a while." He said as I gently leaned forward, his hand lifted my jaw up closer to his face. I smiled and closed my eyes as our lips met in a gentle, slow, and loving kiss. Once we parted, I slid down and rested my head back on his chest, snuggling close. He wrapped his arms around me.

"I love you, Teagan." I whispered as my eyes closed and I started to fall asleep.

"I love you too, Jasmica." He whispered back, closing his eyes and continuing to stroke my hair.

Meanwhile, down in the courtyard, a small army of men started to assemble. Logan, hearing commotion outside his room, woke up and slowly got out of bed, feeling very sore and stiff.

"Holy shit! That was a hell of a ride." Cage said.

"You're telling me. I think we underestimated Kita. She is no ordinary hybrid or Lycan." Logan replied. His head was pounding.

"Well, she is a tri-brid, I guess I should have expected a harsher impact." Cage said. *"Yeah, well, if she can do that to us, how are we supposed to protect her? Especially when she is my mate. I can't have her out shining me."* Logan replied.

"That shouldn't even be an issue you are thinking about. Plenty of Lunas are stronger than their Alphas. They must be, to protect their people as well as their mate, if they were to get hurt. That is just your damn ego talking. Damn that vampire side." Cage said.

"Well, it bothers me." Logan said as he stood up to dress himself.

"Don't let it! When I am on my game in training, it may be different. Don't worry about it. We got this." Cage replied.

"We better." Logan said as he opened his door and looked out.

"Better go see what is going on and what the plan is." Cage said.

"Yeah, I'm on it." Logan replied and he took some

Tylenol with water. Cage did not allow Logan to feel or think about the fact that someone else was holding Jassy right now. He knew she needed the help and Logan was needed elsewhere.

Logan walked out into the courtyard to see a tent set up with Doceo and Vex standing under it. They were leaning over a table, looking at something. Men were scurrying around the courtyard and Warketh was standing on a stack of crates with his megaphone, shouting orders at them.

"Aye! Are ye all total numb skulls! Get dose cannons to da peer not on da dragon lift." He barked. "Come on everyone! Get yur heads out yur arses." Warketh continued as he saw Logan coming out into the yard. "Mornin' Sunshine! Did ya have a fun trip?" Warketh said with a chuckle.

"Oh, ya, it was the damn time of my life." Logan said. "What is going on here?" He asked.

"We gettin ready to get Mena back. I'd go to da bosses or' dere and see what dey want ye to be doin'." Warketh replied.

"Alright. Will do." Logan replied.

"Oye! Cum on guys. Pick up da pace! I am gonna be in mah grave before we get loaded up." Warketh complained.

Vex looked up.

"Oh look, Sleeping Beauty is awake." He said with a chuckle. Doc looked up.

"Yeah, yeah, yeah. Stuff it Vex. My head is killing me. I don't need your shit right now." Logan replied as he looked at Doc.

"So, what are my orders, Sir?" He asked, before Vex

could say anymore.

"Well, that depend on how you are feeling." Doc replied.

"I have a headache from hell and I'm a bit sore, but other than that, I am perfectly fine." Logan said.

"You ok enough to lead a small brigade of men to stage a distraction, to get a few Secret Agents into Luna's Castle?" Doc asked.

"Is Kye leading the Agents?" Logan asked.

"Yes, he is. He has handpicked his team to go in and get Mena out." Doceo replied.

"Ok then. I am down to lead my men." Logan said.

"There will be a combination of men and women going, not just ours." Vex said.

"I figured that, but now that we are all on the same playing field, they become my men as we all serve in the same military. Least that is how I figure it." Logan said.

"He has a point." Doceo said.

"True. I just wanted him to be aware it's not just the standard guys and gals." Vex said. Logan shrugged.

"This is the plan. The tunnels are being cleared as we speak, thanks to the Dwarves. So, we will follow them over to the shore where we can set up a base camp. I have been in touch with Queen Lilith Althair of Hammaslathi. She said that she and her daughter are on our side. Her kingdom is split, between Alduin followers, now that he is back, and us, but we are welcome to use their shore to regroup. They will set up a base for us there." Doceo said. Logan nodded.   "What about the rest of our ports?" Logan asked.

"All are useable except Newham, as far as we know." Vex reported.

"Damn! We lost one already?" Logan asked.

"Yes, sadly, but we will get it back. Major Tucket is there now with some men, making plans to retake it." Doceo replied.

"Good, I am glad. If anyone can get it done it is him." Logan said as he looked at the map, studying the markings of the battles that have occurred.

"Are the tunnels built big enough to ship and support the cannons still?" Vex asked.

"Not sure. Stock and his crew haven't said yet. They are checking it out now. Possibly reinforcing things. But the sooner we can get Warketh down there the better." Doceo replied.

"If you are done with me, I'll go relieve Warketh so he can help Stock in the tunnels." Logan said.

"Go ahead. If we need anything from you or anything changes, we will shout or radio you, over." Doceo said. Logan nodded and headed back towards Warketh.

Logan quickly jogged over to Warketh.

"Ok, Old Man, get your ass back in the tunnels. I'll take it from here." Logan said with a bit of a chuckle.

"Ol' Man my arse. I can still kick yer arse any day." Warketh replied.

"Yeah, yeah, get down there. They need you." Logan said.

"Aye got it, Sir." Warketh said as he hopped down, turned on his enchanted boots and took off to the tunnels, under the city and across the ocean to the mainland.

Logan looked over the crew he had. There were all sorts of different races and tribesmen running around the courtyard. He looked over the dragon cargo, the list of ammunition and stock they were taking, and how it is being transported.

"Lieutenant Swayer!" Logan called out. The Elf in front of him stopped, turned, and stood at attention.

"Yes Sir, Colonel Santiago, Sir." He shouted.

"Load about five more cases of ammo on dragon two and three." Logan commanded. "Yes,   Sir."   The Lieutenant said as he saluted and ran off to do what he was told.

"Master Chief York. I suggest you get some more artillery on those ships along with quick repair kits too. We are going into a rough one." Logan said.

"Note taken and will do, Sir." Replied the officer. Logan looked around and watched the men and women running around getting things together.

"We got ear to da tunnels n they look good so far. Still intact. Though we are havin to reinforce da floors as we go, to support dos cannons. So far so good. Over" Stocks voice reported over the radios.

"Well, there is our answer on that." Vex said.

"Ten four, Stock. Keep up the good work. Over." Doceo replied as Kye walked up to the tent.

"You always have perfect timing. How do you do that?" Vex asked.

"Guess it is my sixth sense." Kye replied as he shrugged.

"I'd say it's because we are Demons and watch everything everywhere." Ahz said as he came up to the tent behind Kye. Kye shrugged again.

"Either way, you both have great timing." Doceo said. "Colonel Santiago, please report to the planning area. Over." Doceo said over the radio. Hearing this, Logan came jogging over to them.

"Yes, Sir." Logan said.

"I called you all here so we can go over the plan and make sure we are all on the same page." Doceo said.

"About that." Ahz said. "I think we should send someone to check on Mena's physical state before we get in there." He suggested.

"What do you mean? Like Astral projection?" Akasha asked as she appeared out of thin air, making everyone jump.

"Yes, exactly." Ahz said.

"That's actually not a bad idea." Vex replied.

"It should be someone who can comfort her. While I would love my granddaughter to do it. Sending her in where a Demon is lurking is not a good idea. So, if you all agree, I will do it while you are getting ready to go." Akasha replied.

"I don't know anyone else who would be better for the job." Doceo said.

"Hey, I could do it you know." Vex said.

"I know but your head needs to be focused here." Doc replied as he pointed to the map.   "He has a point, Vex. We know you can do many things, but right now, getting intel and heading up the team to find the children is where we need you most right now." Ahz said.

"I agree." Doceo said.

"I understand. I am just worried about my niece." Vex

replied.

"We all are." Akasha said.

"Not really all of us. To be honest it doesn't really bother me." Kye said, his voice indifferent.

"Demons." Vex said shaking his head.

"Now, as soon as I hear from Stock and Warketh that the tunnels are all clear, we will send you all out." Doc said, rolling out a blueprint of the Bacimorte Castle. "I think the best place to make the distraction is on the front right corner. Here. And the front of the Castle. Here." Doceo pointed.

"We are gonna need a makeshift bridge for both places because of the mote." Logan said.

"Yeah, you know as well as I do the pussyfoots will close the draw bridge, as soon as they are under attack." Ahz said.

"We better make sure the Agents go in there and not the men, or we will lose more people than is necessary." Kye said.

"Definitely! The less men we lose the better." Logan said.

"Agreed." Doc said.

"Akasha. You go project and check on Mena. Then we can regroup. Logan and Ahz, get the men to start building the bridges to get across the mote." Doceo commanded.

"Yes, Sir." Ahz and Logan replied and went to direct the men to start building the bridges. Akasha nodded and headed towards the forest.

"I am going to go head out and see if I can help find your grand kids." Vex said.   "Godspeed, Brother. Be careful." Doceo said.

"I will and Godspeed to you, too." Vex said as he whistled and his Alicorn came down from the sky. He hopped up on her and headed off. Doceo looked out of the tent to watch the commotion of the soldiers and sighed.

"It's going to be a long one." Alpha said.

"Very much so, and stressful too." Doceo replied.

"Yes, but once they are home safe, we can focus more on the war." Alpha said.

"Yes, and training Jassy." Doc said.

"True. One thing at a time though." Alpha replied. Doceo nodded and just stared for a while, waiting on word from Stock and Warketh while Kye meditated beside him.

CONNECTIONS

Akasha finally made it to the woodland and through the forest to the ceremonial circle that she and Jasmica had made years ago. On the ground inside a white stone circle was a pentacle. A white stone star with a round, flat, stone platform on each point of the star and one in the center. Akasha put fresh candles on each platform for the corresponding elements. She stood on the middle platform with a white candle in front of her. She sighed, then held her arms out and taking a deep breath said,

"I call upon the elements to protect me, as well as the God and Goddess, while I move along this astral plane. I ask you for safe passage and a clear strong connection to my niece, Mena." She spoke. She visualized the elements circling her as she rooted her body to the ground. She sat cross legged behind the white candle, closed her eyes, and concentrated on her breathing.

Soon she was looking down on her body as it sat calmly

and protected, in the center of the circle and pentacle on the ground. She checked that her chain was connected securely to her body, around her waist, and to the body on the ground, because without this connection, she could not get back to her earthly body and would be lost, floating in another astral plane, and her earthly body would die. After double checking her connections, she headed towards the Bacimorte's Castle. She moved swiftly. As she approached the Castle, she could see, where humans, Demons and Dark Elves had cast protective defenses upon the Castle.

"Hmm, how am I going to get in here?" She wondered. She circled around the perimeter of the Castle and noticed many gaps in the protective shields. Near the dungeon there was one opening through a window, but before Akasha entered the room, she put her own protective shield in place, so that they could not trap her inside. Akasha then slipped right through. As luck would have it, it was Mena's cell.

Once inside, she slowly approached Mena who was lying on the floor in the dark. She looked worse than Akasha could have ever imagined.

"Mena, Honey." Akasha said softly. Mena did not move a muscle. Akasha watched her for a moment, waiting to see if she was breathing. Her breathing was very shallow. Akasha breathed a sigh of relief. "Mena, Honey. Wake up for me." Akasha said a bit louder. Mena was the only one who could hear Akasha in her present form. Slowly, Mena lifted her head and looked up at her Ohmah.

"Are you here to save me?" Mena croaked.

"No, Honey. I am here to tell you we are on our way. Do not give up, My Sweet." She explained. Mena nodded, as tears started rolling down her cheeks. "I know, Honey. Don't cry. Kyerus and a couple others will be setting out as soon as I return. I need to ask you. How are you healing?" She asked.

"Not much at all, Ohmah. They keep rebreaking bones as fast as they heal. They used my blood to bring back that thing." Mena responded as tears rolled down her puffy, broken cheeks.   "It's ok, Honey. We can fix that. Just hang on. I promise you; we are on our way as fast as we can." Akasha replied.

"It hurts so bad. I don't know how much longer I can last." Mena said sniffling.

"I know, just hang on a bit longer. We will get you home. Can you walk?" Akasha asked. Mena shook her head no.

"I can barely move at all." She replied.

"Ok, we will have someone who can carry you." Akasha said.

"Someone is coming." Mena said quietly.

"Ok, I will take my leave. I love you, Honey. Stay strong." Akasha said as she rushed out the wall and back to her body.

Once Akasha was in her body, she shook her head a little and refocused. She sat with her anger for a moment and collected her thoughts in the safety of the circle. She made sure no Demon, Dark Elf, or anything else followed her back to her body. She performed her checks, grounded herself, and stood up slowly. She went around the circle, thanking and dismissing each element as she snuffed out each candle. She thanked the God and Goddess for her safe travel, and she dismissed them, too. Finally, she hurried back to the courtyard to report her findings to Doceo.

When Akasha reached the courtyard, she could see that

the military were almost ready to leave.

"Doceo!" She called out. Doc was studying a map and getting the latest update on the current events. He turned and looked in the direction of her voice and he saw her running across the courtyard with tears flowing down her cheeks. Once she reached him, he looked at her with concern.

"Mom, what's wrong?" He asked.

"We have more than just an army to worry about. They have Dark Elves and Demons who have placed protective shields up around the Castle itself. How many Mages have you assigned to go?" Akasha asked wiping her face.

"I think two or three." He answered. "I didn't think we would need them." Doceo finished.

She looked at Doceo and shook her head as Kye and Ahz approached them.

"So, I am guessing that things are not so great, by the look on your face." Kye said looking at Doceo. "Let me guess, they have placed magic seals and protective shields up by now." Kye said.

"How did you know?" Akasha asked.

"Remember, Ahz and I used to be part of their army at one time. I figured that they would be putting them up shortly. Especially when Doceo said the Demon Kingdom was entering the war." He said and sighed.

"Well, they are not good at it. There are many spaces between them." Akasha replied. Kye chuckled some.

"Yeah, that is done on purpose, to seal people in when they sneak through. I am guessing, seeing how you are back, you figured that out." Kye said.

"Yeah, I put in my own bracer so it could not close."

She replied.

"Good idea." Doc replied.

"How many Mages would you suggest?" Doc asked.

"At least four Mages and four Demons, plus us, should be enough to break it down to distract them." Ahz replied.

"Both of you?" Doceo asked.

"Shouldn't one of you stay here, just in case?" Akasha asked.

"Nope. If Alduin attacks or tries to stop all of you, then they are gonna need us both to get out." Kye replied.

"Good point." Doc replied. "What is Mena's condition?" Doceo asked.

"Broken." Akasha said trying to hold back more tears.

"How broken?" He asked. She took a deep breath.

"She can barely move. Healing is impossible because they break her body as soon as it heals. She is not only physically broken, but mentally too. She is close to giving up. She needs us there, as soon as possible." Akasha reported. Doceo tried to swallow down his anger as his eyes glowed.

"Everyone needs to move! Double time!" He commanded over the radio.

"Is Vex back yet?" Akasha asked.

"Yup, just got back." Vex said from behind her, making her jump a little.

"Did you find the kids?" Doceo asked.

"Yes! They are in with Toby getting checked over. They seem ok, just dirty and shook up." Vex replied.

"Oh! Thank the Gods, they are ok!" Akasha exclaimed

as Doceo breathed a sigh of relief.   "Well then, I will let you gentleman handle this and I will go tend to the children with Alice. Just holler if you need me." Akasha said.

"Thanks Mom." Doceo said.

"Think nothing of it, Dear." She said as she disappeared inside.

"Where were they?" Doceo asked.

"Hiding from the men in the woods. They did not recognize any of them and didn't know if they were friend or foe." Vex replied.

"Ahh, makes sense. I guess we taught them well." Doc said as his face grew a bit dark as his thoughts went to Mena. "I need you to head up the Mages and Demons that must go over, as there are many traps and shields that are surrounding the Castle walls. We need them taken down so that those going in will only have to worry about what's inside." Doceo ordered.

"Will do. I will go get them now." Vex said.

"No need. I grabbed them already when I was picking those who will go in. They are the best in their fields when dealing with both threats of Elven and Demonic magic or "Dark" magic." Ahz replied.

"Just to double check, I went over them also. Seeing how Ahzreal has been out of the loop." Kye said.

"Well, I will trust you got the best of the best then." Vex said.

"Without getting the elders involved, yes. They are over there by the dragon fliers. Shall we head over?" Kye asked.

"Yes. The faster we get her home the better." Vex said.

"Yes, and she will need to be carried out, carefully." Doceo announced.

"Ok, glad I grabbed Ol' Matoskah then." Kye said.

"Why him?" Ahz asked.

"They don't call him a light-footed, delicate beast for nothing." Kye said with a smile. "He is a powerhouse, but he can be careful, and he protects everything he carries." Doceo said.

"Makes sense. I forgot about him. Damn, I need to catch up on things again." Ahz replied. Kye nodded.

"Well Godspeed, you all. I will catch Logan up on what is going on and you can all meet up before the battle and finalize your plan of attack." Doceo said.

"Sounds good, Godspeed." Vex said as he, Kye and Ahz walked off towards the dragon stables.

"Hey, Colonel Santiago, to the tent. Over" Doceo radioed.

"Ten four. On my way. Over and out." Logan answered. Logan jogged over to where Doceo was standing under the tent, as it started to rain.

"Oh, great! Just what we need." Logan thought.

"Yes, Sir. You called." Logan said as he reached Doceo.

"You will have to converse with Vex, Kye and Ahz when you all reach the beach. They need to carry Mena out and there is Dark magic that needs to be lifted to get into the Castle itself." Doceo reported.

"Ok, sounds good." Logan replied.

"Warketh to da Base." The radios went off.

"Go ahead, Warketh." Doceo responded.

"We can get all da way to da nest. I repeat, we can get all da way to da nest. N our paths be secure n stable." Warketh said.

"Careful War, there may be magic traps." Kye said over the radio.

"Aye we used our goggles and dem damn idiots forgot da floors." Warketh chuckled. "That figures." Ahz said.

"Well, tis good fer us and no one said we was workin wid da brightest bulbs in da tree. No offense." Warketh replied.

"Ehh, non-taken. Since we left, most of them don't know their ass from a hole in the wall." Ahz said.

"Ok, well, that will get you all closer and inside without having to walk into the middle of that damn hell hole." Doceo said.

"Definitely." Vex said.

"Thank you. Warketh and Stock. Keep those paths clear and open down there. Everyone else, do a once over of your units and cargo, then report." Doceo commanded.

"That all you wanted me for?" Logan asked.

"Yeah, and make sure they all come back, if you can." Doceo said.

"I always do my best, Sir. You know that." Logan replied. Doceo nodded. Logan took his leave to make sure everything was in order. Doceo stood waiting for their reports.

Upstairs Jasmica opened her eyes as Teagan's radio went off.

"Comander Avendon here. We are all set. Over." Vex radioed.

"Ten four" Doceo replied.

"Master Chief York here. We are ready to sail." York radioed.

"Ten four" Doceo replied.

"Colonel Santiago. We are ready to ride." Logan reported.

"Ten four" Doceo radioed. "Everyone be safe, be smart and come back safe. May the Gods be with us all. Bring home the package safe. Godspeed to you all." Doceo said as he felt someone looking at him. He looked up and saw Jasmica standing in the window. Logan looked up and saw her too. She was supported by Jeni. She put the radio to her mouth. Doceo nodded at her.

"Ok, y'all let's take to the skies, part the waters, and tear up the dirt. It's time to roll. Godspeed and be safe." Jasmica ordered. Dragons, Alicorns and Pegasus took flight. Anchors lifted in the harbor. Mermaids took off like a torpedo though the water. Hooves and feet drummed through the tunnels. They were all on their way.

Before Logan left, he looked up at Jasmica again. Teagan was behind her, but he could not see him.

"You should say something to her." Cage suggested.

"I just can't right now. You know I am not good at good-byes." Logan replied as he hopped up onto the saddle of his black Alicorn. Logan made eye contact with me. I smiled weakly and mouthed, "Be safe." He nodded and spurred the horse to take off. We both knew this could be the last time we saw each other but it was all part of our duties and war. I knew he would not come near me right now. He never did when he had to leave for battle. I sighed and looked off into the distance.

Once he was gone out of sight, Teagan took over

holding me up.

"He will be ok, Jassy." Jeni said.

"I know. He always is, no matter what it is. He always seems to be ok. I am more worried about my twin right now." I replied.

"We should get you back in bed. Toby would be having kittens if he knew you were up." Teagan said. Jeni laughed.

"It wouldn't be the first time." Jeni remarked.

"True, but I would rather not get lectured by him today." Teagan replied.

"Amen to that. He is too good at lectures." I said and Teagan picked me up. "I can walk you know." I proclaimed.

"I know, but not that fast and, we need to get you back in bed." Teagan replied.

"Ok, fine." I replied.

"That didn't take much convincing." Jeni said.

"It only happens when she is not feeling well. You know that, Jen." He stated.

"Yeah, yeah, yeah. Hush you two." I said in a sour tone.

Just as we crossed the main staircase, Doceo met us.

"Hey you three." Doceo said.

"Hello, Sir." Jeni said as she curtsied.

"Good to see you, Sir." Teagan replied.

"Hi, Dad." I said.

"How are you feeling, my Little Monkey?" He asked.

"Like I have been run over by a truck, then backed over and run over again." I replied resting my head back on Teagan's shoulder.

"I figured about as much. But it will get easier and the effects will fade, the more you do it." Doceo explained.

"I hope so, because I am about ready to beat Kita for it." I said sighing. Teagan and Doceo laughed.

"Hey, that is not very nice you know. I am here to help and protect you." Kita protested.   *"Sorry, Kita. I just hurt."* I apologized. Kita nodded and laid down.

"Did they find the Little Ones yet?" I asked quietly.

"Yes, Honey, they did. I was headed to check on them, after I checked on you. Alice and your Ohmah are with them." He replied.

"Good. I am glad. Can you tell them I love them and will be down to see them soon. Please?" I asked as I started to dose off in Teagan's arms.

"I will." Doceo replied as he kissed my forehead. I smiled weakly. "Best get her back to bed to rest." Doceo said quietly. Teagan nodded. "Thank you both for taking care of her." He said.

"Of course," Teagan replied.

"Always do." Jeni said.

"Ok, kids. I will see you all soon." He said as he headed back down the stairs.

"See you soon, Sir." Both Teagan and Jeni called after him. They headed to Jasmica's room with her softly snoring.

***

Meanwhile, all the military services were headed towards the Fort near Hammaslathi.

Raven, stood on the stairs of Tirion Castle, looked

towards the Secret Palace and saw the men taking off.

"Godspeed, all." He whispered as he, and the few Agents with him, made a fist over their hearts. When they could not see them in the distance any longer, they all moved into the throne room. Vanora was sitting there, still stunned at what her husband had said to her. As the men came in, Verona looked up and saw her son, Raven, and the other Agents come in.

"You are not packed yet, Mother?" Raven asked.

"No, I can't possibly go alone. I was waiting to see if your father came to his senses, or maybe one of you boys." Venora replied.

"Well, we are here to help support Luna's cause." Raven replied. The Agents nodded in agreement.

"Oh! That is wonderful!" She exclaimed. "I always knew you were smarter than all of them." She continued as she kissed his cheek and hugged him tight.

"Well, let's get packing and get going. I'll send word to Luna that we are coming." Venora said excitedly.

"Ok, you do that." Raven replied as he watched his mother scurry out of the room.

"Dominic!" Raven said.

"Yes, Sir." One of the Agents said.

"Take one of the others with you and take inventory at the docks of who will be going with us." Raven commanded.

"Yes, Sir." Dominic replied as he and another Agent, Jock, went off to the docks. Raven sighed, dreading being away from home and what he was getting into the next few months.

"The rest of you. Start packing the carriage and get your things together so we can leave soon." Raven commanded.

"Yes, Sir!" The others responded and went on their way. Raven headed to his room to pack the things he needed for the trip.

Raphael, Ravens assistant, came up to him as Raven came into his room.

"I am going with you, Sir." He stated.

"No Raph. You need to stay here. It's not safe." Raven replied.

"To hell with safe! I have been with you since you were a baby. I will be damned if you go in there alone without someone who is not corrupted." Raphael responded.

"Fine. Just know, I can't blow my cover." Raven said in a whisper.

"I know. Your brother told me already. Once I knew that, I told him I would go help where I could." Raphael said with a wink. Raven nodded.

"I appreciate it, man. I really do." Raven said. Raphael nodded and set to packing.

Down on the docks and in the stable area, Dominic and Jock arrived at chaos. People were running around everywhere, and few military personnel were trying to gain some kind of control over things. Dominic stood on a crate and fired his gun in the air. Everyone froze and looked at him.   "Now that I have your attention. You all need to make lines, quietly, quickly and in an orderly fashion and board the boats and carriages to get to the Bacimorte's Castle. Do you understand?" Dominic asked.

"Yes, Sir." Everyone said as they started to form

orderly lines. The soldiers, who were trying to get things in order, approached him.

"How did you do that?" he asked.

"Practice, and I am not afraid to use my gun." Dominic said. The soldiers nodded as they supervised the people getting onto the transportation vehicles.

As soon as the carriages and ships were loaded, the soldiers and Agents returned to the Castle. Raven was sitting in his office jotting down some notes when Dominic knocked on the door.   "Who is it?" Raven asked.

"Dominic and company." He answered.

"Come in." Raven replied. The soldiers came in.

"Everyone is loaded and ready to leave now, Sir." Dominic reported.

"Ok, set off then. We will be right behind you." Raven replied as he shook Dominic's hand and received a note from him at the same time.

"Yes, Sir." Dominic replied. He and the rest of the soldiers left the room. Raven sat back in his chair and read the note.

"Hmmm, only about 3000 coming along." He thought.

"Not too shabby." Razor said.

"Meh, its less than a quarter of the Tirion Army." Raven replied.

"True, but that is a good thing." Razor replied.

"Indeed." Raven said as there came a knock on his door again.

"Who is it?" Raven said.

"It's Mother." Verona replied.

"Come in." He said as she opened the door and came in.

"Are you ready to go?" She asked.

"I think so. Let me check with Raph." Raven said as he stood and crossed the room.   "Raph…"   Raven   called out.

"Yes, Sir." Raph said as he came in the passage door to the left.

"Are we all set?" he asked.

"Yes, Sir, we are ready to leave when you are." Raph replied.

"Great! Let's get out of this trader's area." Verona said. Raven, Raph, and Verona all headed down to the carriage. Once they were at them and Verona was inside, Raven held his hand out. One of his Ravens flew down, landing on his hand. He attached the small paper to the bird and cooed at him and the bird took flight again. "Can we leave now or are you going to play with your birds all night?" Verona snapped.

"Coming mother dear, I was instructing them where to go, nothing more. They can be very helpful you know." Raven replied as he climbed in the carriage. Verona rolled her eyes as the carriage took off.

WAITING...

I woke with my head on Teagan's chest, and I was still a bit groggy and sore. I carefully got up off the bed, so as not to wake him. He gently grabbed my wrist.

"Where do you think you are going, Miss Avedon?" He asked as he opened his eyes and a smile crept across his face.

"I was headed to the bathroom. Then, I was planning on going downstairs for a bit." I answered, smiling back. He nodded and let me go. I went across the bedroom and into the bathroom. Teagan sat up and looked at the clock on the wall.

"Probably should try to get some food in you. It's almost dinner time." He called out. As I washed my hands, I felt my stomachache and heard it growl.

"Yeah, I think that is a good idea." I answered. I left the bathroom, went through the bedroom, and into my closet to change into different clothes.

Jeni popped out of the passageway, inside the closet.

"Oh! Good you're up. I was just coming to check on you." She said with a bit of a start.   "Yeah, I just woke up. Is dinner ready yet?" I asked.

"Almost. That was another reason I came up. To see if you and Tee would be attending dinner or if you were gonna eat up here?" She asked.

"We will be at dinner, but I could use some help getting dressed, if you don't mind? I'm still sore as hell." I stated with a weak smile.

"Jassy, you know you don't have to ask." She replied.

"I know but you know how I am." I replied.

"Yeah, I know, silly" Jen said. "Let me get you something you will be comfortable in." She added.

"Ok, thank you, Jen. You are the best." I said hugging her gently.

"You're welcome, Bestie. Now go sit on the lounge sofa." She ordered as she hugged me gently in return.

I moved to the center of the room and gently eased myself down onto the lounge.

"Hey honey. Are you ok?" Teagan asked from the other side of the closet door.

"Yeah, I am good. Jen is here helping me. Why don't you head down and let them know I will be down soon, please." I called back.

"Ok Sweetheart. See you down there." He answered.

"Yuppers." I called back. Teagan chuckled and headed out the bedroom door.

After hearing the door click, Jeni came over to me with two tops, one in each hand.   "So…" She said looking at me.

"So what?" I asked as I pointed to the black one in her right hand.

"How are things going with Tee?" She asked as she put the shirt in her left hand back in the closet.

"Good. He is so damn amazing. I forgot how amazing he really is. It's refreshing, but confusing too." I responded, sighing.

"Listen, you know I am always here for you. Do you want my advice?" Jen asked looking at me.

"Yes and no." I replied as we both chuckled.

"Well, I'm gonna give it to you anyway." Jeni said.

"Ok…" I replied, bracing myself. Jeni sat down next to me.

"Cut Logan loose. He is no good for you. We both know it. He only hurts you." She stated.

"But I…" Jen cut me off by holding her hand up. I stopped talking.

"I know you love him. I know he loves you, but only to a point. He can't give you what you need. He hasn't been able to the whole time we have been gone. A mate bond isn't gonna tame that boy and you know it. He has known about it for most of your lives. It has changed nothing. Tee makes you happy and you deserve to be loved and happy and treated like the Queen you really are. Tee keeps you grounded, and you help him fly. You are perfect together and destine to be with each other." She finished. I looked at her and I closed my eyes.

"I know all this Jen. It's just more complicated. Inside."

I said as a tear slid down my face.

"Oh Sweetie. I didn't mean to make you cry." Jeni replied gently hugging me.

"It's not your fault. Tee mentioned things that got me to thinking the same things you just mentioned. I am so confused." I replied sniffling. Jeni pulled away and wiped my tears.

"Girl, you don't have to decide right now. I am just making my case and pointing things out to you." She noted. I nodded.

"Thank you, Jen. You are the best." I replied.

"I know." She replied as we both laughed. "Let's get you dressed" she sadded.

"Ok, sounds good." I replied.

***

Teagan walked into the dining room to see many of the royals sitting at their tables.   "Uncle Tee!" A young group of children yelled, as they ran towards him.

"Hey guys!" He replied. He knelt and the group of kids toppled him over with hugs. "How are you all?" He asked as they all chattered at him at the same time. "Whoa! Whoa! One at time guys. I don't have super hearing." He laughed.

"Okay, everyone, I know you're excited to see him but back to your seats. It's almost time to eat. You can all chat with him after dinner or during if he is sitting with us." Bree said, as she and her husband, Fayte, approached them. She herded the children towards their seats.

Fayte reached his hand out to help Teagan up.

"Thanks, Man." He said taking Fayte's hand.

"No problem, man. I've been there." Fayte laughed.

"I guess they missed me a little." Teagan replied.

"Yeah, I would say so. Good to see you, man. It's been way too long!" Fayte answered. "I know it has been. It's good to see you as well." Teagan replied. Exie approached them. "Hey there, Tee!" She greeted him.

"Hey, Exie." Teagan replied as they hugged and kissed each other's cheeks.

"Is Sis coming to dinner?" She asked.

"Yeah, Jen is helping her get ready." He replied.

"Hell, she could have come in her jammies. I would if Bree would let me." Fayte said and the three of them laughed.

"Definitely. She has had a long day!" Exie replied.

"I think she just wanted to look like she is ok." Teagan replied.

"How is she doing?" Exie asked.

"What happened to her?" Fayte asked.

"She phased for the first time today, Fayte." Exie answered.

"Oh Damn! That is rough." Fayte answered.

"Yeah, it sure is. She is doing ok. Tired and sore but you know her, pushing herself, as always." Teagan replied. Exie shook her head.

"How are you feeling Exie?" Teagan asked.

"Oh, we are good." She said as she rubbed her small belly. "I'm not due for a bit now." She said with a smile.

"Glad to hear it." Teagan replied.

"Yeah, we've been worried about all the stress affecting you and the baby." Fayte said. "Don't want that little bun to come out too early." He said laughing.

"Definitely not!" Exie replied, smiling.

***

After getting dressed in flowing, black dress pants and a black, V-neck top. I put on black, sparkly ballerina flats and came out of the closet to my vanity. Jeni helped me with my hair. Tonight, I wasn't wearing makeup. I was too tired for that. I spritzed myself with perfume and stood up. Jeni held out her arm.

"I know you think you are super women, but just accept the help." She offered. I smiled and nodded, taking her arm in mine as we walked to the door. Josh opened it, hearing our footsteps approaching.

"I can take it from here, Jen." Josh said.

"Ok Josh, thank you. I'll be headed to the kitchen and around if you need me." She explained. I took Josh's arm.

"Nice and slow, Hun. We don't need you getting too tired or falling." He advised me. I nodded and smiled a little smile. We walked to the top of the stairs and Josh scooped me up in his arms.

"I can walk down them." I protested.

"Not today. You need to keep your strength up to eat." Josh replied.

"Ok fine, but at least put me down so that I can walk into dinner, please?" I asked.

"I can do that." Josh replied as he carried me down the stairs to the back entrance of the dining hall. He gently set me down, making sure I was stable, before opening the door. He held his arm out, I took it, smiled, and he escorted me into dinner. As I walked in with him, I saw my family all together, laughing and talking, and Teagan fit in with them perfectly. It warmed my heart to see them all relaxed. But a twinge of pain came over my heart, not seeing my twin or her husband amongst them. Her three children were sitting quietly among the others, waiting on their food.

"Josh, I need to see my niece and nephews over there, first." I said pointing towards them. He nodded as we changed course and moved towards them. Once I was closer to the children, I saw Mena's oldest, Trey Jr, whom we called JR. I could see his violet eyes were red from crying. He was only eight years old. The twins, Selena, and Tyler were only four, and they were now all alone in this big room, without their mother or father. JR was looking at the floor when my pants came into his view. He looked up and a smile came across his face. He stood up and hugged me tight, which hurt, but I held in a yelp, hugging him back just as tight.

"I am so glad you're ok, Auntie Jas." He said with his face pressed against me. I smiled and squatted down, so I was eye level with him.

"I will always be, OK." I said wiping his tears away from his face.

"I missed you so much." He replied.

"I have missed you as well, My Little One." I said smiling. Selena and Tyler hopped on my back, hugging me. "Uff" I said feeling more pain but not letting it show. "There are my other two Little Ones." I said smiling through it all.

"Hi's Auntie!" They exclaimed.

Teagan noticed me with the kids and excused himself from Exie and Fayte. He headed towards the children and me. He took the twins off my back.

"Hey, you two Little Monkeys, easy on your Auntie." He said smiling and hugging them both. I smiled. Selena looked at him and Tyler started to tear up.

"Who is you?" Selena asked.

"I am your Uncle Teagan. It's nice to meet you." He said politely. She looked at me for assurance. I nodded my approval; she smiled and hugged him.

"Otay." She said happily. "No cry, cry, Ty. Him is safe." Selena said to her twin, Tyler, touching his face. I smiled to myself, remembering how Mena used to do that to me, and I to her, when we needed reassurance. I closed my eyes as JR touched my cheek.

"It will be ok, Auntie. We will find Momma. Right Uncle Teagan?" He asked.

"Right." Teagan said with a nod. I took JR in my arms and hugged him again, holding back my tears. He hugged me back and held his tears also.

"How about we have some dinner at our own table tonight?" I suggested.

"Yes, please!" The kids answered.

"Josh, can you…" I began.

"Already on it. I'll get them to set up a table for five." Josh replied and scurried off to tell Jeni and the staff.

As the table was set up, Alice noticed and leaned over to Doceo.

"What is going on? Have we done something to upset Jasmica?" She asked. Doceo looked at his wife a bit confused. She gestured to Jasmica, Teagan and the children sitting at their own table.

"Ohh," He replied. "No, My Sweet. Mena's children are close to Jasmica. I am sure she is trying to make them feel better because their parents are not here. If she were angry, trust me, we would know." Doceo replied.

"Oh, ok Dear. I was worried for a moment. Shouldn't they be with all the family?" She asked.

"They have been, all day. As you know, they have been asking for her, so I think it is best to let them be. She can bring them more comfort right now than we can." He replied.

"Ok, My Love." She replied.

Teagan pulled out my chair and I sat down. The kids sat between us. We both helped the Little Ones with their dinners, as they told us about their day. They also filled us in on what had been going on before, and after they were rescued. We laughed and made jokes and the time flew by. After dinner, I went with them into the playroom and colored with JR while Selena and Tyler played with blocks on the floor with Teagan.

"Auntie?" JR asked.

"Yes, Hun?" I replied.

"Can we go somewhere to talk?" He asked.

"Of course, Buddy. Just let me tell Teagan we are going for a walk." I said with a smile. He nodded as we stood up.

"Hey, you three. JR and I are going for a walk. Will you guys be, ok?" I asked.

"We be fines." Selena piped up.

"I is goods. I godziwa. Rawr!" Tyler said as he knocked over some blocks and they laughed.

"I think we are good, Babe. I mean, Hun." Teagan said bashfully smiling.

"Ok. We will be back." I said holding out my hand to JR. He took my hand, and we left the room. He moved in closer, putting his arm around me and I put mine around him. We walked down the hall to the swing, under the gazebo, at the end of the hall. The ceiling of the gazebo was glass so you could look at the sky.

"So, what is up, Little One?" I asked as we sat, snuggling up on the swing, rocking and looking up at the stars.

"Do you think they will really find Momma?" He asked.

"I know they will." I said, brushing a blonde curl out of his violet eyes.

"Will she be, ok?" He asked.

"I hope so, Buddy. I really hope so." I replied. He nodded and went quiet for a moment.   "Auntie" he said.

"Yes, Hun." I replied.

"Will you take care of us if not?" He asked. I sat up and looked him in his eyes.

"I will always take care of you three and keep you safe, no matter what. I am here for you all." I said and tears fell from both our eyes. I hugged him tight.

"Shh, it will be ok." I said trying to sooth him as he started to cry harder. "I know, Baby. It will be, ok. I am here.... Shhh,, let it all out.... Auntie is here." I cooed softly, rubbing his back, and trying to comfort him. Inside, my heart was breaking for them all. I knew they would find my twin, but I wasn't sure she would be, ok. I wasn't sure she was even alive anymore, but I had to keep believing she was. Uncle Vex is right, she is tough and strong. I still ached inside thinking about her. Once JR had calmed down, he yawned.

"I think it is time for bed, Little One." I suggested.

"Yeah, probably a good idea." He agreed. I smiled.

"Let's go get the twins and get you all into bed." I said as we wiped our faces and stood up.

We walked back down to the playroom. When we walked in, I saw Teagan laying on the floor with Selena and Tyler. They were using him as a pillow and all three were sleeping quietly. I smiled and picked up Selena. She wrapped her arms around my neck and went back to sleeping quietly. As I picked her up, Teagan woke up.

"Hi" I whispered. "Can you grab Tyler so we can get them to bed?" I asked.

"Of course," Teagan replied as he rubbed his eyes with one hand and shook his other arm to wake it up. He scooped up Tyler, who fussed a little bit.

"It's ok, Little Man. Go back to sleep." Teagan said softly as Tyler rested his head on Teagan's shoulder and went back to sleep. JR took my hand, and we walked up to their room. JR opened the door for us.

"You go get your jammies on and brush your teeth while we get your brother and sister into jammies. Ok, Buddy?" I said to JR.

"Ok, Auntie." He replied and went off to get ready for bed. I gently placed Selena on her bed, got her pajamas out, undressed her and redressed her in her pajamas. Teagan laid Tyler down and came over to move Selena for me.

"I can do it, Babe. You have carried them enough tonight." Teagan said softly, and I nodded. He moved

Selena, putting her in her bed, tucking her in. She woke up and looked at him.

"Beddy time?" She asked.

"Yes, Sweetie. It's bedtime." He answered.

"I needs Teddy." She replied.

"Ok, let me find him." Teagan replied and looked around the room. I changed Tyler into his pajamas, and he too woke up.

"Auntie, me sweep now." He protested.

"I know Ty, but you need jammies on." I answered softly.

"Otay" he said, helping me by moving his arm into the sleeve of his footed jammies. I zipped them up and he crawled into his bed with his dino plushie. I tucked him in and kissed his forehead.

"Good night, My Little One. I love you." I replied.

"Nini Auntie. Wuv you toos." He responded as he snuggled down into his bed.

I walked over to see what Teagan was looking for.

"Whatcha looking for?" I asked.

"Teddy bear for Selena" He replied. I looked around and couldn't see it.

"Did you check under the bed?" I asked.

"Nope." He replied. He looked under the bed and sure enough, he emerged with a teddy bear in a pink, sparkly tutu. "Here you are, Darlin'." Teagan said as he handed it to her. She smiled.

"Tank you" Selena replied happily, snuggling her bear. I came to her and kissed her forehead. She wrapped her arms around my neck, kissed my cheek and I hugged her tight.

"I wuv you, Auntie. Nini" she said as she let me go.

"I love you too, My Little One. Good night." I replied. JR came back into the room and got in his bed. I went over and tucked him in as Teagan said good night to the twins. He smiled and snuggled down into his bed.

"You know I am old enough not to get tucked in, Auntie." He explained.

"Nope, you're not." I replied.

"Yes, I am. I am eight." He protested.

"Very true, you are, but you are never, ever, too old to be tucked in. Sometimes we all need a good tuck in before bed." I said smiling.

"Really, even you, Auntie?" He asked.

"Yes, even I do, some nights." I said smiling.

"Oh, ok then." He replied. I kissed his forehead, hugged him, he kissed my cheek and hugged me back.

"Good night, My Little One. I love you." I told him.

"Good night, Auntie. I love you too." He replied. Teagan came over.

"Night buddy. Sweet dreams." He added.

"Night, Uncle Tee." JR replied.

As Teagan and I were about to leave the room, Selena sat up.

"Auntie" She called out.

"Yes, Sweetie." I replied.

"Would you swing da swong?" She asked.

"What song, Sweetie?" I asked.

"The lullaby you wrote for us." JR replied.

"Plwease, it would helps." Tyler chimed in.

"Ok, but then it's time for sleep." I replied. They all three nodded as they got comfy in their beds again. I sat down in the rocking chair, in the middle of the room, cleared my throat and softly I started to hum the melody and I sang....

"Hush now, hush now
My Little Ones,
The stars are glowing, mood is hung
Hush now, Hush now
My Little Ones,
Close your eyes and
Let sleep come.
Hush now, hush now
It's time to roam
The dream realm is calling you home.
Hush now, hush now
My Little Ones
You're safe and warm
Embraced til morn.
Hush now, hush now
My Little Ones
Run fast through forests, swim in seas
Hush now, hush now
My Little Ones
Climb up to cliff tops and follow your dreams
Hush now, hush now
My Little Ones
Don't be afraid of what shall come.
Hush now, hush now
My Little Ones
The stars are glowing n moon is hung

Hush now, hush now
My Little Ones
Close your eyes and
Let sleep come."

Once I was done, I noticed all the kids were asleep. I smiled and quietly walked out the door, closing it softly behind me.

"That was beautiful, Babe" Teagan said.

"Thank you." I replied.

"You wrote it?" He asked as he came up to me, facing me, and placing his arms around my waist.

"Yes, I did. When JR was born. He would not calm down, so I started humming the melody and then the words just came to me." I replied as I put my arms around his mid-section.   "Well, I have said it before, and I will say it again. One day you will make one hell of a mother." Teagan said smiling.

"Aww, thank you." I said as I looked up at him and leaned in closer. He leaned down, taking my chin in his hand. We got closer and our lips met, and the world faded away completely. My body heated up. I could feel butterflies in my stomach and fireworks going off in the background. Kissing Teagan was different than Logan. Logan's kiss was electric and full of lust. Where Teagan's kiss was both lust and love. It made me whole. It felt right, throughout my whole being. As our lips parted from each other, I smiled, and I opened my eyes. He was smiling back.

"Damn, I missed that." He said quietly.

Suddenly, we heard someone clear their throat in the hallway. I peeked around Teagan. He let me go and we turned towards the voice.

"Sorry to interrupt you two but, Jassy, your father has asked you to come see him for a moment." Josh said with a smile.

"Oh, ok." I replied. "I guess I'll catch up with you later, Tee." I said smiling.

"Yeah, I'll see you in a bit, Hun." Teagan said. I walked away with Josh.

"Damn, our dad has bad timing." Kita said.

"Yeah, sometimes." I replied.

"Damn it!" Teagan thought.

"I agree. I was like, finally! Then nope, not happening." Conri laughed.

"I just want her to be mine again." Teagan replied.

"I know man, me too but we must bide our time. Things are not that simple anymore." Conri counseled.

"Before I didn't mind when she would be away from me, because I knew she was coming back." Teagan replied.

"I know. Trust me. The last thing I want is anyone else touching our mate, but at least you know she is only going to see her dad. So, it is not like anyone will try to seduce her." Conri reasoned.

"Your right, man." Teagan said.

"Go for a swim. It will help." Conri suggested. Teagan nodded and headed towards the water.

***

I made it to my father's office and knocked before going in. I walked in slowly and saw him sitting at his desk. He smiled at me when he saw me come in.

"Hey there, My Little Monkey. How are you doing?" he asked.

"I am ok. Still very sore, but ok. I can feel myself getting stronger, especially after eating dinner." I replied.

"Good, I am happy to hear it. How are the kiddos doing?" He asked.

"They are hanging in there." I replied and I plopped in the chair. "The twins seem unphased, for the most part. JR is worried but trying to keep it together and be strong." I replied. Doceo nodded.

"He is a tough little guy. Even though he doesn't have to be." He replied.

"Yeah, well it's his stubbornness and need to be strong for his siblings, that keeps him going, I think. He and I went for a walk, and he broke down." I said, looking down at the floor. "I figured he would open up with you. You two have always been close." He said smiling.

"Yeah, he is My Little Man." I said smiling. "How are you holding up, Dad?" I asked, looking at him.

"I was just about to ask you the same question." He said with a chuckle.

"Great minds think alike." I replied.

He came around the desk, turned the chair next to me towards me, and sat down. I turned my chair towards him, sat back and put my hands in his, smiling as I looked at him.

"I am tired, My Little Monkey, and worried." He replied.

"I can tell you are tired. I am worried too. This is not where I thought we would be right now. I am so worried about Mena. I don't know if I can sleep." I explained.

"I can understand that Honey, but you need to keep up your strength. She is going to need you when she gets back. Plus, you have training to start as soon as possible when you are strong enough." Doceo replied.

"I know." I said as I stood up, walked over to the window, and looked out.

"Something else is bothering you. What is it?" Doc asked as he stood up, and walked up behind me, looking out the window over top of my head.

"I…" I paused, closing my eyes.

"You what?" He asked.

"I am not sure what to do right now?" I replied.

"About?" He asked.

"Teagan and Logan." I whispered and a tear ran down my cheek.

"Ahh… Well, let it take its course. Enjoy your time with them and let your heart guide you. That is all you can do, My Little Monkey." He replied.

"What do I do while I wait for them to get Mena?" I asked, turning around toward him.   "You pray, and you keep getting stronger. You keep going. I know it is hard, but we will get through this." He said as he pulled me into a hug. I hugged him back and broke down completely for the first time in a long time.

"Let it out, Honey. I am right here." He said rubbing my back. Doceo's eyes welled up. He could hear the pain in my cries. "Shh, it will be ok, My Little Money. Let that pain go." He said softly as he held me and gently petted my head. I started to calm down, looking at the pink tinge on his white shirt.

"I think you are gonna need some bleach." I said with a

little chuckle.

"Yeah, nothing new there, Honey. You feelin' better now?" He asked, trying to look into my eyes. I looked up at him and our eyes met.

"Yeah." I said, nodding and wiping my eyes.

"Good. It will be ok. We will get through this." He reassured me and I nodded. He leaned in kissing my forehead. "Good. Now go get some sleep." He said with a smile.

"Ok, Dad, you, too. I love you." I replied.

"I will. I promise. I love you, too." He replied. I walked out of his office and Josh helped me to my room.

HAMMASLATHI

Back on the mainland, across the sea, a desert and barren land sat quietly. The wind whipped across the land, picking up dirt and sand, and blowing it here and there, hitting the scattered buildings that dotted the landscape. Logan could barely make out the shoreline below. As he and his horse came closer to the ground, he was met by extreme heat. It was like running into a wall. Hammaslathi was a desert and felt as hot as the bowels of hell.

He landed on the beach, looked around and recalled that this was where the old base for Hammaslathi was, years ago. He saw a few scattered, rundown buildings left standing.

"Damn it! I forgot how hot this place was." Vex exclaimed.

"Yeah, even a fan wouldn't help this place." Logan replied, wiping his forehead.

"You will get used to it." A light and crisp voice said. They turned and there, standing in the heat, was an elegantly dressed women with a parasol. She was six-foot, one-inch tall, thin, broad shoulders with long, white hair that fell over them. Her very narrow, ocean blue eyes, seemed to almost glow in the shade of the parasol, as she stared at them. She smiled, making her bright white fangs show clearly. The skintight dress showed off every curve and muscle and a gold crown sat upon her head and sparkled when the sun hit it.

"Lilith! Pleasure to see you, as always." Vex replied with a large smile, as he took her hand and kissed it.

"Yes, glad you all made it safely here, Colonel Santiago." She said, nodding at him. Logan nodded back. Just then the rest of the troops started to arrive, and ships started to dock in the harbor.

"I take it this is the area of the base?" Vex asked.

"Yes, of course. My troops will be out immediately to help you set up. It's a bit run down, but with some dusting, you will be good to go. Everything still works, to my knowledge." She replied.

"Thank you. We truly appreciate it, and your support." Vex replied.

"No need to kiss my ass, Vex. You know we will always stand with you and your family. I would rather die than go back to living under…" She stopped abruptly as she saw both Kye and Ahz land.

"There is no way…" She said quietly as Vex looked at her with concern.

"Are you ok?" He asked.

"My… MY SON!" She half yelled and gasped.

Hearing this, Ahzreal turned towards his mother,

sighed, and started to walk towards her. Kye followed, unsure what would happen when Lilith reached her son. Tears ran over her high cheek bones and down her thin face. They hugged each other.

"I thought you were..." She said, her voice shaky.

"Dead. I know. Everyone did. It's ok, Ma. If my sperm doner couldn't kill me, how in the hell do you think anyone else could." He replied.

"True." She admitted.

"It's ok, I am ok." He said reassuringly.

"I am so happy to hear that. I have missed you so. You will have to meet your sister soon." She stated.

"I have a sister?" He asked.

"Yes, I was pregnant when you left, remember?" She asked.

"Oh yeah. Well, glad the pregnancy went well." He replied.

"Thank you. Hello Kyerus." Lilith replied. Kye nodded. "Well, we can catch up later. I know you have work to do. Come see me anytime at the Palace. I trust you remember your way?" She asked.

"Yeah." Ahz answered as he turned and walked away from her. Kye rolled his eyes and walked in the opposite direction.

Lilith turned back toward Vex.

"I'm sorry. Things have happened so fast. We have not had time to warn you." Vex said trying to comfort her.

"No, no. Your brother explained it all when he asked for our help. I had just thought he might be a bit more, receptive." She responded, looking a bit hurt.

"A lot has happened Lil. Give him some time." Vex said as he patted her shoulder.

"Yes, of course. Sorry. The men will be out soon. If you need me, they can bring you to the Palace." She stated.

"Thank you and take care." Vex replied. Lilith nodded and headed back towards the village and the Palace.

"That was fucking awkward." Logan said.

"Yeah, well, he and Lilith didn't end things on a very good note." Kye replied.

"Seems like he is bitchier than usual." Logan replied.

"Both of us will be. This is the last place either of us wants to be. When we left, we swore never to return! Now we have no choice." Kye said as his eyes glowed brighter under his hood.

"Damn. That sucks, man." Logan said.

"Let's get this bullshit done so we can leave. Get the top people together. We can meet in ten." Kye replied as he walked away from Logan towards the water where Ahz was standing.

Logan went to go get Stock and Warketh.

Vex went into the main command center. It was a large two-story brick building with many rooms off each side. The stairs were on the left-hand side of the room.

"Well, Lilith was right. This place needs some dusting." He said and he coughed.

"Sorry bout dat, Sir." A deep gruff voice said. Vex jumped when he turned around and saw a large muscular mass standing behind him. Greasy black hair covered some of its face and laid on its shoulders. When it turned towards him, he could see it was a female, with deep green skin. She had large brown eyes and a wide nose with a bull ring in it. She gave him a bit of a smile which exposed her large, razor-sharp, pointed teeth. Vex was taken aback for a moment as he had not been around Orcs in some time. He took a deep breath, which was a big mistake. The smell of stagnate water, wet earth and body odor filled his nostrils.

"What is your name, Soldier?" He asked, trying not to gag from the smell.

"I Major Daisy." She replied.

"We have little time to clean. But the Peons will get to it now." She said as she turned and made a motion and a bunch of Orcs and demons of all shapes and sizes came charging in around Vex and started cleaning. Vex backed out of the room, coughing.

"I guess they started cleaning without the windows open?" A high-pitched voice said.

"Yeah…" Vex replied as he looked up to see a six-foot, red woman with large wings standing there in a tight black leather outfit. Her slanted, glowing red eyes were focused on him. Her pointed nose was sharp in contrast to her full lips, which were covered in black lipstick. He watched her for a moment as her long arrow ended tail, swung behind her.

"Ahh, Second Colonel Nessess. Good to see you." Vex said as he stood in front of her.

"Nice to see you as well, Commander Vex. I must apologize. We were not on top of cleaning things up. We had some upheaval in the area that we had to deal with." She replied.

"I can imagine. Well, we are supposed to be meeting here to finish up plans for the retrieval. But I am guessing that will have to wait for now." He replied.

"Oh, they will be done quickly. You underestimate us, as always." Nessess replied rolling her eyes. "By the way, is Jasmica here?" She asked.

"No, its best she is not here. She would be a liability." He replied.

"Bullshit! She is the only one, out of all you men, that has her head out of her ass!" She proclaimed. "Did she at least approve the plan?" Nessess asked.

"No, but the Dark Prince did." Vex said. "And I don't appreciate your tone at all! I am your superior!" He demanded. Nessess rolled her eyes.

"Until I get confirmation from, Lieutenant Jasmica. We do nothing but clean and leave." Nessess replied.

"You will do as you are told!" Vex demanded.

"Wanna bet?" She challenged.

"The Dark Prince will hear about this as will Queen Lilith." He threatened.

"I bet they will. Good Luck without us." Nessess said as she walked away.

"Second Colonel Nessess." Logan said as he saw her.

"Tsss." She said as she walked on by him, Stock and Warketh.

"Second Colonel. Your Colonel said something to you! I suggest you respond correctly." Ahz demanded as he and Kye walked up to them.

"King Ahzreal!" She said as she dropped to her knees "I am so sorry, Sir." She stuttered, looking at the ground.

"Stand up. I am not the King here anymore, but I suggest you respect your superiors, or I will make sure you do not disobey again. Am I clear." Ahz replied. Nessess nodded and she stood up.

"Oh! You will listen to him, and not to me? I am above him!" Vex said confronting Nessess.

"Vex, she doesn't owe you shit, and you know it. Demons are different than everyone else. Orcs are not the brightest and Demons hold few allegiances. I don't even listen to you, and I work for you." Kye said.

"What do you mean? You do what I tell you, Kye." Vex replied.

"No, I do what Jasmica and the Dark Prince tell me. You are just the messenger boy." Kye chuckled.

"I ought to put you in the brig right now!" Vex yelled as he held a radio phone in his hand.

"Hey! Calm down!" Logan yelled. "We are here to do a fucking job!" Logan stated. "Who are you talking to?!" Logan asked.

"My brother, reporting Nessess's insolence." Vex answer.

"Oh Jesus! Give me the phone." Logan commanded.

"No, get your own." Vex said walking away from him.

As Logan was about to go after Vex, his own phone rang.

"Who the hell?" He asked. "Colonel Santiago here. How can I help you?" He answered.

"What in the hell is going on over there?" Jasmica's voice came over the phone.

"A clusterfuck of power hungry idoits." Logan replied.

"Jesus, I am coming over there and fixing this shit!" She replied.

"No Jassy! You stay put. I will put you on speaker. It is too dangerous for you to be here. Do you hear me?"

Logan demanded. There was a long pause… "Jassy, are you there?" He asked as he heard a sigh.

"Fine, I will stay here, but I have a few choice things to say." She replied.

"That's fine but you must stay put!" Logan replied.

"Ok." She replied.

"We will get the computers set up and I will call you back. Give me half an hour?" Logan asked.

"Ok, don't be late!" She said and hung up. Logan hung up and kicked a trash can that was near him.

"FUCK!" He yelled as he walked away in a circle and ran his hand through his hair, frustrated.

"What did she have to say, Colonel?" Nessess asked. "We need to be set up in twenty-five minutes! Get your asses moving because she is pissed." Logan commanded. As orders were being shouted out, the Privates, Seamen and Agents ran around following orders and setting up, as fast as they could.

***

Back in the war room, Jasmica paced quietly at the front of the room. Doceo and Alice sat quietly.

"Do you think they will be ready on time?" Alice asked.

"Well, they better be. Because they don't want her to come over there. She will be kicking ass and taking names if she does." Doceo replied. "She does not take kindly to their quarreling among each other, nor do I. Especially when there is something to be done." He replied.

"I thought you said she wasn't to go over yet." Alice protested.

"Yeah, just because I tell her not to do it, doesn't mean she won't go. She is more stubborn than I am." Doceo

213

replied chuckling.

"Oh Dear. That is not good." She replied.

"Actually. It can be a very good thing. Somehow, she knows when not to listen and when to listen." He replied. "She came here when she was young and was raised for this. She has been trained to be a warrior and a leader." Doceo replied.

"But what about being a lady?" Alice asked.

"Akasha covered that because Luna was never around her." He explained.

"That's very sad. Her own mother was not there for her." She said with sympathy.

"Luna always has had something against Jassy. No one knows why. She would always favor Mena over Jassy, and Exie over them both, but she came out amazing without her." He replied as he watched Jasmica reading the reports as they were coming in.

"By the look of it, she could take over now." Alice stated.

"Pretty much, yes. In the end, that is the plan." He replied smiling.

The video call rang and came up on the large middle screen, as Jasmica came to take her seat by her father. He answered.

"Hello. Glad you all could get things straightened out. I will turn it over to my daughter now." Doceo said.

"Thank you, Dad." I replied. "Now, before any of you say anything. I am fine. I don't want to hear the bullshit. You are there to do a mission, NOT bicker like children. Am I clear?" I asked. They all nodded in agreement. "Get your shit together. I am in no mood for this. We are at war and as higher-ranking officials; we are meant to be the examples, not the ones arguing." I said shaking my head.

"Yes Ma'am" They replied.

"Kye, I got the intel you sent over. It looks like the lunch, guard change, will be the best time to cause an issue. Most of the guards will be in the mess hall eating, so they will not know what is going on." I stated.

"I agree with that." Kye said.

"Should we get someone to lock the exits?" Vex suggested.

"I wouldn't. At least not the main one. They will suspect something if that door is locked." Logan replied.

"I agree. If possible, side doors, but we need to keep it low key for our insiders." I agreed.

"We have people inside already?" Vex inquired.

"Yes. Teagan made sure of that before Raven even left." I replied.

"Oh…" Vex retorted a bit snippy.

"Ok, the main forces should be focused on the front of the Castle and the right side, away from the dungeon." I stated. "Stock, those tunnels all clear still and undetected?" I asked.

"Yes, um." Stock replied.

"Ok, so Kye, you and your men hit those tunnels and the entrance at the same time the attack is under way." I commanded.

"Yes, I know. That way they are all over there and not in the dungeon. This is not my first rodeo darlin'." Kye replied. I smiled and nodded.

"Now the Mages and Ahz. I need you all around the back and left side, breaking barriers. Take along a few dragon flyers to block any attacks coming from them to our men on the front." I ordered.

"Yes, I will take the Mages on the ground." Vex stated.

"No! I will! Dragons and I do not do well together, remember?" Ahz stated.

"Oh right. Ok then. I am up with the flyers." Vex said.

"Ok, we will need a group spaced out around the town to make sure we do not get boxed in." I commanded.

"We got that covered." A young centaur called out from the back.

"Thank you Frix. Now, we should do this in daylight, not night." I stated.

"WHAT?!" Everyone said at once as Kye smiled. He knew this would be their reaction.

"Calm down. When did you all think lunch was? Just think about it. We are going into mostly Vampire territory. They are weaker in the light. So, they will not see it coming. We are good at disguising ourselves and blending in. Therefore, they probably will think nothing of it." I concluded.

"That is madness." Alice stated.

"Now wait a minute. Let us think about it. She makes a good point." Vex replied. Doceo nodded.

"It's true. No one would expect us to attack in daylight. They know we are going to come for Mena, but they have more soldiers on at night then the day." Kye replied.

"Seems they have already decided we are coming at night then." Logan deduced.

"So, we catch them off guard." Ahz replied.

"Aye, I like it." Stock replied.

"But what about getting Mena out of the tunnels?"

Matoshka asked.

"That shant not be a problem. They lead right back ear." Warketh replied.

"So that is why you all have been watching them like a hawk." Nessess replied.

"Aye, we be needin da tunnels and not needin any surprise visitors." Stock replied.

"Make sure your resources are readily available so that you can get her out of there as soon as you get to the light." I commanded.

"Why don't we put her on a ship, sail it to the harbor and take off from there? That way, if anyone is following, we can get her off land." Ahz suggested.

"I have no objections to that." I replied.

"Ok, sounds good. Can we trust you all to do your jobs now and divide up the teams accordingly?" Doceo asked.

"Yes, Sir" They replied.

"Good, Godspeed and get it done. Bring my girl home!" Doceo said as he hung up.

"Do you think they will be ok without you?" Alice asked looking at Jasmica.

"Let's hope so, for everyone's sake." I replied as I left the room to go get more intel.

"She doesn't socialize much when she is like this, does she?" Alice asked.

"No. You get used to it. She has a job to do, and she does it well. We have taught her not to take any shit from anyone." Doceo replied. Alice nodded.

***

"Well, you eard dem. Let's get to it!" Stock said, as the

screen went black.

"Ok, you get men together to guard throughout the tunnels, Stock and Warketh." Logan commanded.

"Master Chief York, have your fastest vessel ready to go, by the tunnel entrance at dusk. Make it look like a patrol." Vex commanded.

"Aye, aye, Sir." Master Chief York replied.

"I'll brief the men who are not here, and we will head into the tunnels towards Pernrith, immediately." Kye said.

"We will be right behind you, underground, and in the air. We will exit the tunnel before we get to Pernrith, regroup, and set it all in motion." Logan said as he motioned for Frix to follow him.

"Won't it takes days to get there?" One young Orc asked.

"Naw, be usein' magic rails kid." Stock replied.

"Yes, Nessess get your people together. Ahz will take the ones who cannot fly, and I will take the flyers with me." Vex commanded.

"Ok." She said with a shrug and walked off to gather them up.

"The rest stay here and keep things safe." Logan commanded.

"Let's move out." Vex commanded. They all headed out to gather their troops.

THE RETRIEVAL

Mena sat quietly in the corner of her dark, dingy room. The only light coming in was from the window and hallway. The smell of blood, bodily fluids, and rotting flesh surrounded her. She had no tears left in her to cry, as she stared at the corner of the room where her husband's rotting head sat on a spike. She could hear the cries of others being tortured and knew, sooner than later, that it would be her turn again.

She turned her head quickly hearing the key in the lock and the door creaked open. A small woman came in the door that closed and locked behind her. The woman placed a plate on Mena's small table to her left that was bolted to the wall. Mena looked at the plate. It had a piece of stale bread, cheese, and something that barely resembled meat. The woman placed a glass on the table and poured some rancid, blood wine in it.

"Thank you, Ellona." Mena said quietly. Ellona walked

quietly but quickly over to her. "Here. I stole you some good food from the kitchen." Ellona whispered, and she handed Mena a fresh, small roast beef sandwich, an apple, and a bottle of blood water.

"It's not much, but it is better than what they gave you." She said with a smile.

"Thank you. I appreciate it, more than you know." Mena replied gratefully.

"Eat up, quickly, before they come to get me." Ellona instructed.

Mena nodded and ate it quickly. It had been so long since she had eaten proper food that was not expired. She was more than grateful for the kindness Ellona had given her when she started working in the dungeon kitchen. Ellona tossed the rotten food and drink out the window so Mena wouldn't get in trouble for not eating.

"How are you holding up?" Ellona asked.

"I am hanging in there." Mena replied, though she could not bring herself to smile.

"It will be over soon, I promise." Ellona assured her.

Suddenly there was a loud bang outside that shook the whole dungeon.

"What the hell was that?!" Mena asked.

"I am not sure!" Ellona replied. Outside the cell, in the hallway, soldiers were yelling, and you could hear their boots hitting the stones, as they ran towards the noise to see what was going on.

"Man your battle stations! We are under attack!" One man yelled down the hall. Soon the commotion in the hall quieted.

"Hey! Let me out of here!" Ellona yelled. But no one

was around.

"I guess you are stuck with me." Mena said quietly.

"I guess so." Ellona replied as she stretched up to look out the window on the door.   "Damn, this is going to be easier than taking candy from a baby." She said with a smile and a wink at Mena.

"What do you mean?" Mena asked.

"Just trust me, ok?" Ellona asked.

Mena nodded as Ellona pulled a radio out from under her apron.

"This is Kitchen to Underground. What's your location?" Ellona said into the radio.

"We are inside and headed to you. Over." A familiar voice responded over the radio. "Ten four! Move quickly. We are without guard. Over." Ellona responded.

"Ten four. Over and out." The voice answered.

"You are with us?" Mena asked.

"Of course! You didn't think they would let you rot and die in here, did you?" Ellona asked.

"No, but I didn't think we could infiltrate things so fast." Mena replied. Ellona chuckled. "Maybe not the military, but the Special Agents have no issue with doing that. We are like chameleons. We blend in well, quickly." Ellona replied.

***

Meanwhile, outside the Castle, Ahz and his Mages had strategically placed themselves around the outside of the Castle and started to break the barriers down.

"Ok, keep calm and steady everyone. On the count of three, get to work. When I say go, you all take off." Ahz commanded and Vex nodded. "One… two… three!" Ahz said. The Avedonians waited to see the flyers in the air. The barrier dissolved. "Steady all." Ahz commanded. Once he knew it would hold, Ahz yelled, "NOW!" Vex took off with the dragon flyers and flying demons.

Seeing this, Warketh yelled,

"FIRE!" As the cannons rang out, Logan yelled,

"ATTACK!"

The men ran and placed their homemade bridges across the mote and charged across them, with ladders in hand. They placed them against the outer walls of the Castle and started scaling the Castle walls.

After hearing the first cannon hit the wall, a soldier came running into the dining hall.   "They are here! Man your stations, soldiers!" He yelled. There was a mad rush towards all the exits.

"Good. They came to us." Luna said with a large smile.

"Your highnesses, you must take action and get to a safe area" The General said.

"We will go to the towers to watch. I am sure it will not last long." Alduin replied as he held out his hand to Luna. She took it and he led herup the stairs to the tower, with the Bacimortes following, to watch the battle.

"This should be a snap." Alduin thought.

***

Men flooded out of the castle gate to fight on the mucky, muddy shore. Cannons fired upon the walls of the Castle.

"Load 'em again!" Warketh commanded.

***

"Get those cannons ready. Quickly now!" One soldier yelled from on top of the wall. Civilians ran into the castle and into their homes to take shelter, and Luna's soldiers ran out across the draw bridge. The Avedonian forces were more than ready for them. Arrows and fire rained down from above and across the ground. Luna's forces were running across the street and they either exploded, or the bridge collapsed beneath them. Those who made it across, began hand to hand combat with the enemies.

Swords and shields clanged against armor as both sides fought for their lives. Cries of agony filled the air from the wounded, and the cries and bursts of fire from the dragon fliers and Demons could be heard too. Occasionally the shot of a gun was heard ringing through the air.
    "Steady now, everyone. Hold firm and give them hell!" Vex commanded as they continued breaking down the shield and fighting the other fliers that emerged from the ground. "Hang in there, all. Not much longer!" Logan commented to those on the ground.   "Medics, get the wounded out of here, quickly. I want them to take no prisoners today!" Logan commanded, as the onslaught continued.

As the battle distraction continued, Kye and his men came out from the tunnel. They cautiously moved in the shadows to get to the hallway that Mena's cell was in. One guard came running around the corner. Kye swooped around behind him, pulling out his dagger, and slitting the man's throat. He lowered him to the ground and two of the other Agents moved the body to the corner.

"Wow! These guys are either really stupid or planning a trap that leaves their prisoners unguarded." Matoshka whispered.

"I'll take the first, for one hundred!" Kye said with a quiet chuckle.

"Kitchen to Underground. I need a sign. Over." Kye

said over the radio. Hearing this Ellona peaked out the window in the door, stuck her arm out as far as she could, holding and waving a white handkerchief for them to see.

"Got it Kitchen, almost there. Over and out" Kye replied.

They rushed down the hall to the door. Once Ellona saw Kye's eyes appear on the other side of the door, she pulled in her arm.

"Can you walk, Mena?" Ellona asked.

"Not really." Mena answered.

"OK, let me get these chains off you." Ellona said.

"Kye, I need something to get these chains off." She told him as the door popped open.

"Must I do everything myself?" Kye sighed and huffed. He grabbed the chain and melted off one of the links and freed Mena.

"You're up, Bear." Kye replied.

"Ok." he replied and Matoshka came in. "I know this may hurt, Miss Mena, but I need to pick you up." He told her.

"Ok, Mr. Arrowheart." Mena replied.

"Try not to make too much noise." Ellona advised.

"Why not? I'm up for killing some more people today." Kye replied. Ellona gave him a dirty look and Kye shrugged and walked out of the cell.

Carefully, Matoshka picked up Mena's frail and broken body. She tried to hold in a scream of agony by releasing a low moan of pain. Once she was settled in a position that was good for both her and Matoshka, they all started to make their way back to the tunnels. As they moved down the wide hallways you could feel the walls shaking and dust falling from the stones, as the cannonballs hit the walls outside. Ellona lifted the hatch to the tunnels, the other two Agents went down first. Mena was passed to them; she could not hold in her moan of pain. As it came out, it echoed in the dungeon and in the tunnels below. Everyone stopped for a moment, as they heard the clang of metal coming towards them.

"Move now! Quickly!" Kye ordered. Matoshka hurried down the ladder, followed by Ellona.

"Bear. Get moving with Mena. Get her out of here now! Run! You two go with him! We got this!" Ellona ordered. Matoshka took Mena quickly, which made her moan again.

"Sorry, Miss Mena." He said as he started to run.

"Just run." Mena croaked, as tears ran down her cheeks. The three started running down the tunnel. Kye ran to the outside wall and left a message only Alduin could read. He then ran back to the entrance to the tunnels where Ellona was waiting. He started down the ladder and closed the hatch above but not before he placed a charm on it so only Alduin could open it. **If** he found it. He continued down the ladder.

"Come on! They haven't made it here yet and I bought us some time." Kye ordered as he and Ellona ran after the other three.

***

In the tower, Luna looked through the spy glass as did Alduin.

"Where is she?" Luna screeched.

"Who?" Angie asked.

"Jasmica! I do not see her anywhere!" Luna yelled.

"I have not seen her or the Dark Prince, for that matter." Tony replied.

"I have only seen Vex and Logan." Marcus said shrugging. Luna took Marcus's spy glass and looked at Vex, studying him.

"Why would they not come to defend their Kingdom?" Alduin asked. "Wait a minute. What is that trader doing here!?" He demanded as he saw red.

"Who?" Angie asked.

***

"We have the package out of the hole. Headed out. Over." Ellona's voice came over the Avedonian radios.

"Retreat!" Logan yelled.

"Get your Mages and let's get out of here." Vex commanded.

"Pack 'em up boys! We is headed home." Warketh demanded. As the Mages grabbed onto their fliers, they were still taking fire from Luna's forces.

"Let's give them some cover!" Vex demanded.

***

"Ahzreal!" Alduin yelled as the whole castle shook and the ground trembled. Hearing this Ahz looked right at his father and gave him an evil grin. Alduin came out onto the roof, keeping eye contact with Ahz. Ahz threw a ball of fire at Alduin that missed him and hit the tower he was just in. He stood, looking around, laughing.

"I see you are still an inadequate shot." Alduin shouted. Ahz came flying directly at him, took his claws and caught Alduin's right cheek, landing near him.

"You think that will…" Suddenly, Alduin felt extreme pain in his right cheek and fell to the ground yelling. Vex doused the fire enough so people could escape. Screams were heard from the tower as Luna and the rest emerged with the same scratches on their faces.

"Most interesting." Ahz said, standing above his father. "I was not aiming for you, only your whore and her minions. So, I hit my mark." Ahz cockily remarked, grinning evilly as Luna and the Bacimortes emerged coughing from the tower.

"You will regret this!" Alduin yelled.

"No! It is you that will regret it!" Ahz replied as fire came out of his muzzle while his eyes and the runes on his body glowed brightly. Alduin started toward Ahz. Ahz merely jumped up and flew out of the way.

"That mixed blood has made you slow, Old Man. I would get ready for hell to come for you all. But that is just me." Ahz cockily said. He took off but not before he saw Vex taking off from near Luna. Ahz was gone before anything else could be said.

One Escapes Yet More Arrive

The Avedonian military ran back to the tunnel and underground railway knowing they had completed their mission, but they were not out of danger yet. They still had to get the Princess safely away from here and to the Secret Palace. The cloaking of the tunnel system by the Mages was working perfectly. Matoshka gently placed Mena on one cart and buckled her in so she would not fall off. Her face now carried the same bleeding scratch as Alduin's. He was still panting as tears were running down Mena's cheeks. He sat next to her and held her gently, trying to comfort her, and hoping he could ease her pain.

Once Kye and Ellona caught up with Matoshka and the other two Agents, they all rode in the same car. A smell of rotting flesh filled the area.

"Uhh, what is that smell?" The smaller agent asked.

"Don't worry about it. Just know, it needs to return with her." Ellona replied as she set a parcel next to her.

"Please tell me you didn't?" The other Agent asked.

"He needs to be whole and deserves it as much as any one of us." Ellona replied. Kye rolled his eyes.

"Just shut up, all of you! Now start this thing. That is an order!" Kye commanded. At that point the smaller Agent turned on the car and it whooshed down the tracks, back towards Hammaslathi.

"Kye, do you think a sleep spell might help her get through this part? She is in a lot of pain." Ellona suggested. Kye nodded and spoke an incantation. Mena gently fell asleep on Matoshka.

They could hear other cars coming behind them. Kye looked back and saw it was their external ground forces and cannons.

As they came up beside them, everyone made sure they were not being followed and then they cheered.

"We are safe inside and on our way. Go ahead and fly to base everyone." Logan commanded over his radio.

The tracks branched out into eight lanes with a median in the middle. Kye looked to his left and he saw Logan, who gave him the thumbs up with a nod. Kye nodded back to say, 'good job'. Warketh cheered loudly as he rode on their right side.

"Full speed ahead all! Let's get her to the coast!" Kye ordered. The cars sped up to full speed towards the Hammaslathi coast and the base.

***

Back in Pernrith they were still running around like chickens with their heads cut off. Soldiers were returning from chasing the ground troops, empty handed. In the throne room, Alduin was pacing angrily and shouting at everyone.

"How could this happen?!" He barked. "What have you all done to me?!" He yelled.   "Nothing, my love, but bring you back to life." Luna replied unsteadily. He charged at Luna, hit her, sending her flying across the room, to land on the ground, and slide across the floor, hitting the wall. This resulted in hurting him too. He stood there, shocked, as Angie ran over to check on Luna. He then sat down and thought for a moment.

"Well, that was uncivilized and brutish." A female voice said from the other side of the room.

"Verona!" Angie shouted as she ran over to her and hugged her. The two women embraced.

"And Raven?" She said, shocked.

"Yes ma'am." Raven replied.

"Well, that is a surprise! Though I am not sure we should trust him. He is part of them." Luna replied as she slowly stood up and made her way over to them.

"I am no more part of the Secret Service. What can I say really? I don't side with ignorant idiots." Raven replied.

"I am not sure you can be trusted mut." Luna replied glaring at him.

"My son is nothing but Loyal to me and the cause. You turn him away. You will turn all away. You know damn well I can make that happen, Luna." Verona threatened.

"Well... what I mean Verona is..." Luna stubbled over her words some. "Just know I will be watching him closely."

She finished and she stood to the side.

"No need, I assure you. He will be more then helpful in any way he can be. Isn't that right, My Dear?" Verona asked.

"Of course, Mother anything you need just ask and I shall do it…" Raven answered as he raised his eyebrow and looked at Luna seductively.

"Even kill your brother and father?" She asked him.

"If need be, then so be it." Raven answered confidently.

"Well then, I guess you are right, Verona. You brought the right son with you." Luna replied.

"Yes, but it looks like we missed the party." Verona said.

"Better late than never." Tony replied.

"The more help the better, at this point." Marcus said shaking his head.

"Well, we have brought you a couple thousand well trained men and women. I do hope that it will help. Plus, Raven has many useful skills from the Secret Service and a couple of their men." Verona replied.

"Yes, definitely. I'll let the General know immediately, so they can get stationed and help with the cleanup." Marcus said with a smile.

"Thank you, Marc." Tony said as Marcus took his leave.

"Now you two must meet our new King and ruler." Luna said as she hurried them over to Alduin. "My love, I want you to meet our new allies." Luna said as she approached him. Alduin sat on the small throne and was muttering,

"How can this be?" He looked up. "What are you

nagging me about now?" He asked, raising his voice.

"I want you to meet Verona Ringclaw and her son Raven. Both are wonderful contributions to our cause." Luna explained.

"Ahh, yes. I have heard much about you." Alduin replied, sizing them both up. Verona looked him over and gave Luna a skeptical look.

"I guess he will do for now." She said with a sassy, yet disgusted tone.

"How DARE you?!" Alduin bellowed as the walls shook.

"Forgive my mother's ignorance. She knows no better, as she has been married to a beastly creature for years now." Raven said as he stood between Alduin and Verona. Luna trembled seeing this rage come out again.

"Oh, I see. Well then, I will excuse it this time, ONLY." He said as he sat back down. Raven looked around.

"Looks like this place took quite a hit." He commented.

"Yes, but the cowards retreated." Luna said with a proud grin as she sat beside Alduin. *"Wow! Can people really be this stupid?"* Razor said.

"Apparently." Raven replied.

Alduin was still lost in thought as he mumbled.

"How? How? How?" repeatedly.

"Not to intrude on your thoughts but, how what?" Verona asked.

"Well, as you can see, we all have scratches on our faces. However, the only one who was actually struck, was me. I am wondering how I am so weak and how what happens to them affects me?" Alduin questioned.

"Hmm." Verona thought for a moment. "Luna did you

use only Alduin's blood during the ritual?" She asked.

"We had to use some of ours as well. Because the first attempt failed." Luna replied.   "YOU WHAT!?" Aldiun bellowed as he stood up and picked up the empty throne chair, flinging it across the room.

"Well, that explains it! You have mixed blood, which will weaken your present form." Verona replied.

"Whom else did you use?" Alduin asked as he did his best not to strangle Luna.

"Well, yours, Ahzreal, Mine and Mena's." Luna replied.

"Was everyone in the circle who's blood you used?" Verona asked.

"Of course not! You know that mutt would kill me as soon as look at me." Luna hissed back.

"Well then, one of the bloods is holding a curse, and you all got in the circle. Doing so linked him to your own life forces. Any ideas?" Verona replied.

"It's Ahzreal's Blood!" Alduin screamed as he fell back in shock to the small throne chair, which broke under his weight.

"I cursed him long ago. Dammed him!" Alduin answered.

"That is your issue. You will never be pure again. The more of your life forces that die, the less strength you have." Verona deduced.

"Can I be killed now?" Alduin asked.

"Yes." Verona replied. Alduin sat in shock as he stared at Verona, her words sinking in. "Might I suggest you be careful in making sure those, who brought you back, are in their best health." Raven suggested.

"Yes indeed." Alduin replied.

"I would also suggest a better place to reside. This place is a mess and not to safe." Raven said as he looked around.

Just then Marcus and the General came running into the room.

"She is gone!" Marcus yelled.

"Who?" Verona asked.

"Mena and her husband's head are both gone." The General replied.

"WHAT!?" Luna screeched. "How could you let this happen?" She scolded the General.   "I am sorry, Your Highness, but all the men were needed to defend the Castle. We could not spare them on the prisoners." The General replied.

"UGHH! I am surrounded by idiots!" She ranted as she paced.

"We cannot figure out how they got in, or out." Marcus said.

"There is no hole in the wall?" Luna asked.

"No, your highness but Chomp has picked up some Demonic magic that was used. We were wondering if possibly King Alduin could come see if he can figure it out?" The General asked. Alduin sighed.

"Fine." He replied with irritation in his voice.

Alduin, Luna, Verona, Raven, the Bacimortes and the General, all headed to the dungeon. They walked down the stairs and through a few hallways to Mena's cell. Alduin sniffed.

"Yes... there has been some Demonic magic used

here..." He said as he walked around the tiny room. "It's...Familiar." He continued, walking down the hall, following the smell. He walked into the main connection of the corridors and stopped above the hatch. He then continued to the wall straight ahead. Alduin said a few words and the image of Kye appeared in front of them in front of a hole in the wall. Kye was flipping them off. Above Kye's head it read,

"CHECKMATE. You Lose." Alduin growled and hit the wall, breaking a large hole through it.

"KYERUS!!!" He bellowed.

"I think it is time to take your advice." Alduin said as he looked at Raven.

"Where would you suggest?" He continued.

"How about your old battle Castle? No one would expect it." Raven advised.

"Hmmm... I like the way you think. Get packed! We leave tonight!" Alduin ordered. "But what about..." Luna said as she was cut off.

"We leave tonight! Understood?" Alduin said in a stern tone.

"Okay." Luna said looking down at the floor. They all walked up the stairs away from the dungeon.

"Well, this should be easy." Raven thought.

"We still need to be cautious. They may be dumb but not carless." Razor advised. *"True."* Raven nodded and started up the stairs after them.

HOME

The screeching of brakes was heard as the carts slowed down on the metal rails. Mena's eyes floated open as she smelled the rubber and saw the sparks coming out from the sides of the cart. Matoshka unhooked her buckle.

"Ok, Miss Mena. I need to pick you up again. Deep breath." He instructed her. She breathed in as deep as she could, and he gently lifted her. She felt sharp pains run through her body and tried not to cry out in pain. Tears filled her eyes and flowed down her cheeks.

"What is the quickest way to get her there?" Logan asked.

"Flying." Kye replied.

"We can't have her on a horse. She can't hang on!" Vex replied.

"I can carry her." Ahz replied.

"Are you sure?" Vex asked.

"Yes, give her here, Bear. I must talk to Jassy and Akasha about some things." Ahz replied.

"Nessess you hold down the fort here with York and Ellona. We all need to get back." Logan replied.

"Indeed." Vex replied. Kye, Logan, and Vex mounted their horses.

"We'll meet ye back at da homestead." Stock said. Logan nodded in agreement.

Matoshka handed Mena off to Ahz.

"Shh, sleep now." Ahz said to Mena and she drifted off to sleep.

"Do you have her?" Matoshka asked.

"Yeah, safe and sound." Ahz replied as he got on the boat, carrying Mena. The men led their horses onto the boat. Matoshka took the head and followed them on his own horse. The boat pulled up anchor and moved out towards the ocean.

"Who is going first?" Vex asked.

"Go ahead Vex. Once you are up, the rest of us will all take off at once. That way if anyone is watching, they will not know who has what." Kye answered. They all nodded. Once they were in position, he kicked off the boat and into the air. When everyone saw it was clear, the others followed suit, into the night air. It was cold and crisp against any exposed skin.

"Jassy is gonna lose her mind." Cage said.

"No, she is going to be crushed first, then she will lose it." Logan replied.

"Either way, she is going to need us." Cage replied.

"More than either of us know." Logan said as he urged his horse faster.

"Keep her warm Ahz. The last thing she needs is hyperthermia." Logan warned as he started to see steam coming off Ahzreal's back.

"I am not a damn car! But I got it covered." Ahz replied. Logan chuckled as they flew faster.

***

In the Secret Palace, things were proceeding as a normal evening. They all sat down for dinner. Everyone was trying their best not to discuss what was happening on the mainland. I sat in my chair at the table, pushing food around with my fork and staring into the fireplace.

"Jas, you need to eat something." Teagan said.

"I am not hungry." I replied. "Dad, may I be excused, please." I asked looking up at my father, Doceo. He sighed and nodded yes. I stood up and quickly walked out of the room. Teagan stood and tried to follow me, but Doceo stopped him.

"Let her be right now, Son. I think she needs some time." Doc said. Teagan hung his head and sat back down.

I ran outside to the garden, facing the direction of the mainland. Finding that no one was following me, I sighed and walked out to an area in which I could see only sky. That way I could see if anyone was coming by air, and I could look at the stars. Slowly, I sat on the grass, feeling my heart ache as tears started to flow from my eyes. My friends and family were at risk, along with my people and I could do nothing but wait. It hurt me more than anything to know that it was out of my hands.

I sat quietly. Then I heard someone come behind me.

"Panda?" Shadow's voice called out gently.

"Hi, Howls." I replied as I wiped my eyes.

"What's wrong? Are you hurt?" Shadow asked in a bit of a panic, as he sat beside me.

"I am not hurt, at least not physically." I replied.

"That is a good thing, after yesterday." He said with a bit of a smile. "They will bring her home safe. Things will be ok." He confirmed as he lifted my chin. I nodded.

"I hope so. I don't know what I would do without her." I said as more tears slid down my cheeks. Shadow wrapped his arms around me and held me as I cried softly.

"It's ok, Panda. I got you." Shadow said softly and he let me cry. He gently rubbed my back. I cried for all those I had lost, for the pain, for my niece and nephews, for my twin and family and for the confusion. I cried for it all. Shadow just let me cry. He didn't talk, he just continued to hold me and rub my back and let me cry, as long as I needed to.

***

Slowly, the Palace came into Ahzreal's view.

"Okay, slow and steady." Logan commanded everyone. Ahzreal nodded.

"You all go ahead and get Toby. She needs the hospital, stat. I felt her stop breathing a few times and had to juice her back to life." Ahz responded.

"Got it!" They replied and headed quickly towards the ground.

***

"Toby!" Vex yelled as he came running in the front door of the hospital unit. "Vex! Happy day! You are back!

Are you ok?" Toby asked.

"Yes, I am fine but get ready, stat! My niece is not far behind, and she is gonna need all you got. She is in a bad way!" Vex explained.

"I will go get Doceo!" Logan said as he ran in.

"They are in the dining room." Toby replied.

"Just grab Doc. The rest will have to wait. This place will be too full, otherwise." Toby warned.

"Got it!" Logan said as he ran towards the Palace dining room.

"I'll get the horses settled." Kye replied as he walked back outside. Vex nodded as he helped the staff bring out the gurney for Mena.

Ahz landed as gently as he could and softly placed her on the gurney.

"Sweet Lord in heaven above." Toby replied as he blessed himself.

"I know. Do what you have to and clean her up, so the family doesn't have to see her this bad." Vex said. Toby nodded as his team, and he rushed her inside to the operating room.

"I am going for a bath and to speak with Kye. I hope she makes it, but I have had to revive her a few times already." Ahz said as he hung his head.

"Thank you for everything Ahzreal." Vex said as he headed inside, doing his best not to think about the worst.

***

I was unsure how long I had been crying but suddenly Teagan's voice came from behind us, as he cleared his throat.

"Uttumm, Sorry to disturb you both but I have news for you, Princess." He said. I turned and looked at him, my cheeks stained red and my eyes blood shot.

"Oh, good he was just comforting her." Teagan said.

"Thank God! We don't need anyone else to keep her safe from here." Conri replied.   "What is it Tee?" I asked.

"She is home." He said. I bolted up from the ground and started to walk towards him. "Where?" I demanded.

"Jassy, wait!" Teagan called as I started moving towards the Castle.

"Where is she?" I asked again when Logan appeared in front of me.

"Logan. Where is she?" I called out.

"Jassy, wait." He said as he placed his hands on my shoulders, and I stopped.

"What is going on? I want to see her." I demanded.

"I have to warn you, she is in the worst shape I have ever seen her." He explained.

"Okay. I still need to see her." I replied.

"We will bring you to her." Logan said and looked at Teagan.

"Should I come as well?" Shadow asked.

"Probably be a good idea." Logan admitted. Shadow followed behind Logan and I.

I walked quietly and as quickly as I could.

"Are you ok?" I asked him.

"Jassy, I am fine. You know I always am." Logan replied.

"Ok, I was just checking." I explained. As we all came around the corner, I saw my father sitting in a chair with his head in his hands. I broke away from them and ran over to him.

"Dad. Are you ok?" I asked. He stood and pulled me in tight.

"Honey, you don't want to go in there." He assured me.

"I do! I am not a child! I need to see her! She needs me!" I stated. "How long has she been here?" I asked.

"She has been in and out of surgery for hours. I am waiting on Toby to come talk to me." Doc replied.

"I need to see her, Dad." I demanded.

"Just know, My Little Monkey, that it is bad." He replied as he held the door open for me.

I walked through and the door and laying in a very large bed, was a mangled woman. Her face was almost unrecognizable to me. Tears just burst out from my eyes.

"No..." I whispered. My whole body trembled as I walked closer to her. Her long copper blonde hair was all knotted and dirty. She looked weak and pale. Tubes and wires were coming out of her in every direction. I walked up to the side of the bed and gently moved her hair out of her swollen eyes. She slowly opened them.

"Twinny..." She croaked out. I nodded.

"Yes, it's me. You are safe now." I said quietly, as tears streamed down my cheeks. I climbed onto the bed next to her and gently held her as she started to sob.

"It was so horrible." She said.

"I am so sorry, Twinny. I could not get you out sooner. I promise I will get her for this." I said through tears.

"You can't go there unless it is to kill her, or she will hurt you, worse than she did me." Mena said.

"Promise me you will not go there until you are ready, please." She pleaded.

"I promise, Twinny. I will not go until I can kill her. I swear." I replied looking into her eyes.

"How are my babies? Please tell me they made it." She asked.

"They did. They are safe and sound." I replied.

"Good." She said as she lay against me. Logan came into the room.

"Jassy, Toby is gonna give his report, if you want to hear it." He said.

"I can tell you already." Mena replied.

"I will stay in here. Thank you, Logan." I said. He nodded and walked back out the door.

When he had left, I turned to her.

"You're going to be ok, right?" I asked.

"I am afraid not, Twinny." She replied. "I will never heal completely and as long as my blood is flowing, Alduin will live and be stronger. I will never make it through his death." She replied.

"No... no, I can't lose you, Twinny. There must be something we can do?" I said as I held her tighter. We both cried.

"I am afraid not. This is the end of the line for me. But I need you to do somethings for me, okay?" She asked.

"I will do anything for you, Twinny. You name it." I replied.

"You get stronger, and you make those bastards suffer, and then you kill them. Then come back and raise my babies like they were your own. I cannot see them like this. This is the last way I ever want them to see me." Mena said as she gently touched my face with her broken hand, wiping the tears away.

"I understand and I will, Twinny, I promise." I replied. She nodded as she took a deep breath, and she gave me the best squeeze she could.

Logan came in hanging his head. I could tell she was telling me the truth.

"Now, there is one more thing I must ask of you, and this will be the hardest thing." She stated.

"What is it? Anything you need, I will do it." I replied. She gave the best smile she could.

"I need you to kill me and let me go." She declared. I trembled as I could see in her eyes, she was serious.

"I… can't…" I cried.

"Twinny you have to. I don't want to suffer anymore. I have already died a couple times on the way here, and it is only a matter of time before it happens again. Please." She begged.   "You can do this for me. I know you can. You have always been the stronger one." She urged. Inside I was screaming, as tears ran down my cheeks.

"Please, Twinny." She asked again. I hung my head as she touched my cheek.

"Ok, Twinny…I will talk to Dad and let him know your decision." I complied, gently holding her hand to my face as I looked into her eyes.

"Thank you, Twinny." she said.

"You rest and I will come back soon." I told her, as I

gently laid her on her pillow. She nodded, closed her eyes, and I walked out of the room with Logan behind me, closing the door.

Doceo caught me as I fell into his arms when my legs gave out. He picked me up and carried me up to his office. I bawled like a baby. My heart was breaking. Her words rang in my ears.

"Daddy, please tell me it's not true." I begged.

"I am sorry, Honey. I can't say that." He replied as he sat down on the couch, placing me on his lap and gently rocking me.

"Please, there has to be something we can do." I begged.

"I am afraid we have done all we can do, Little One." Toby said from the other side of the room. I stood up and overturned a table full of paperwork and just screamed. Vex and Logan stood near Toby, Doc stayed on the couch, hanging his head. Logan got two drinks ready and brought one to me and one to Doc.

"I think you both could use this." He said, handing one to each of us. I downed the drink and threw the glass into the fireplace.

Everyone hung their heads as the liquor burned its way down my throat. I looked at Toby.   "Are you positive there is nothing at all that we can do to help her?" I asked, my eyes begging him to come up with something.

"I am so sorry, Princess. There is nothing that can be done." Toby replied with tears welling up in his eyes. I turned and walked towards the fireplace and stared at it for a moment.

"Then I must do what she asked." I stated.

"Listen Jassy, if you can't, I can. I will make it quick and easy." Logan replied.

"No Logan. I must do it. It is the least I can do for her." I said and I hugged him.

"I understand, but I will be there with you, I promise." He said as he kissed my forehead.   "What are you two talking about?" Vex asked.

I looked back at the fire. Closing my eyes.

"Mena asked me to end her life for her, to kill those who did this to her, to raise her children." I said breaking down again and dropping down to the floor.

"Whoa! Whoa! That would be murder." Vex replied. "You cannot be considering this?" He exclaimed. I glared at him.

"Why not! She is suffering! Should her children be put through hell watching their mother die? Should she suffer even more than she has already? You all have told me she is going to die, so there is no difference if it is now or months from now, if she makes it that long." I demanded. "Am I wrong?" I asked.

"You're not wrong..." Vex replied. "It was just a shock, is all." He said running his hand through his hair.

"What do we tell people? That saw her alive?" Vex stated.

"She didn't make it through the flight, and we could not get her back in surgery." Doceo responded.

Doc got on the floor next to me.

"Are you sure you can do this, Little Monkey?" He asked looking into my eyes as the tears went down my cheeks again. I nodded yes.

"Yes, it is what she needs, and I would do anything for her, as she would for me." I replied. He nodded.

"Toby, get her the injection she needs." Doceo ordered. Toby walked out and headed to get the injection ready.

"Logan, please bring her to the place she and I used to watch the sun rise, in the meadow, on the cliff, above the ocean." I asked.

"I will go get her and start heading there." He replied, leaving the room.

"You two go. Say your goodbyes. I will be along shortly to meet with Logan and Twinny." I told my father and Vex and they left the room.

Once they were gone, I sighed.

"You can come out now." I said as Kye and Ahz appeared from the shadows.

"We made sure Shadow got back to his room. Though he is worried sick about you, as is Teagan." Ahz said. "How did you know we were there?" He asked.

"I grew up with this guy around all the time. I've more than learned to sense it." I replied looking at Kye.

"You ok to do this, Little One?" Kye asked. I nodded.

"I'll deal with the emotions when it is over." I said as I headed downstairs to get the lethal cocktail needle from Toby.

WE ALL LOSE TODAY

I walked by Selena, Tyler, and JR's room. They were still sleeping and dreaming happily. I walked in and covered them back up and placed Selena's bear next to her. I walked out and went to my room. I changed into a comfortable outfit of leggings and a top. I looked at the picture of Mena and I, being silly, that sat on the dresser.

"You must do what you need to do." The voice of the Moon Goddess came through to me. I nodded and walked out of my room and headed towards the hospital wing.

***

Logan was at the hospital wing and went into Mena's room. They had given her a bath and washed her hair. She laid there in her favorite leggings and t-shirt. She jumped, surprised to see him.

"It's ok, Mena. It's just me, Logan." He explained.

"Ok." She replied, a bit confused.

"I am here to take you to watch the sunrise with Jassy." He explained. Mena understood and nodded slowly.

"Thank you, Logan. She knows I like sunrises when I am awake. Sunsets are better but I will take what I can get, at this point." Mena commented, trying to make a slight joke. Logan chuckled.

"Well, we can arrange that, if you would like to say your good-byes today." He suggested.

"I think I would like to spend the day on the cliff in the meadow, with Twinny." She answered.

"Well, once your father has come in, we shall be on our way." He replied.

"Ok. That sounds good." Mena said, still in a lot of pain.

Doceo walked in with Vex next to him.

"We have heard your request." Vex stated, before Doc could say anything.

"Yes." Mena said. She never really cared for her Uncle Vex, but dealt with him when she had to.

"Could you both leave for a moment so I may talk to my daughter alone, please." Doc requested. Logan and Vex left the room. Doc came around and sat in the chair by the bed.

"Are you sure this is what you want, hun?" He asked.

"Yes, Dad. I wish to spend the day with my Twin, in the meadow, and at the end of the day, to leave this plane of existence." She explained, as solidly as she could. Doceo agreed.

"If that is your decision? Given the circumstances. I shall allow it. I am gonna miss you, kiddo." He replied, as tears welled up in his eyes.

"I will always be with all of you, you know that. We shall meet again. I will have a party waiting for you on the next plane." She said with a weak smile. A tear trickled down her cheek.

"Give them hell, Dad." She stated.

"I will, don't you worry. I love you, kiddo." He replied and he leaned down and hugged her one last time.

"I love you too, Dad." She replied, returning the hug. He stood, smiled the best smile he could muster, and walked out of the room, holding back his tears.

Logan came back in with Toby.

"You ready to go?" He asked.

"Yes." She replied. Toby unhooked the machinery.

"It's been an honor knowing you. Godspeed, Hon." Toby said as he stepped back.

"You too, Toby. Take good care of them all." Mena said, then nodded to Logan to pick her up and he did.

"I will. I promise." Toby replied as he opened the door. I was standing in the hall with my father when Logan brought her out. I gave her a bright smile and I swallowed all the pain I was feeling.

"You ready for a day out?" I asked.

"I am, Twinny." She replied.

"I see great minds think alike." I said as I noticed we were wearing matching outfits.   "Indeed." She agreed.

"I'll start up the path." Logan said.

"Ok, I'll be right behind you." I replied.

Toby walked up to me and handed me the single

needle, filled with what I needed to help Mena pass.

"She will just go to sleep and that will be it. When are you planning to do it?" He asked.   "After the sunset. That is her favorite time of day." I replied.

"I will head up there once it is dark. Will Logan be with you?" He asked.

"No, just her and I. That is how it always is when we hang out up there." I explained. He nodded.

"I will bring Logan and Teagan with me to the cliff to retrieve both of you." Toby replied. I nodded and turned to my father, hugging him tight.

"You got this. I love you both." Doceo said as a tear slid down his cheek.

"We love you too, Dad." I replied as I wiped the tear away. Turning away from him I gripped the syringe in my hand and left to go up the cliff. I wiped my tears as I caught up with Logan and Mena and I put on my best smile.

"Hey, you two move fast." I commented.

"Yeah, he has those damn long legs." Mena joked. We all laughed.

"If I left it to you, we would miss the sunrise." Logan replied.

"Fair point." I replied, almost having to jog to keep up with him. When we reached the meadow, on the cliff side, by the ocean, the sun was just starting to come up in the distance. It was a grassy area with wildflowers, and you could see for miles. Nothing but ocean in front of us and trees to the right and left. The wind blew softly through the trees as the ocean waves broke below. There was a small sitting area with a small pillow pile couch where we would lay and watch the sun rise or set, look at the stars, and just talk. It was our not-so-secret place that we went to when we wanted to just do our, "twin thing", as my other sisters would say. A small table sat next to the pillow pile where we would place things we brought up, or that someone brought us, while we were there.

Logan gently sat Mena on our little pillow pile. I placed the syringe on the table and gently sat next to her as she rested her head on my shoulder. I put my arm around her shoulders.   "I will have Jeni bring you guys food, later." Logan said as he went to leave.

"Logan, stay with us for the sunrise." She requested.

"Sure thing." He replied and he sat down on the other side of Mena. Everyone was quiet as the sun broke over the ocean. The clouds were lighting up with oranges and reds as the blue came in lighter behind it. Only the sound of the wind and the ocean could be heard. A tear slid down Mena's cheek.

"So beautiful." She said quietly.

"Yes, it is." I replied.

"You two, enjoy your day. I will see you later." Logan said standing.

"Take care of yourself." Mena replied. Logan hung his head and headed down the cliff side path.

We sat quietly, letting the sun warm us and the damp dew dry.

"Is there anything you want to do, Twinny?" I asked.

"Nope. Just sit and talk. Update me on things I have missed." She requested.

"Ok." I said as I began to update her on all the happenings that had been going on since we last saw each other.

***

Logan got back to the Palace door and wiped the tears from his eyes. He could feel the pain Jasmica was feeling, as well as his own sorrow. He had known Mena her whole life. The two were not close, but it still bothered him.

"This pain is killing me. I feel like a woman, crying so much." Logan said.

"Yeah, it is one of the bad things about a mate bond. But at least you can understand what she is going through right now." Cage replied.

"I don't think I could do that for my own family." Logan replied.

"She doesn't want to, but sometimes you do what you must do. How would you like to be in her shoes? To have to not only kill your closest sister, but to condemn your own mother to death. She is stronger than any of us ever could have dreamed." Cage said.

"I know. I never dreamed she would have to do any of this." Logan replied.

"Me neither. Now get inside and report to Doc and tell Jeni to bring them some food." Cage replied. Logan took a deep breath and opened the side door and walked inside.

Ahz stood outside the Dark Prince's office and nodded as Logan approached and opened the door. Doceo sat in a chair facing the window, in silence.

"Uttumm." Logan cleared his throat.

"Yes, Logan." Doc replied, as he kept staring out the window.

"They are safely up there. I am going to brief Jeni and have her bring them some food today." Logan said. Doceo just kept staring out the window. Logan remembered that

Doceo acted like this when Jasmica had gone missing. At least he was still talking, a little this time. Logan turned to leave.

"Logan…" Doc said.

"Yes?" He replied.

"Brief Teagan. Both of you will have to go get them tonight. I will wait for them here." Doc instructed.

"Will do." Logan said as he left the office to inform Jeni and Teagan of what was going on. He met Alice and held the door for her. She acknowledged him and went to Doceo. She sat by him and was holding his hand. Logan closed the door behind her.

***

Mena and I sat together, and I held her, most of the day. We ate a small brunch and after an early dinner of Mena's favorite foods, we reminisced, laughed, told stories, and sang songs with the radio that had been brought up. The sky was starting to grow darker. Pinks, purples, reds, and oranges covered it as the sun started to sink below the waves. It was like the ocean was swallowing the sun for the night.

"You know if you ever need me, don't go to my grave." She instructed.

"Why?" I asked.

"I won't be there." She stated.

"Well, where will you be?" I asked.

"Here, waiting to hear all about what is going on." She said with a smile. "Promise you will come sit with me and keep me up to date." She requested.

"I will. I promise." I said as I tried to hold back tears.

"Bring the kids sometime too. They will like it here." She requested. I nodded and we watched as the last of the sun dipped under the horizon and the stars started to shine brightly above.

"It's time, Twinny." She said calmly. I took a deep breath.

"Are you sure? I don't know what I am gonna do without you." I said as a tear slid down my cheek.

"Yes. You will live, Twinny. I will always be with you forever, in your heart and in spirit all around you. You will never be alone. Remember that, ok." She assured me, as she touched my face and wiped the tear away.

"Ok." I replied taking another deep breath.

I leaned over and got the syringe from the table. My hands trembled as I took her arm in my hand. I placed the tourniquet around her arm and found the vein.

"Deep breath." I said and we both breathed deep as I put the needle in her vein. My hands shook as I released the tourniquet, pushed the plunger down, and the liquid went into her arm. We both breathed out. I took the needle out and set it back on the table and held her in my arms. As her eyes got heavy.....

"Twinny..." She said.

"Yes, Twinny." I replied.

"Thank you... I love you, always." She said quietly. I nodded.

"I love you too. Always." I replied as her eyes closed and she gave a small smile. I could feel her take her last breath,

"Twinny..? Twinny...? Twinny...?" I asked crying harder each time I said her name. I checked for a pulse and found none. A slight wind blew. I just held her tight and cried, as I waited for the boys to come.

Soon I felt a strong hand on my shoulder, and I turned to see Teagan, Logan, and Toby there. Toby got down and checked Mena's vitals. He looked up at me and he nodded.

"She is gone." Toby said. I clung to her more, crying harder than I thought I ever could.   "You have to let go of her, Honey, so we can take her back down." Teagan said softly.

"I will take Mena and you get Jas, Tee." Logan said as they pried us apart.   "Twinny… NO you can't take her! Twinny!" I screamed and cried as Logan picked up her lifeless body. Teagan caught me before I could get to Logan and Mena.

"Shhh…. It's OK." Teagan said as he held me. I was yelling and saying inaudible things.

"I know, Honey." He comforted me and picked me up because I was so weak, I could not even stand. Teagan started down the path, carrying me as I cried. Logan was behind us, carrying Mena, whom Toby had covered with a white sheet. Toby walked down the path behind us all.

Doceo, Alice, Vex, Kye and Ahz were standing at the entrance to the Palace. As they saw us, tears started to flow from everyone's eyes. We went past them. I was inconsolable and did not even notice them.

"I will bring her to her room." Teagan said. Doceo agreed.

"Bring Mena down to the morgue, Logan. I will prepare her and her husband for their burial." Toby ordered. Logan nodded. Toby stopped and looked at Doceo.

"I am so very sorry I could not do more." Toby said.

"You did the best you could. At least she is free and at rest with her husband now." Doceo replied.

"I'll let everyone know of the loss and that we will not be conducting meetings for the rest of the week." Ahz said.

"Thank You, Ahzreal." Doceo said as he patted him on the shoulder, trying to hold himself together.

"Let's get you to bed, Brother." Vex said to Doceo. Alice and Vex helped him to his room.

"I've said it once and I will say it again. No one wins in war." Kye said as he and Ahz looked on.

"So true…" Ahz replied.

Life Changing

I woke up in my room on Teagan's wet chest. My eyes hurt and stung. It had been two days since Mena died and I had done nothing but lay in bed, cry, and sleep. The side passage door opened and in walked my father. I looked at him. He smiled gently and opened his arms as he had done every day since Mena passed. Today I got up and went over to him and hugged him tight. As I did, we both cried again.

"It's going to be ok, My Little Monkey." He said as he sniffled a little.

"I still don't know how..." I replied.

"It will be." He said lifting my chin. "I know you are hurting but there are three little ones who need you now, more than ever." He said wiping my tears. I nodded in agreement.

"Do they know yet?" I asked.

"No one knows except those that were in on it. We have kept it quiet until we could tell the Little Ones." Doceo replied.

"Thank you. Let me take a bath and I will go with you." I replied.

"Ok, Honey. I will meet you downstairs in half an hour, ok?" He asked.

"Ok." I said as I nodded.

He let me go and walked out of the room. I took a deep breath. Teagan walked up behind me and put his arms around my waist.

"Just breath babe. You got this." He said as he kissed my head. I nodded, giving him a weak smile as I walked towards the bathroom. I turned on the shower, disrobed, and stepped inside. I just let the water run over me and cried some more, knowing that there were now three little ones depending on me.

"We can do this." Kita said.

"It's so hard Kita. I am not ok, and I am far from fine." I replied.

"Yes, we are, but we also know how to do what needs to be done." Kita answered. I agreed.

"It is hard to be strong all the time." I said feeling the ache in my heart.

"You don't have to be strong all the time. You have people that have got you. You just need to realize that and talk to them when you need to. No one expects you to be strong all the time, my dear." Kita advised.

I took a deep breath, rinsed myself off and stepped out of the shower to dry off. I took my hand, wiped the mirror, and stared at myself for a moment. Remembering all the similarities between me and my twin.

"Give me the strength to do this, please." I said quietly, as I closed my eyes and hung my head. I grabbed my clothes and dressed myself, put my hair up in a ponytail and came out into the bedroom. Logan and Teagan were standing there waiting for me. I gave them a bit of a smile as I went to my vanity, sprayed myself with perfume and slipped my flats on my feet.

"Time?" I asked.

"You have about five minutes to get down there." Logan said.

"Well, better late than never, I guess." I replied.

"He ought to be used to it by now." Teagan replied.

"Yeah, I know I am." Logan said with a bit of a chuckle.

I smiled a bit and just walked towards the door which opened, and Josh was on the other side. He joined them behind me. I moved quickly down the stairs and towards the front entrance. When I started down the main staircase, I could see my father standing at the bottom with Alice. "Where are they?" I asked.

"They are in the side living room, over there. The other living room has your sisters and our family in it." Alice said.

"I figured we could tell one and then the other." Doceo suggested.

"I will tell the kids. They don't need a lot of people around when they find out." I replied. "So, we will tell the girls then." Alice suggested. I nodded in agreement.

"We can all meet back in with the kids, after you tell them." Doceo suggested.

"Sounds good. I will be in with the kids." I told him.

"Ok, Honey." He said and he kissed my forehead. "You guys, go with her." He instructed Teagan, Logan, and Josh. They nodded and we parted ways.

Doceo and Alice opened the door to the right living area, quietly. Inside sat Exie, her boyfriend Chaos, Lady, Bree and her husband, Fayte, with their children, Akasha and Dior, John and Delya with Shadow and Joseph. They were all talking and laughing. For a moment, Doc and Alice just watched them and enjoyed the moment of happiness. It relieved some of the sadness and grief. Alice took Doceo's hand, and they entered the room. Vex came in behind them and sat in the back of the room, nodded to Alice and Doc. Doceo cleared his throat.

"Utt umm. Can I have your attention please?" He asked, doing his best to keep his voice steady. Alice squeezed his hand as everyone quieted down to give him support and to listen.

"I have an announcement. It is bad news." He said pausing. "It's about your sister, Mena." He said as murmuring started.

"Is she ok?" Exie asked.

"Where is she?" Bree asked.

"I haven't seen Trey either." Lady mentioned.

"It is with a heavy heart that I have to tell you all that neither of them made it here to the Secret Palace." Doceo said trembling a bit.

"What do you mean? Are they prisoners?" Exie asked.

"No, Sweetie. They have been killed." Doceo said, his voice wavering as he tried not to cry.

"No!" Exie cried as tears started to fall and Chaos put

his arm around her. Tears started running down Bree's cheeks, as her kids and Fayte all embraced.

"Are you sure?" Lady asked.

"Yes, I am positive. We have their bodies." Alice replied as Lady fell into her mother's arms, crying. Akasha and Dior came up to Doceo and hugged him. Delya and John hugged. Shadow and Joseph hung their heads.

"Where is Jassy?" Lady asked.

"She is with the kids right now, telling them. We will meet her soon." Alice answered. The room that had been full of joy had now dissolved into pain and grief.

***

Across the foyer, I stood in the other living room watching the twins play and JR was watching tv. I allowed them a few more minutes of play time before I had to drop a bombshell on them that would change their young lives, yet again. Selena spotted Teagan and ran up to him.
"Uncle Tee!" She yelled.

"There is my girl." Teagan said as he picked her up and hugged her tight. He took her to sit in the chair with him.

"Uncle Logan is here too!" Yelled Tyler as he toddled up to him.

"Hey there, Buddy." Logan said picking him up and carrying him to the other chair and sitting with him.

"Auntie!" JR said as the twins looked at me, got down and ran over to me. I squatted down and gave them a group hug.

"Hi, Little Ones. How are you?" I asked.

"We are goods." Selena said smiling big.

"That is good. How about we all go sit down. I must talk to you guys. Ok?" I suggested.

"Ok." They said as they went running back to the couch. I sat in the middle of them. JR on my right, Tyler on my left and Selena on my lap, facing me. I took a deep breath.

"Well, I have some bad news." I said slowly.

"No, Auntie. Please no." JR said.

"I am sorry, Buddy. Momma is not coming back." I said trying to keep myself together.   "No! No! No!" JR said as he pulled away and started hitting the couch.

"What you mean Auntie?" Selena said as her little eyes started to well up with tears.   "Baby Momma went to heaven with Daddy." I replied. Selena and Tyler both burst into tears and fell against me. I held open my arm and JR fell against me too. "I know babies. I am so sorry." I said through falling tears of my own. I held them all the best I could, as they cried and clung to me, like they would never let go.

Josh, Logan, and Teagan all wiped their eyes as the rest of the family came through the door, still sniffling and crying. I looked at them, and my sisters came over to the kids and me. We all hugged together, and we cried. Everyone in the room, whether trying to hide it or not, was crying and felt the pain of that moment. We did our best to comfort one another. The announcement was then made to the public.

I held the kids until each of them had fallen asleep. I slept in their room, on the floor. They woke up from time to time, crying out for their mother. I comforted them and put them back to sleep. The next morning the nanny came in and found me asleep on the floor.

"Miss Jasmica." She said as she shook me gently. "Are you ok, Miss Jasmica?" She asked as my eyes fluttered open.

"Yes, I am fine, I slept in here with them last night, Ana." I replied.

"Oh ok. Well, I am here now. Poor dears." Ana said.

"Yes, please dress them for the funeral today." I said as I walked out of the room.

"Yes, Miss." She replied. We didn't use our nannies much but when things got busy, we had to.

I knew I had to get myself ready for the funeral too. Jeni met me in the hallway, on my way to my room. She pulled me into a tight hug.

"I am so sorry, Jassy." She said.

"Thank you. How are you doing, Jen?" I asked.

"I am hanging in there. How are you doing?" Jeni asked in a worried tone.

"Well, I feel like a piece of me is missing and I have a huge hole in me. But I am still breathing, so here I am." I confessed.

"Oh Jas, I am sorry." She replied. I nodded.

"I need to get dressed and I am gonna need your help more than ever for this. I am now the kid's guardian, so I will need help with them too." I explained.

"No worries, I got you, always." Jeni replied.

"Thanks Jen. Ana is dressing them now." I said.

"Okay, good. Let's get you ready then." She said as we walked, arm in arm, to my room.

Time For Goodbye

I dressed in a black, knee length dress with three quarter length sleeves. It was plain and simple with black tights and heels. I put waterproof mascara on, and the jewelry my twin and I had always worn together. My hair was down in curls. I sprayed myself with some of our favorite perfume and walked out to my balcony and sat quietly, thinking, and still feeling lost.

I felt a hand on my shoulder and looked up to see my father, Doceo, standing there and I put my hand on his.

"Hi, Dad." I said quietly.

"Hi, Honey. How are you holding up?" He asked.

"I'm here." I stated.

"Me too." He said quietly. "Do you want to say anything today at the funeral or would you like me to do the eulogy?" He asked.

"I will speak." I agreed.

"Okay, Honey. I will see you downstairs in an hour, OK?" He asked.

"OK. Are we all going as a family?" I asked.

"Yes, I think that will be best." He replied. I nodded and squeezed his hand. He squeezed mine then turned and left me alone again.

I went into my room and grabbed paper and a pen and started to write. I wrote and then scribbled it out.

"What is wrong? That sounded good." Kita said.

"It is just not what I want to say." I replied.

"Don't over think it. Just let it flow." Kita advised. I nodded and sat there with a blank page in front of me when Logan came in the room. He stood there watching me as I looked out into the sky.

"Writer's block?" He asked. I sighed in response.

"Yes, I just can't find the right words." I replied as I stood and turned towards him.

He gave me a bit of a smirk. Then walked over to my bookcase and grabbed my photo album that was labeled Me and Twinny. I watched him flip through it until he stopped and took a photo out of it. He closed it and walked over to me, handing the photo to me. I took it and looked at it. It was a picture he took of Twinny and I sitting in our not-so-secret place, with our arms around each other. We never knew he was there. We didn't know until he gave it to us with the phrase, "Always Together, Forever" across the top.

"That is my favorite picture of you two." He said as his eyes welled up a little.

"I hope it will inspire you up there." He said smiling a little smile. I closed my eyes, nodded, and hugged him.

"Thank you." I whispered.

"You're welcome, Babe. Now let's get you down there." He replied. I nodded again as we both started towards the door.

As always, it opened and there was Josh, and this time Kye was standing there too.   "Come on, Little One. I know where I am needed most today." He replied as he came up and kissed my forehead. I smiled as we walked down the stairs. People joined us, as we continued to walk downstairs. First was Jeni and Teagan, then the three kids, with Logan picking up Tyler and Teagan picking up Selena. I took JR's hand and we continued to walk. Lady joined us and Bree, Fayte, and the kids. Continuing to head downstairs, Exie and Choas joined us. Once we got to the final staircase, I could see my father, stepmother, Alice, my grandparents, Akasha, and Dior, along with other family members. We all came together in the middle of the landing and walked out of the Palace and across the courtyard together. Servants and soldiers lined up all the way around the courtyard with their heads bowed.

We all took a deep breath as we left the courtyard and proceeded into the city, walking quietly. People followed behind us to the graveyard on the hill. I could see the chairs were set up, as we approached, there were two coffins, with our flag draped over them, and the most recent picture of Mena and Trey together set up between them. Flowers lay on the coffins and around them, with a podium in front of that. We took our seats in front. Doceo leaned over towards me.

"Do you want to go first, or you want me to?" He asked.

"You can go first, if you want to?" I replied. He nodded and sat back.

The priest and priestess came to the front and performed a simple blessing that said that they would both be welcomed into the next plane of life, along with a short ceremony. It was not a huge funeral mass. We all dabbed our eyes and sniffled some. Doceo stood, and walked up to the podium and cleared his throat.

"Uttumm. Thank you all for coming today." He started. "The support and love you all are showing, and have shown my family through this tough time, has been appreciated and not gone unnoticed." He said in a formal tone as he paused. "Trey was a strong and brave man. He fathered my beautiful grandchildren and made my amazing daughter, Mena, very happy. He loved his family fiercely. He will be truly missed by our family." Doc said as he paused again trying to be strong. "Mena was a beautiful soul. She loved hard and was a strong woman. She and her twin, Jasmica, were almost inseparable and she was close with all the family. She had an infectious laugh that seemed to brighten the room. She was a wonderful mother, wife, sister and daughter. We are truly missing her and feeling the effects of her loss. She will be forever in our hearts." Doceo said, swallowing hard. He nodded to me as he started to leave the podium.

I wiped my eyes and stood quietly. I walked up to him, and we hugged. He went back to his seat with his head hung. Then he looked up at me. I approached the podium and sat the picture Logan found for me on it and took a deep breath. I looked around at everyone and closed my eyes, as I breathed out.

"I have to say, my twin, Mena, and I were inseparable. I didn't know Trey as well. But what I did know of him, he was kind, generous and sweet. He would do anything for his family and loved all our family a lot." I started. "My Twin was a special person all around. She and I had a special bond which we developed in the womb. It was never shaken and never broken. We knew each other's pain, happiness, fears, and everything in between. We laughed, fought, and loved each other unconditionally. I look at all the beauty she brought to my life, and I can't imagine how I will go on without her. She was my rock, when I needed it, as I was for her. She wiped my tears and brought the smile back to my face when I needed it. She challenged me when I thought I couldn't do something, and she reminded me of who I was when I might have forgotten. When I was down, she helped me back up, and showed me my strength when I was weak. She always had an ear to listen, a shoulder to cry on and she was a friend to laugh with. She was an amazing mother, who would do anything for her children and family. She loved us all without a second thought. There was nothing she would not do for ALL her family. As we are here today remembering her, she would want us to laugh, and remember the good times. To celebrate her and her husband and the wonderful things they gave to us, while they were here. We were all blessed to have had such amazing souls in our lives. No one can ever replace them. We will have this hole in our lives forever, but together we shall get through and support each other. Our love for them will always be strong. Their spirit and love will be felt throughout the rest of our lives." I finished my eulogy, walked down, and sat next to JR.

JR leaned over and hugged me tight and cried. I held him tightly. Then Selena and Tyler came over and clung onto me. I held them all, as people filed by us to say their good-byes.

The rain started again. No one ran, we all just sat in the rain and cried together. When it came time, I took the kids up to the caskets to say 'fare well' to their parents. Once they had done so, I sat back down. Lady took the kids back to the Palace and I sat there alone, and still. Everyone had gone except myself, my father, Alice, Ohmah and Kye.

I approached the caskets again. Tears slid down my cheeks as I knelt next to Mena's Casket.

"I still don't fully understand it all, Twinny. I don't know why we had to be separated, but I know it had to be. I keep waking up, hoping this has all been a bad dream that I will wake up from. I am so lost without you, but I am keeping it together for Tyler, Selena, and JR. I miss you so much, already. I was not ready for this. We had too much left that we planned to do. I know you will be by my side in spirit, but it is not the same. I love you always and forever. This is just goodbye to your body. We will meet again, I know, but I still really needed you here." I said as I cried harder. "I love you so much, My Twin. Please give me the strength to keep going because I don't know how anymore." I asked as I felt the wind gently blow and I could smell her perfume and I smiled. I looked up at the sky as the rain hit my face and wiped my tears away. "Thank you, Twinny. I understand. I will avenge you and end this." I replied as the rain stopped and the last bit of the sun peaked through, shining on me.

Doceo, Akasha, Alice, and Kye all walked up behind me. I stood up and turned around to look at them and nodded.

"I know you are hurting, My Little Monkey. But it is time." Father said to me.

"I know. Teach me so I can end this…" I said to them. They all nodded, and we started back towards the Palace. As we walked back, others followed us. They had waited until I was ready. It was time for my training to start. It will soon be time for me to lead them. Only I could end this war that had already taken so much from all of us.

GLOSSARY

Alicorn: A horse with a horn and wings

Bracers {on arms}: Arm guard made of leather to cover inside surface of archer's arm.

Centaur: A being that is human from the waist up with a horse body.

Demon: A fallen Angel that has magical powers.

Drow Elf: Also known as a Dark Elf they live under ground with dark skin and glowing eyes. They rely more on Technology than their magical abilities.

Dwarf: Stocky humans that are under four feet tall. Both men and women have beards, and they reside underground in the mountains. They usually are miners, blacksmiths, and jewelers. Use magic but mostly technology oriented.

Duergar Dwarf: Another name for a Dark Dwarf.

Elf: A magical being that lives mostly in forested areas and have magical abilities and have infra-red vision. There are many different kind see High elf, Drow elf and Wood elf.

Fairy/Fae: A magical being that is tiny in statue, they look like humans with wings. They use magic and are nature based.

High Elf: The aristocrats of the Elven people who are more magic driven and tall.

Hardtack bread and pottage: A biscuit or cracker with thick soup or stew with vegetables and meats available.

Katana: A long Oriental sword.

Lycan: Also known as Werewolves a shape shifter that turns from a human to a wolf like form and back.

Mages: wielders of magic, spells, and potions. Generally, Elves and Demons but can be witches and wizards if human.

Merfolk: Mermaid and Mermen; Beings that are human from the waist up and fish fins from the waist down.

Microbraided: Multiple tiny braids all over the head.

Orc: A being made from the earth that is large, with green skin, large eyes and teeth. They have a very bad odor that is a combination of sweat, swamp and mud.

Pegasus: A horse with wings.

Rune: A mark or letter of mysterious or magical significance from the Germanic alphabet.

Stout: another name for a strong dark beer.

Unicorn: A horse with a horn on its forehead.

Vampire: A being that is undead who feeds on blood and alcohol.

Wood Elf: Elves that live in the woods who rely more on technology than their magical powers.

About the Author

Jessica is a very creative person who struggles with many mental health obstacles which can cause her to struggle to write at times. But even with these struggles she pushes on and continues to write and enjoy making content that she hopes you all love as much as she loves writing it. This past year she lost her furbaby "monkey" in January which took a big toll on her. Writing has helped her overcome it. She spends as much time as she can with her mother, who is her best friend. Her faith keeps her strong and grounded as she overcomes all the odds.

You can find her on social media:

Facebook: www.facebook.com/JessicaBenjaminsBooks

X: Jasmica87

Instagram: jessicabenjamin87

TikTok: jessica_benjamin_87

Thread: jessicabenjamin87

Website: http://jabbooks.wixsite.com/mainsight

www.ingramcontent.com/pod-product-compliance
Lightning Source LLC
Chambersburg PA
CBHW070606170726
48291CB00003B/720